More Praise for

Trial by Fire

❋

"[A] very riveting, sensual story." —Barbara Vey, *Publishers Weekly*

"Jo Davis turns up the heat full-blast with *Trial by Fire*. Romantic suspense that has it all: a sizzling firefighter hero, a heroine you'll love, and a story that crackles and pops with sensuality and action. All I can say is keep the fire extinguisher handy or risk spontaneous combustion!"

—Linda Castillo, National Bestselling Author of *Overkill*

"Jo Davis set the trap, baited the hook, and completely reeled me in with *Trial by Fire*. Heady sexual tension, heartwarming romance, and combustible love." —Joyfully Reviewed

when alex was bad

jo davis

HEAT

HEAT

Published by New American Library,
a division of Penguin Group (USA) Inc.,
375 Hudson Street, New York, New York 10014, USA
Penguin Group (Canada), 90 Eglinton Avenue East, Suite 700, Toronto,
Ontario M4P 2Y3, Canada (a division of Pearson Penguin Canada Inc.)
Penguin Books Ltd., 80 Strand, London WC2R 0RL, England
Penguin Ireland, 25 St. Stephen's Green, Dublin 2,
Ireland (a division of Penguin Books Ltd.)
Penguin Group (Australia), 250 Camberwell Road, Camberwell,
Victoria 3124, Australia (a division of Pearson Australia Group Pty. Ltd.)
Penguin Books India Pvt. Ltd., 11 Community Centre,
Panchsheel Park, New Delhi - 110 017, India
Penguin Group (NZ), 67 Apollo Drive, Rosedale, North Shore 0632,
New Zealand (a division of Pearson New Zealand Ltd.)
Penguin Books (South Africa) (Pty.) Ltd., 24 Sturdee Avenue,
Rosebank, Johannesburg 2196, South Africa

Penguin Books Ltd., Registered Offices:
80 Strand, London WC2R 0RL, England

First published by Heat, an imprint of New American Library,
a division of Penguin Group (USA) Inc.

First Printing, August 2009
1 3 5 7 9 10 8 6 4 2

HEAT is a trademark of Penguin Group (USA) Inc.

LIBRARY OF CONGRESS CATALOGING-IN-PUBLICATION DATA:

Davis, Jo.
When Alex was bad/Jo Davis.
p. cm.
ISBN 978-0-451-22702-7
1. Married people—Fiction.   2. Adultery—Fiction.   3. Triangles (Interpersonal relations)—
Fiction.   I. Title.
PS3604.A963W47 2009
813'.6—dc22   2009004599

Printed in the United States of America

Acknowledgments

My heartfelt thanks to:

Roberta Brown, my awesome agent and a fabulous lady. From e-press to major movie deals ... wow, we've come a long way together. I can't wait to see what surprises hide beyond the next bend in the road.

Tracy Bernstein, my terrific editor, always an anchor in the face of my uncertainties. I'm grateful that you saw the diamond in Alex, and encouraged me, as always, to just get the work done and quit obsessing over everything I can't control.

Joel Gotler, my tenacious book-to-film agent and all-around cool guy. Your support of my work humbles me, and I'm one lucky author to have you on my side. A big wave as well to Thomas DeTrinis, for taking care of the details behind the scenes, and for being such a sweetheart.

Cathy Schulman, Academy Award-winning producer and president of Mandalay Pictures, for believing in Alex's story and taking it to a level I never dreamed possible. Every author fantasizes about that call, and the reality still rocks my world. Should Cinderella get to attend the ball, you may have to revive me first.

I dedicate this book to all of you. Who knew a bad boy like Alex would spark such a grand adventure?

when alex was bad

One

✳

Olivia Quinn knew she was losing her husband when she discovered his knockout junior partner caressing his crotch by the azalea bush.

Until that moment, the party had been rather uneventful.

One of those fabled life-altering moments that seizes a woman by the throat, squeezes the air from her lungs. Blows her to dust. Refuses to allow her to cower one second longer behind a safe cocoon of denial.

Groaning, Alexander made a halfhearted attempt to peel the vixen off him. "Jenna, no."

The flame-haired beauty only laughed, a soft tinkle in the darkness as she pressed her breasts to his bare chest. Fondled the bulge in his swim trunks. "Why not? The others are by the pool. No one will see, darling."

"My wife—"

"Doesn't take care of you, baby," she crooned. "She doesn't give you what you need. I can make you feel all better."

Damn, that hurt like a bastard. Even if Olivia could speak, she couldn't deny the charge.

Her husband dipped his head, brought his mouth down hard on Jenna's. Cupped her firm breasts through the skimpy bikini top, brushed her nipples with his thumbs. A blond god in the moonlight, seduced by a fiery goddess.

Alex, why?

But she knew the answer. They'd shared an explosive sex life once. Had fucked like rabbits, whispering their wildest fantasies. Some included wicked things they'd do to one another, and a few they'd actually tried and perfected. Light bondage, spanking and such.

But she'd loved nothing more than fucking Alex while spinning a tale of him sinking his cock into another beautiful woman. Or a handsome man, young and vulnerable. Her erotic stories sent him over the edge every single time.

Fifteen years and two busy careers later, they shared a home in an exclusive gated community, a Jag, a Mercedes and a healthy 40I(k). Mutual respect and love. Yes, despite the gut-wrenching scene before her, she had no doubt her husband still loved her. The proof was in the small, everyday things money—and great sex—couldn't buy.

The way Alex's green eyes lit when she walked through the door at the end of a late evening at the restaurant. His fussing when she tried to lift something too heavy, his serious consideration of her opinion in all matters. A true partnership between soul mates.

But the fantasies and the scorching heat were gone.

Or were they?

Watching them kiss, Olivia's nipples tightened to eraser points. A warm tingling had begun between her thighs that she hadn't noticed a few moments ago. She shifted, making sure to keep well hidden behind the shrubs. Her pussy was hot, soaking wet, as confusion assailed her.

For God's sake, Alex's tongue was stuffed down another woman's throat, a coworker who'd obviously been pursuing him for a while, and Olivia could only writhe, turned on at the idea of his long, thick cock stuffed into his would-be lover's cunt. Giving in to his torment, letting her have what she'd been dying for.

Alex broke the kiss and set Jenna from him, gentle but firm. "No. I can't cheat on Olivia. I won't."

Olivia's heart stuttered. Her husband was gazing at his junior partner with wretched longing etched on his angular, handsome face.

He looked breathtakingly beautiful . . . and completely miserable.

Jenna ran a manicured nail down his cheek, across his lower lip, and smiled. "Oh, I think you'll stray all right, my gorgeous stud. And when you do——"

"You're wrong," he rasped.

"Gotta run. See you Monday. Don't forget we're working late on the Boardman defense. I'll wear the black skirt you like so much." She started to leave, then snapped her fingers as though remembering something. "Oh, and Alex?"

"What?"

"I won't be wearing anything underneath."

Jenna walked off and left Alex standing there, staring after her swinging hips. Swiping a hand down his face, he exhaled a world-weary sigh and headed back toward the pool and their guests.

For several minutes, Olivia stood silent, contemplating the reality of the situation. She was losing her husband. Though Alex was putting up a brave fight, he'd soon buckle under the weight of dark, forbidden desires. The need to explore his sexuality, his untapped fantasies, with or without his wife.

By the last guest's departure, Olivia had formed a radical plan to save her marriage.

One guaranteed to rock Alex's world and put the spice back into their sex life for good.

Or to destroy her husband, and their love, by using his own demons against him.

. . .

Holy Christ, what a narrow escape.

Alex Quinn stepped from the shower, glad to wash the stink of chlorine off his body. Along with the tantalizing aroma of Jenna Shaw's perfume lingering on his skin, wrecking his control. Damn, what a lush mouth. Opening for him, sucking his tongue. A tall, lithe wet dream inviting him inside to take what he wanted.

What he wouldn't have given for her to suck his cock, too. Jesus, he'd wanted to fuck her. Almost had. Right there in the shadows mere feet from his own party. From his *wife*.

The idea lifted his unsatisfied erection a notch.

"My God," he whispered, horrified. "What am I doing?"

Using the towel, he swiped a spot of steam off the bathroom mirror and stared at his reflection. Hated what he saw: a forty-year-old lawyer in his physical prime yet desperate with unquenched lust. Shadows haunting his green eyes, guilt eating his soul.

He was sick to death of working himself into the ground. All work, no play. Tired of coming home to the status quo, to the ghost of his marriage. Of being alone, invisible to the woman he'd once loved with an all-consuming passion. Loved still. Didn't he?

Olivia doesn't see me anymore, doesn't know me.

No matter how late he worked at the office, hoping she'd be here when he got home, she was always busy with her upscale restaurant. Giancarlo's, her family's namesake, was the toast of fine dining in St. Louis, and rightly so. Olivia had worked damned hard to make it a success, and Alex was extremely proud of her, even if he did occasionally urge her to delegate some of the responsibility to her staff.

I'm the owner, Alex. Isn't my career just as important as yours?

No way would he begrudge her independence, but . . .

God, I'm so lonely.

Yes, he thought the sun rose and set on his wife. Always would. But he wanted to feel *alive.* To experience all of the wild pleasures life had to offer, before he became too old to enjoy them. He wanted nasty, forbidden, blistering hot sex with someone who appreciated him. Couldn't get enough of him. If not now, when?

No easy answers.

And Monday would arrive all too soon.

Pulling a pair of silk boxers over his deflating penis, he walked into the bedroom. To his surprise, Olivia wasn't asleep. For a moment, he allowed himself to drink her in.

She was propped up on a couple of pillows, reading a romance novel. Olivia, reading? Searching his memory, he couldn't recall the last time he'd seen her pick up a book. Truth be told, she usually came home from the restaurant a couple of hours after he went to bed. Alone. So he really had no idea what her other interests were anymore.

Dim light from the lamp on her side of the bed cut the gloom. Caught at the raven hair tumbling past her slim shoulders and framing a delicate oval face graced by full, sensual lips, a blade of a nose, and wide blue eyes. Her classic beauty struck him like a fist in the stomach, as always.

Too bad they never made time for one another anymore.

As if she'd heard his thoughts, Olivia glanced up from her book and pinned him with a laser blue gaze so very intense, a flicker of panic seized his gut. Had she seen him and Jenna tonight?

But the notion was dispelled as she flashed him a small, secretive smile. Marking her place, she laid the book on the nightstand and patted the bed beside her. "Join me, handsome. I need to talk to you."

Talk. Woman Code for *Your ass is toast.*

So she had seen. He spread his hands in appeal. "Liv, I'm sorry."

"What for?" Giving him a puzzled frown, she tossed back the covers. "Come to bed, Alex. Lord, you're strung tight. What's wrong?"

"I-I—" He broke off, unsure of what to say. Shit, he'd nearly blown it! "I'm sorry you didn't seem to enjoy yourself tonight. It's never been much fun for you, making nice with my partners and employees. But they've come to expect the annual Quinn and Quinn spring pool party." Shrugging, he gave Liv a weak smile and joined her in bed.

Congratulations, asshole. Now you're a liar as well as a cheat.

"Oh, I don't mind." She dismissed his apology with a wave. "I like your associates—you know that. I need to talk to you about something else. Something important."

Wary, he cocked his head. "Anything, sweetheart."

Scooting around to face him better, she nibbled her lower lip as though weighing a heavy decision. Suddenly, her worry cleared, mind obviously made up. "Alex, do you remember the weekend we married?"

He closed his fingers over hers. "Of course I do. We went to Puerto Vallarta. It was lovely, but not nearly as exquisite as you." Corny, but at least it wasn't a lie.

Her azure eyes sparkled. "And you were the blond god of my dreams. Remember where we made love for the first time as husband and wife?"

"We made love a lot in those days." He laughed, the sound a little sad and wistful to his ears. He hadn't meant for his loneliness to slip out. "But yeah, I remember. We walked down the beach, a mile or so away from the resort. We wanted each other right in the open with the ocean pounding the shore a few yards from us. No matter who might happen along."

"And it started to rain."

"But that didn't stop us, did it?"

Liv squeezed his hand, looked straight into his soul. "Somewhere along the way, something did," she said quietly.

A shaft of pain pierced his heart. "Liv—"

"Remember the fantasies we used to share in bed?"

He nodded, wondering where she was going with all of this, and more than a bit nervous. "We made up a ton of them. They were fun. Exciting."

"Ooh, yes. Our role play added sizzle, don't you think? I mean, making love with you is always wonderful, don't get me wrong. But when we role-played our most secret desires, we *fucked*. Down and dirty, delicious fucking," she mused. "Be honest. Have you, before or since, experienced such intense orgasms as when you pretended to bury your cock in another lover?"

His prick twitched, coming to life again. Shit! What the hell was she driving at?

"No, I haven't." He stared at his calm, serene wife. "But those scenarios were safe because I was really with you. We played the game *together.*"

"So why did it end, Alex?" She ran a hand down his cheek. "Why don't we share our darkest fantasies anymore?"

"I don't know, baby. I guess there just wasn't anywhere left to go with them."

Jesus, that hurt most of all. Even if Liv hadn't seen him kissing his junior partner, she sensed their distance. Knew their once unbreakable bond was fading, her husband on the verge of turning from her. Had they really reached the end of the road sexually? Had they become little more than friends with benefits?

"What if," she said slowly, "I told you there's one avenue left unexplored? That I know exactly how to rekindle the spark, get things back on track for us?"

Alex blinked. "If you have an idea, I'd love to hear it."

"The plan is risky," she cautioned. "We'll both be required to let go of our taboos. Open our marriage to new experiences, ones that will either backfire or heal us as a couple. What I have in mind could transform you into a very happy, sexually satisfied man."

Her seductive words poured over him, quickening his pulse. "Good God, Liv. Are you suggesting . . . "

"That you act on your desires. That you allow yourself to indulge in the wicked pleasures you've only dreamed of, guilt-free." Liv's hand strayed to the slit of his boxers where the head of his throbbing cock peeked through. Swirling the tip with one finger, she continued. Lured him with her siren song.

"Look how hard you are at the mere suggestion. Truth is, I get hot and wet just picturing my sexy husband entering his lover. Knowing he has my full blessing to fuck her or him into oblivion. One partner this time, perhaps a ménage à trois the next. Would you like that?"

"Y-yes. I mean, no," he groaned, assailed by the images she awakened. His dick was on fire, ready to detonate. "Liv, baby, I can't." But he'd already been considering it, hadn't he?

"Why not?" Pushing down the front of the boxers, she grasped his penis. Stroked.

"There's nothing in this for you. I get all the benefits and you get hurt." Closing his eyes, he spread his legs to accommodate her attentions. Lost himself in her touch.

"Not if we do things my way. Besides, if we keep going as we have been, I get hurt, anyway."

Alex no longer had to agonize over whether she'd seen him and Jenna groping one another. Liv had been watching. . . .

The breath left his lungs as the truth hit him like a runaway truck. He opened his eyes, read the unmasked emotion in her blue ones.

Olivia was *aroused* by what she'd witnessed.

Rather than letting their marriage die, she'd chosen to participate in their sexual reawakening as a couple. To give him the freedom to explore . . . and then what?

"Your ground rules?" he gasped. Her hand pumped him, slow and steady. Bringing him near to orgasm.

"I'll allow your liaisons, with any lover you wish, so long as you are honest about being married. Also, I don't want to know beforehand when you plan to seek your pleasure. This gives you the thrill of being naughty, you see."

"The catch?" God, he was going to explode.

"After each encounter, you'll confess to me," she purred. "In detail. Every caress, every word. Then, my love, I'll exact your punishment. That is the price you will pay for our pact."

"Wh-what?"

"You'll willingly submit to whatever discipline I choose, and no, I won't tell you what the punishment might be. I'll only say that the encounters you pursue give me permission to enjoy myself likewise. You're the gambler here, so you take the chances and live with the consequences. One thing more." Her lips hitched up in a small smile.

"You get seven confessions total. After the last punishment is delivered, our pact is done and we must make a decision on where to go with our marriage."

"What do you mean?"

"Maybe we'll want to continue our pact for another seven confessions, same rules." Increasing the pressure of the strokes, Liv looked him straight in the eye. "Or we might embrace a whole new sexual lifestyle *together.*"

Alex moaned, unable to stave off the orgasm. Cum boiled in his drawn-up balls, shot from the base of his spine so hard it shook his body. Semen spewed over her hand, his boxers, the sheets. On and on, thick and hot.

When he lay spent and panting, Liv leaned over, placed a loving kiss on his lips. "Do we have a pact?"

The monumental impact of his answer made him tremble

in fear. And anticipation. One way or another, their lives were about to change forever.

"Yes, sweetheart. We do."

*   *   *

The restaurant would survive without her for a few days. Finally, when it was almost too late, she understood that.

But Alex loved her.

Olivia repeated the mantra throughout the bright Monday, which stretched on, interminably long. The silence was broken only by a pair of delivery men, who glanced at her in curiosity more than once as she had them erect her new purchases in the downstairs media room.

She declined to reveal what the items were for, but suspected they knew all the same. After a generous tip, they left, averting their gazes.

Bored, she donned her bikini bottoms and went to sun in a lounger by the pool. Normally, she'd be more cautious about sunbathing topless, but the lots on their right and out back were wooded, part of hers and Alex's property, and their widowed neighbor on the left, Bill Strickland, had died a couple of months ago, leaving no children. The sprawling mini mansion stood sad and empty, and what might become of the place was anyone's guess. Their gated community boasted a burly security guard and a group of snoopy, blue-haired old retirees who watched everyone that came and went like beady-eyed hawks. Hell, they probably knew tae kwon do.

So, no worries.

Which was why, a few minutes later, she was shocked as shit

to open her eyes and see a man staring at her over the top of Bill Strickland's fence.

Squeaking in alarm, she snatched a towel over her breasts. His eyes widened and his head ducked out of sight. Before she could find the words to admonish him, the man's distressed voice drifted from her deceased neighbor's yard.

"Gosh, lady, I'm sorry! I-I wasn't expecting . . . I mean, I didn't . . . damn."

For some reason, his stammered apology enchanted her. Soothed her fright. He truly seemed as surprised as she by the encounter, and dreadfully embarrassed to have been busted ogling her.

Relaxing a little, she called out. "Are you a friend of Bill's?"

A pause. "I'm his nephew, Jason Strickland."

Ah. That explained things. "You're in town to take care of his estate?"

"You could say that," came the muffled reply.

"This is a tad awkward, shouting through the fence, don't you think? Come over if you'd like, Jason. The gate is unlocked."

After a moment's hesitation, footsteps shuffled through the grass. The latch clicked and the gate squealed open. Liv turned her head to see the man walk tentatively inside. Nervous, he wiped his hands on faded jeans slung low on his hips and sporting holes in the knees.

"I'm really sorry," he said, color staining his cheeks.

A young man, Liv noted. No more than twenty-three or so. Shaggy, sun-kissed brown hair fell to strong shoulders, not too broad. He had a lean build, hard with muscle but not bulky. His navy T-shirt was new, unlike his jeans, and emphasized his flat, almost concave, stomach.

And holy cow, was he a looker. High, supermodel cheekbones, a boyishly handsome face. A perfectly sculpted mouth.

"You gave me a start, that's all. Come, Jason, sit down." She gestured at the lounger on her right, which Alex used when they relaxed together. Strickland approached, sharp gaze taking in his surroundings warily, as though he expected to be jumped.

Curious, she wondered at his story. Why hadn't Bill ever mentioned his own nephew?

Jason sat on the edge of the lounger facing her, hands clasped between spread knees. He made an attempt to appear nonchalant, but the tense set of his posture gave away his discomfort. He was poised for trouble and seemed totally unaware of the fact, as though the survival instinct was ingrained into his DNA.

Liv held out her hand. "I'm Olivia Quinn, but most people call me Liv. My husband, Alex, is working right now, but I'm sure he'd love to meet you."

Jason's eyes widened a fraction. He stared at the offered hand for a couple of seconds before enclosing her palm in his. "I . . . thanks. I don't know how long I'll stay in the neighborhood, but I'd like that."

His hand was strong, callused, the nails clean. These were the hands of a working man who'd known little luxury. The bruised look in his lovely mocha brown eyes hinted at secrets, pain, and hard-won knowledge beyond his years.

If she had her guess, Jason Strickland had been hurt. Badly.

"Forgive me for being so forward, but Alex and I believed Bill died without an heir." At his pinched expression, she relented. "Now it's my turn to apologize."

He gave her a small smile. "No, it's fine. I was Uncle Bill's only living relative. I had no clue he left everything to me, and his lawyer had trouble tracking me down. I never realized Bill gave a shit about my welfare." He shrugged. "His absentee nephew was a better option than letting the state take it all, I guess."

So young to be so cynical. Poor man.

"What will you do now?"

He shook his head, gaze dropping to his battered tennis shoes. "I don't know. I've always dreamed of having a nice place to hang my hat. But that mausoleum doesn't feel like home. I'll probably sell."

Reaching out, she patted his knee. "I hope you'll stay while you figure out what you want to do. My husband and I would enjoy having you around."

Jason's gaze went to the hand on his knee. Traveled up to linger on the towel covering her breasts, and on to her face. She sucked in a breath at the heat in his eyes. The longing.

"Then maybe I'll have to stay," he whispered. Getting to his feet, he took her hand from his knee. Kissed her fingers. "It's been a pleasure meeting you, Olivia. I'd like to get to know both of you better."

Her pulse pounded, tingling warmth moistening her sex. Had Jason meant to imply he'd be open to more than neighborly friendship? Letting go of her, he skirted the lounger and headed for the gate. On impulse, she called after him.

"Lunch with me tomorrow?"

He froze. Glanced over his shoulder. "What time?"

Triumph surged in her breast. "Eleven thirty."

A ghost of a smile tugged at his lips before he answered. "I'll count the minutes."

With that, he disappeared through the gate.

"So will I, dear Jason." She grinned to herself. Oh yes, the chemistry was there, and if Jason was willing . . . this young man might play a vital role in their future.

The wait for Alex no longer seemed unbearable as it did before. She had no doubt he'd fuck Jenna tonight, and there were several others in their acquaintance Liv knew would be thrilled to bed him. Her magnificent husband was seething with suppressed sexual desires that had gone ignored for far too long.

If she knew Alex as well as she'd always believed, he'd be very eager to share his confessions and receive his punishment. Soon he'd come to crave his discipline from Liv as much or more than taking his lovers. Then she'd enact phase two. A bold plan.

The survival of their marriage depended on it.

Two

Monday passed in a haze. After the post-party discussion with Liv, Alex tossed all of Saturday night. And last night, too. His sleep-deprived brain hardly registered what Jenna or any of his associates said to him during the course of the day—except for one pissed-off man who would not be ignored.

And with good reason.

"Tell me, Alex, why the *fuck* you assigned Jenna Shaw to assist with the Boardman trial. Over *me?*"

Alex leaned back in his office chair and gazed at Ken Brock, one of Alex's senior partners and six feet two inches of lean, mean hard-ass. He steepled his fingers, striving to appear unperturbed in the face of the hard onyx stare that made prosecutors tremble, and heaved a deep sigh.

"Come on, Ken, I went over my reasons in the meeting. You were busy finishing up the Briggs murder trial, and the other partners are all in the middle of big defenses." Truth, every word.

"The Briggs trial wrapped this morning, just like I told you it would. You could've waited for me."

Also true. Dammit.

Alex stood and rounded his desk, unwilling to have the angry black man towering over him. He affected a casual pose, leaning one hip against the corner of his desk and folding his arms. "Time is money and all that, so I chose not to wait. Besides, this is Jenna's first big case. It's a good opportunity to get her feet wet."

Ken barked a bitter laugh. "Yeah, man. Something's getting wet and I'll bet my Rolex it's not her feet."

Alex's stomach gave a sick twist and his expression froze. "All right, that's enough. I'm done with this conversation except to promise you'll get the next big client. Take the rest of the day off, Ken. You've earned it."

Ken bristled at the curt dismissal. He opened his mouth to protest, but must've thought better of continuing the argument. The cold look he shot at Alex before he spun and stalked out suggested the reprieve was temporary.

The remainder of the day went downhill from there. Papers were shoved in his face, clients demanded to be placated, court dates had to be set, more money was piled in his bank account.

And Jenna Shaw badly needed to be fucked.

Ken's assessment was dead-on.

Half the firm had to know she wanted him and intended to have him. She hadn't exactly been subtle about her mission these past few weeks, though at least today she'd had the sense to keep the sly invitations discreet, for his eyes only.

A glimpse of the dark red triangle under the short black skirt as she uncrossed her legs while discussing case notes. A flash of creamy breasts as she leaned over his desk to point out an argument the prosecution might make against one of their clients.

All goddamned day he'd been hard enough to hammer railroad spikes.

He and Jenna were slated to work late. Very late. And Liv *knew* what might happen. Even approved.

I can't do this.

What on earth had made him agree to Liv's proposal? Temporary insanity, amplified by her low, seductive voice as she worked his cock. Painted the most erotic picture he'd ever imagined.

Sitting behind his huge mahogany desk, Alex swiped a hand down his face. Frustration and despair ate at him. He glanced at his watch. Seven o'clock. There was still time to slip out and head home before Jenna came around with the Boardman files. Grabbing his suit jacket, he decided he'd call his junior partner on her cell. Explain that he hadn't felt well—

The door opened, and Jenna stepped into his office. She did not have a file or anything else in her hands. Her glorious coppery hair was no longer secured in the demure twist at her nape, but hung in shiny waves over the shoulders of her white blouse.

"About the Boardman case—"

"I'm sorry, Alex. I seem to have left the files at home by accident," she said, all wide-eyed innocence. Slowly, she walked toward him, five feet, ten inches of feline grace. Stalking her prey.

Shrugging, he feigned indifference. His dick didn't receive the message. "No problem. We'll come in early in the morning and go over the notes before Henry Boardman arrives."

She made a face. "Didn't Danielle tell you? Mr. Boardman called and changed his appointment to seven a.m. sharp."

"No, she didn't." Crap. Staring at Jenna, Alex wondered whether she'd had a hand in Mr. Boardman's change of plans. Danielle, his new secretary, had gone home at five, so he couldn't question her. Damned convenient.

"Well, then, we've got no choice. We'll have to go over the files tonight so we can be ready to present his defense."

"I'd offer to go get them and bring them back here, but I don't have my car." She sighed. "My sister dropped me off, then kept my wheels to borrow since her car is in the shop."

Oh, that was neat and tidy. He had to give the she-devil credit for a well-executed conquest. "I'll give you a lift home; then we can just go over them there. No need to drive all the way back to the office when your place is practically on my way home," he heard himself say. *Idiot.*

Their gazes locked. She'd won, and knew it.

Her berry-ripe lips turned up, a sly smile of victory. Reaching out, she cupped his cheek. Leaned in, brushed his mouth lightly with hers.

"Perfect."

Caught, a fly in the black widow's web.

The drive to Jenna's condo was fifteen minutes of sheer torture. She made sure of it, reclining in the supple leather passenger's seat of his Jag, tiny skirt hiked to the top of her toned thighs. Her long legs were spread, body angled just enough for him to see the shadow of the curls nestled there. Waiting, begging for his touch.

Eyes closed, head tipped back, she appeared not to care. The poke of taut nipples against the fabric of her blouse, the pungent scent of arousal gave her away.

"Which unit?" he asked, pulling into the complex. His hands shook on the wheel and his throat had gone tight. Sweet Jesus, he couldn't lie to himself. He was about to fuck someone other than his wife for the first time in nearly two decades. He'd be lying if he said he wasn't nervous as hell.

She pointed at the last building on the right. "There. The empty space is mine. Go ahead and park in it." As he pulled into the space, she fished a paper from her purse and handed it to him.

"What's this?" Opening the driver's door, he peered at the sheet. Oh, boy. "Test results?"

"I'm clean. Thought you should see."

He cleared his throat. "Ah, good to know. I . . . I haven't been with anyone but my wife in fifteen years. We're both clean."

She just gave him a smile as she retrieved the paper.

In short order, he was following Jenna into her spacious, third-floor condo. The place was sleek and sexy, like the woman herself. Done in modern decor, light tints of blue and beige, mirrors and glass everywhere.

Tossing aside her purse, which she'd grabbed as they'd left, she turned to Alex. Parted his suit jacket and smoothed her palms on his chest. "You like?"

"Yeah," he said hoarsely. "I like a lot."

They both knew he wasn't referring to the furniture.

She cupped his sex through his pants, slim fingers squeezing his already aching erection. Moaning, he shifted his stance to give her better access.

"What, no gallant protests of fidelity? After weeks of resisting, you're finally ready to stop fighting me?"

"Y-yes." Sharp teeth grazed his earlobe.

"Why? I want to hear you say it," she demanded, pushing the jacket off his shoulders. It fell to the floor, and she began unbuttoning his shirt.

"Because I-I want you."

"You can do better, stud. I'm waiting." His shirt joined the jacket. She unbuckled his belt, went to work on his fly.

"I have to slide my cock into your hot pussy before the anticipation kills me." He almost told her about his arrangement with Liv, but this was simpler, cleaner, and no less the truth. "I've wanted to do your luscious body from the second I hired you, and I can't resist anymore."

God help me.

Something dark and dangerous flashed in her topaz eyes, there and gone so fast he must've imagined it. "And why should you? Poor neglected baby, let me make you feel good."

Taking him by the hand, she led him into the living room to stand in front of the sofa. Grasping the waist of his pants, she tugged them down, boxers and all. His shaft sprang free, ready and eager for whatever games she had in mind. Indeed, she seemed to be taking the dominant role, a role normally his, and the idea shot a thrill down his spine.

If Jenna wanted to control him tonight, he'd let her. Now that his fate was decided, he'd do whatever she wanted. Let his lover devour him whole.

"Sit down while I put on the music." After throwing his cock a hungry look, she walked over to a wall panel, slid it open to reveal an expensive stereo system.

While she busied herself with her selection, Alex removed his pants and shoes. He was totally naked, sitting on an associate's sofa, harder than he'd ever been. Maybe he should feel guilty despite the agreement he'd made, but that emotion had vanished. Instead, he felt . . .

Drugged. Naughty. Free.

Jenna returned to stand between his knees as soft strains of Chopin wafted from across the room. She undid her blouse, parted the material to reveal the full, pale breasts he'd dreamed of tasting. The peaks were rosy, taut nubs tempting him. He stared as the blouse and skirt hit the floor.

His gaze traveled down the plane of her flat tummy to the dark red nest of hair. From his position, her pink little clit and the slick folds of her bare pussy lips were visible, plump and inviting. Wet for him.

Kneeling on the carpet, she ran her palms up his thighs. "So big everywhere. Muscular and fit. I insist on a man who takes care of his body."

"Baby, you're the gorgeous one."

Apparently pleased by his compliment, Jenna grasped his cock around the base. Flicking her smoldering gaze to his, she licked the broad, flushed head of his penis. Dipped the tip of her pink tongue in the weeping slit, collecting those first telltale drops.

The initial contact electrified every nerve ending. Paralyzed Alex in a fog of need, leaving him at her mercy. Her pretty mouth surrounded the head, suckled as though craving nourishment only he could provide. Inch by agonizing inch, she swallowed the length of him. Gasping, he watched his iron-hard shaft disappear between her lips. The most erotic sight he'd ever beheld.

One hand manipulated his balls with expertise as she sucked him, a double whammy of pleasure. Unable to help himself, he groaned, jacking his hips upward. With a low, husky laugh, she released him and straddled his lap.

"You need this, big boy?"

"Oh yeah."

Grabbing a handful of blond hair, she yanked back his head. "Beg."

"Jenna, fuck me. Please, baby, *fuck me. . . .* "

She sank onto his rigid penis the same way she'd sucked him, slow and deliberate. He spanned his hands at her trim waist. Reveled in the slide of her fiery sheath gripping his cock. Down, down until she took all of him. Skin to skin, locked together.

So goddamned good. So fucking nasty.

Dark, forbidden delight.

"*This* is what you've craved, dear Alex. What you need that no one else can give you, even your lovely wife." Her voice was triumphant, her eyes glittering pools.

But Liv made this possible, he wanted to cry in denial.

"Yes," he whispered instead. Easier to agree. He couldn't think, not with Jenna's clit rubbing the length of his rod. Her hot channel squeezing as she rode him faster, harder.

"Fuck!" she cried, bouncing up and down on his lap, slamming onto his cock again and again. "That's it, take what you deserve."

He did. His hips pistoned into her sweet cunt, flesh slapping in delicious, noisy rhythm. A familiar quickening seized his balls, gathered in the base of his spine.

"Ahhh, God!"

He exploded with shattering force, pumping into her on and on, filling her with his release. She joined him in climax and they shuddered together for a full minute before Alex finally collapsed into the cushions, sated and spent. For now.

Grinning, she flicked the end of his nose with one bloodred nail. "The Boardman files?"

"Ugh. Must we?"

"Mmm. If you're very efficient, we might dispatch with business and have time to play before you have to go home." She cocked her head. "Unless you'd like to stay?"

"I can't. You know I love Olivia." He took a deep breath. "In fact, she—"

"I've heard that song before." She chuckled knowingly.

A chill gripped his heart. "Jenna, after tonight, this can't happen again."

Cool topaz eyes bored into his, unconcerned. As though she knew something he didn't.

"We'll see, loverboy. Don't bet the farm."

. . .

Carrying her glass of wine through the French doors and onto the second-story balcony adjoining their bedroom, Olivia's heart ached.

Midnight, and no Alex.

In fifteen years, he'd never been this late. Then again, he'd never been given carte blanche to explore his sexuality. *Neither have I.* How would he react when he discovered what part of his eventual punishment entailed?

A movement from next door caught her attention. From her perch, she had a perfect view as Jason strode toward his pool. Gloriously naked. Lights shimmered in the water, danced across his back and chiseled buttocks. A bit of breeze stirred his hair as he stared over the grounds, perhaps taking in his change of fortune.

He dove into the pool and began to swim laps in strong, steady strokes. Back and forth, as Liv watched, intrigued anew by the young man. Excitement about their impending lunch date grew, and she couldn't wait for tomorrow.

Twenty minutes later, Jason hauled himself out of the pool and pushed his dripping hair away from his face. Liv fixated on his flaccid penis and round balls, wishing she weren't so far away. Even from this distance, it was apparent the man was endowed.

Suddenly, his chin lifted. His gaze found hers, and they simply regarded each other for a moment. A connection sizzled between them. Raising a hand, he waved.

"Good night, Olivia," Jason called. "See you tomorrow."

Smiling, she waved back. "Tomorrow."

Jason disappeared inside. Her smile vanished as she heard the hum of the garage door opener. Nerves screaming, she discarded her silk robe and went downstairs. She must look her best to greet Alex, and the skimpy blue nightie that barely covered her rear would do.

At the bottom of the stairs, she stopped and drank in the sight of him. He'd turned on a lamp in the living room and set his briefcase on his favorite easy chair. His jacket and tie were missing, his thick golden hair mussed. He hadn't yet noticed her watching. Still as marble, he gazed into space, looking lost.

She must've made a small sound, because his green eyes snapped to where she stood. His handsome face was wretched with guilt.

"Olivia. I have a confession."

"I know," she said calmly. "Come with me."

Steeling herself with purpose, she spun on her heel, leaving him to follow.

"Liv, it's late. Why don't we—"

Spinning, she cut him with a cool glare. "Did Jenna eat your watch along with your cock?"

He paled. "I—"

"You agreed to my rules, correct?"

"I did." He let out a shaky breath.

"Are you going to renege, now that you've gotten your rocks off?"

"No. I gave you my word."

"Good. Let's go."

She led him into the large media room, turned the lights on dim and set aside her wine. Studying Alex, she savored his stunned reaction to the new contraptions gracing the center of the room.

"What is that thing?" He gaped, pointing to a weblike device suspended from the ceiling. "Some sort of torture sling?"

"Good observation. I strap you in and you'll hang there, just like a bug in a spiderweb. The other toy is pretty self-explanatory." She gestured to a pair of posts connected to a base. A black padded cuff hung from the top of each post by a short length of chain, and another set of cuffs, for his ankles, graced the bottom.

"Jesus," Alex muttered. "What do you want me to do?"

"Take off your clothes and go stand between the poles. Next, fasten your ankles."

Silently, she congratulated herself on remaining calm. This wasn't in the least about jealousy or revenge, which he'd understand in the next few weeks, but about sexual awakening. She must handle this exactly right, or all would be lost.

Alex shed his clothes and went to stand between the posts. His bewildered look nearly made her relent, but the rich scent of sex drifting from his naked body spurred her on.

Fastening the cuffs around his ankles, he waited. Liv had to use a small stool to reach his wrists, but secured them with no problem. Surveying her handiwork, she nodded in approval.

"You're already half-erect." She laughed softly, cupping his balls. "Does being at my mercy excite you?"

"Yes," he said honestly. "Everything about you excites me, Liv." To prove his point, his shaft began to harden. His testicles drew tight in her grasp.

"Not Liv, *Mistress.* When you come to confessional and receive your punishment, I'm Mistress to you. Is that understood?"

Unable to hide his shock, he cleared his throat. "Yes . . . Mistress."

"Excellent." This was an important adjustment between them. First, it established her position of authority. Second, it enabled him to disassociate from Liv, his wife, and connect with their new roles, encouraging him to speak freely. Caressing his penis, she lowered her voice to a sultry whisper. "Make your confession, my love."

Alex closed his eyes for a few moments. When he opened them again, they brimmed with warring emotions. Guilt, lust, gratitude.

"Jenna and I were supposed to work late, but she'd left our most important case file at her condo and said she didn't have her car. A transparent ploy, but I took her home, anyway."

"Was she commando under the black skirt, as promised?"

"Yeah. In the car, she spread her legs. Kept giving me glimpses of her pussy."

"My, your cock is getting hot just from telling me." The heat of him branded her fingers. She reveled in the power she held over him. "Is that when you knew you'd give in to her?"

"No, Mistress. I knew Saturday night I didn't stand a chance if she kept after me." His mouth trembled.

As much as the truth stung, Alex's admission was a vital step. "Continue."

"When we got to Jenna's condo, she undressed me. I didn't resist this time. She led me to the sofa. I sat while she put on music and then sh-she . . ." He swallowed with an audible gulp.

"She went down on me. I was afraid of going through with it

at first. But something dark inside me took over. Watching her suck me was so incredibly erotic. . . . And knowing you gave me permission to surrender, even more so."

Just the progress she'd hoped for. "That's right. Our bargain gave you leave to be bad. You must let go of your old taboos and feel no shame, my love. I'll help you embrace our freedom, understand?"

"I'm trying." He groaned as she stroked him.

"After she sucked you, what happened?"

"She straddled my lap and sank onto my cock," he breathed, losing some of his trepidation and speaking more easily. "Her pussy felt so good, hot and wet. She fucked the shit out of me, and I couldn't stop myself from shooting into her. Didn't want to."

Liv's sex throbbed just imagining them together. God, Alex had enjoyed sex with another woman, and it turned her on! And he, in turn, was getting off on telling her about the encounter.

"Afterward, we went over the case files for a couple of hours. We didn't even bother to get dressed. When we finished working, Jenna started playing with me, getting me hard again. I took her against a mirror on her bedroom wall, with her legs wrapped around my waist. There was a mirror on her dresser behind us, so I could see the reflection of my ass flexing as I pounded into her."

Ooh, how delicious. Her cunt grew moist. "I'll bet you came even harder than before."

"God, yes." His cheeks flushed, his jewel green eyes fever bright. "Still, I couldn't get enough. I took her to bed and ate her sweet pussy for a good long while."

She felt the wetness trickle down one thigh. "Do you love Jenna?"

Alex blinked in surprise. "No. I wanted her, but that's not the same."

"All right," she said, relieved. "Then what happened?"

"Nothing. I came home right after that."

"Will you take her again?"

"I don't know. Maybe." He sighed, and the shadows returned. "Probably. She's pretty stuck on me, and persistent."

Liv shook her head. "Don't divert the responsibility to Jenna. If you had wanted to discourage her, you'd have done it by now," she pointed out, careful to keep her tone factual. "You don't yet have her out of your system. Under the circumstances, I'm not surprised, nor do I blame you."

"Yes, you're right. I wanted her and I gave in, so the responsibility is mine," he said quietly. "Th-thank you, Mistress."

"All right, Alex. You've had your first day of pleasure, and you've made your first confession. You've done well."

"Thank you, Mistress."

"Now you must receive your punishment."

Three

✳

How he could possibly be hard after two mind-blowing orgasms, Alex couldn't fathom. He had to admit, despite his initial fears, Liv's bargain was a stroke of genius. He'd known her almost half his life, and he could tell she was highly aroused by his encounter with Jenna. He'd gotten off sharing the story, too.

Bam, just like that, Liv had added a liberal dash of red-hot pepper to their salsa. So to speak.

Transfixed, he watched Liv pick up a small, bracelet-sized leather strap from the coffee table. Christ, he hadn't noticed the array of whips and belts lying there! As she approached with the device, a sneaking suspicion formed.

"You're not going to put that on me?"

"Oh yes. I'll fit this cock ring around the base of your penis and behind your balls. It will help maintain your erection during this phase of your punishment."

This phase? Alex shook in his restraints as Liv—no, Mistress—tightened the Velcro ends of the strap in place. The leather bit into him, squeezing. Uncomfortable pressure, raising his package, flushed and vulnerable, to her wishes. He liked this, he realized, being restrained and at her mercy.

God, his wife looked so fucking sexy. Shiny raven hair framed her beautiful face, tumbling past her shoulders. Her pert breasts nearly spilled from the tiny blue nightie, nipples puckered in excitement. The silky material hardly covered the creamy globes of her ass, and the smooth skin between her thighs was damp.

"You will not come until I give you permission," she said. Returning to the table, she selected a small riding crop. Settling the handle into a firm grip, she gave it an experimental whip in the air.

The resulting crack made Alex cringe. If Mistress was inclined, she could beat him bloody with that thing, with very little effort.

"You look so worried." She laughed softly, walking over to him. Using the tip, she lifted his testicles. "Hmm. I'll have to use just the right amount of force not to leave marks. The skin is so delicate here."

She stepped back a couple of feet, readying to strike. Alex clamped his lips together, heart thundering, determined not to cry out. He deserved this.

The first snap of the leather strip caught the left side of his balls. Fiery pain shot through his groin and he gasped, arching in the restraints. Giving him no mercy, she struck again. The next snap lashed his raging penis, sending bolts of pain to every nerve ending. But the agony also gave rise to a strange, sweet quickening.

The wave spread from his groin to his limbs, forcing him to comply. To accept. Two more lashes to his penis, another to his testicles. Heat coursed through his veins, pain and ecstasy swirling together, lighting his body like a torch. She was relentless, the blows raining down in rapid succession.

"Ahh, God!" He was going to explode.

The whipping stopped. Panting, trembling with the effort of staving off his orgasm, he focused on her face. Lovely, powerful in her self-assurance.

Tapping the quirt in one palm, she studied him thoughtfully. "That will do. I must say, I'm quite pleased with your responsiveness."

He tried to catch his breath. "You said . . . this was the first phase."

"I'm getting to the rest." Her lips turned up. "When I proposed our arrangement, you worried you'd have all the fun, basically leaving me to pine. You can see how wrong you were."

"Definitely," he agreed.

"You'll see more clearly in the next few weeks," she whispered, brushing his turgid shaft. "While you are playing with your lovers, I intend to select one for myself."

Alex stared at her, mouth gone dry. "Who?"

"I have a candidate in mind, and you'll meet him soon enough." Reaching between his legs, she released his balls and penis from the strap, tossed it aside. "So, remember, every time you sink that big rod of yours into another, my young lover is doing the same to me. I might even ask him to join me in administering your discipline. You may come now, my love."

With a yell, he exploded. His cock pulsed to his heartbeat, a thick fountain arching from his body. Splattering the carpet. His brain spun, overwhelmed by the extent of her plans for him. For them both.

As the last spasms wrung him out, he sagged in the bonds.

Bone tired, but looking forward to tomorrow and the day after more than he had in years.

He couldn't wait to explore more of his newfound sexual freedom. Even more, he was chomping at the bit to experience what Liv had in mind for his next punishment.

Another man. Between her sleek thighs.

Damn her! A male third had long been one of his most treasured fantasies—second to a female, which Liv, of course, would never allow. Too many cat claws in a confined space—not a good idea. But a man? Though he'd always been attracted to men as well as women, he'd never acted on the desire. Now Liv would use that knowledge to drive him crazy. Tempt him beyond reason.

Tempt him into seven kinds of delicious sin.

. . .

Jason Strickland prowled the vast, empty tomb his uncle had called home, forcing down the debilitating self-doubt that haunted every second of his days and nights. Jumping at shadows, staring into dark corners, heart pounding. Waiting. Taking comfort only in knowing that the agony of suspense would be mercifully brief.

He'll find me.

The sick thing was, part of him wanted to be found. Wanted to be punished.

Jason took no joy in his opulent surroundings or newfound wealth. He didn't dare. Nothing lasted. Happiness was an illusion, an oasis always just out of reach for a dying man.

For a man who was no longer sure where he belonged.

Oh, God. He paused in the monstrous marble foyer, hands clenched into fists. "It's not over," he told no one. "You got out, but he'll track you here, hundreds of miles from Los Angeles.

He'll learn who and what you really are, and when he does, you're a dead man."

Cocky, stupid little sonofabitch, look at you now.

"Stop it, Jase." He had to, or he'd drive himself insane. He had a job to do.

As if to underscore his turbulent thoughts, the phone rang. He didn't have to wonder who was on the other end—no one else knew where he was. He crossed to the bar and picked up the receiver, gritting his teeth.

"Yeah?"

"Line secure?"

"What do you think?" He held the phone in a death grip, thankful Reginald couldn't see him sweat. "Figured I'd have heard from you already. Must be getting slow in your old age."

"Thought I'd give you time to settle in, given your bereavement and all." The man sounded anything but sympathetic.

"Why, that's mighty white of you, boss." His boss was as ebony as the ace of spades and huge enough to pound Jason into the dirt without straining a muscle.

"Fuck you, kid."

"Take a number."

A short, humorless laugh. "That's what I like about you, Jason. Impulsive to the last. Then again, that little flaw is how we're asshole-deep in this fucking pile of goat shit, isn't it." A statement, not a question.

His colossal failure. He didn't need a reminder. "You're the one who pulled me. I know I fucked up, but I was handling—"

"Kid, I've been hearing that crap from my men since you were watching the Powerpuff Girls and eating SpaghettiOs, what, about three years ago?"

"Goddammit, Reginald—"

"Focus on our subject. I want to know every move he makes. If he breaks wind, I wanna smell it. Can you handle *that?*"

"He's covered," he said tightly, rubbing his temple. "I'm tailing him every chance I get." He ought to be doing more, and hoped Reginald would let it go for now.

"Don't fuck this up."

"And to think I forgot to get you a card for Boss's Day."

"You want hearts and flowers, model for Victoria's Secret."

"Eat sh—"

The bastard hung up.

Slamming down the phone, he paced the living room, dying to wreck something. Lose control.

Thank God for the lunch plans with his new neighbor.

He should have told Reginald about it. About living next door to Alexander Quinn, his subject's hotshot defense attorney . . . and therefore, a man who bore watching closely.

Surprise, surprise. Ain't it a small fucking world?

Getting involved with the Quinns was not a good idea. But he needed a distraction to calm his nerves, and God, what a distraction. A gorgeous, black-haired wet dream with a killer body and perfect breasts peaked by rose-tipped nipples. Wide, electric blue eyes brimming with sultry invitation.

He'd never been much into women, though he suspected this was due to lack of opportunity and experience. He'd serviced a couple, on his master's orders, propelled by duty, not by choice. How would it feel to explore his desires freely, to find out what he—Jason, not the sex slave—wanted?

Christ, he was a head case. She'd only asked him to lunch, not to *be* lunch. Smiling at himself, mood somewhat lightened, he went upstairs to dress. Meeting Olivia yesterday had brought him out of his funk enough to go out and buy some decent clothes. After lugging his bags home from the mall, he'd spent a long time removing each item and caressing the fabric, getting reacquainted with having things that belonged to him. Readjusting to his former world of relative normalcy.

In his walk-in closet, he stood debating. He settled on a pair of dark jeans and a stretchy black ribbed T-shirt. The shirt hugged his chest and abs, showing his hard work at keeping fit. Last, he pulled on a new pair of Red Wings. His old, ratty tennis shoes had hit the garbage.

Leaving the closet, he glanced at his SIG lying on the corner of the dresser. He picked up the hand cannon, hoping to take comfort in handling it again, but after the past year, he knew better.

More often than not, the real enemy lay within.

Placing it back on the dresser, he ran a hand through his hair. He realized it could use a trim, but his former master had hated it long, and so Jason had decided to let it grow.

At least he no longer looked like what he'd been a year ago— a naive boy with his head up his ass. An idealist with dreams of glory.

Shaking off the thought, he jogged downstairs, wondering whether to ring Olivia's front doorbell or go to the back where they'd met yesterday. A quick glance out his patio door answered the question. His knockout neighbor was by her pool, setting a canopied table for two. Watching her, a weight lifted from his heart. No one had ever gone to any trouble to welcome him in friendship, see to his pleasure.

No one.

He hurried to meet her, crossing his deck and pushing through his gate. Unlatching hers, he stepped into the Quinns' sculpted yard and shut it behind him. She looked up, her warm smile matching his.

"Jason. I'm so glad you came." Her blue gaze swept him from head to toe, heating every spot it touched. "You look wonderful, and I swear you're a different man wearing that big smile."

"Well, you put it there," he said, closing the space between them. Taking her hand, he chanced a light kiss on her cheek. "Thank you for having me over."

"My pleasure."

The low, husky statement, rife with double meaning, trailed an invisible fingernail straight down his spine. Olivia hadn't objected to the slight contact. Wouldn't object to more, if his guess was correct. The idea snaked around his balls, stiffened his cock.

Pulling away, she gestured to the chair next to him. "Have a seat. I hope you like white wine and Caesar salad topped with grilled chicken. I don't normally eat a heavy lunch."

Slaves don't normally eat lunch at all.

Squashing the stray thought, he allowed himself to enjoy the moment. "The salad looks almost as delicious as my hostess." Jesus, he couldn't believe he'd said something so lame. He'd just compared a gorgeous woman to lettuce. Fucking idiot.

But she beamed at him, unaware of his fumbling. "Thanks, you're too sweet. Shall we?"

Sweet? No, he'd never been innocent in any way. Full of himself, carrying a load of misplaced confidence for which he was paying dearly? Oh yes. Undone, he poured the wine while she served their salads in ceramic bowls, and belatedly wished he'd thought to bring something for Olivia. A small token, like flowers. His social graces were lacking, since he'd been out of circulation for a while.

He speared some lettuce and chicken, took a bite. The flavors burst on his taste buds, a succulent delight. Would Liv taste even better?

"This is fantastic," he said, waving his fork at her. "You're quite a cook."

She took a sip of wine and nodded. "I appreciate the compliment, but the kudos really go to my head chef."

His brows shot up. "You employ a personal chef?"

"At my restaurant. I own Giancarlo's, on The Hill."

"Wow. Sexy *and* a savvy entrepreneur. Guess I won the neighbor lottery." He drank some of his wine, studying her with open curiosity. "I can tell by your voice how much pride you take in your restaurant. Must be nice to have something that's all yours, nurtured and thriving because of your efforts."

Now her smile was sad. "Sacrifice causes other things to fall by the wayside. People get left behind."

"One person in particular?"

"My husband, Alex," she said, confirming his suspicion.

Jason set aside his wineglass, laid his hand over hers. "Your work took over your life, and he became lonely." He was careful to keep accusation out of his tone.

"Yes. We've grown apart."

"Has he . . . cheated on you, Olivia?"

"He has now."

His chest ached for her. Empathy for another person was new to him, and he didn't like the way it hurt. But nothing could've prepared him for the shocker she delivered next.

"Alex only did what I urged him to do."

He blinked, unsure he'd heard right. "What?"

"My husband was on the verge of turning from me, so I took matters into my own hands. I made him a proposition he couldn't refuse. A high-stakes game in which we win or lose everything."

"How does it work?" Jason leaned forward, intrigued.

"Alex gets seven encounters with any lover he desires, but after each one he must confess to me in detail and accept whatever punishment I choose."

"My God, Olivia," he gasped. "But you get nothing from that arrangement!"

"Not true." Her blue eyes pinned his, and she hesitated. Speculating. Perhaps sizing up his reaction. "In return, I'll take any lover I wish. What's more, my lover and I can use Alex in every way, punish him together if we like."

Jesus Christ! His cock was hard and straining behind his zipper. He couldn't keep the hunger off his face if he tried. "And your husband agreed to all of this?"

"In a heartbeat." She sent him a sly grin, sadness replaced by determination. "He received his first punishment last night."

Olivia's frankness, the heat of her arousal, startled him. No small feat for a man who'd believed nothing else could surprise him. "You're not angry with him?"

"I was fully prepared to be," she admitted. "But when he began to describe the things they did . . . I got so caught up in imagining them together. Picturing my beautiful Alex sinking his cock into another lover. God, it turned me on like never before. By including me, we shared the experience together. There's no longer any reason to deny what we only used to fantasize about in bed."

Jason's own cock throbbed painfully. Before he could find his voice, she pulled her hand from his and slapped it against her cheek, eyes round.

"Listen to me. I can't believe I told you all of that. You must think we're both crazy. Or worse, sleazy pervs."

"Olivia, I know all about sleazy," he said quietly. "And trust me, two people trying to rekindle the spark to save their marriage by sharing mutual pleasure isn't it."

No, Olivia's bargain with her husband was incredibly erotic. Designed for pure, sensual bliss. This lovely lady had no idea what sleazy perverts really existed, and Jason hoped she never met any.

She reached out, ran a finger over his lower lip, studying him for a long moment. He held his breath, his body electrified by her delicate touch. He'd never known such a caress. Then she withdrew, retrieving her fork.

"Thank you," she said.

"Any time."

They finished their meal as Jason listened to his new friend describe Alex. His mouth watered as she painted a picture of a tall, blond Adonis with dancing green eyes. He'd known Alex was a smart defense lawyer with his own successful firm, but her accolades about the man's warm and caring personality, his charming magnetism, made him sound like a dream.

They'd been so happy once. Could be again. Jason found himself wishing to be a part of . . . what? What did he know of relationships, or happiness in any form?

"Want to take a dip in the pool?"

Warm and relaxed from the wine, he waggled his brows at her. "Your pool or mine?"

She laughed. "Mine. Race you."

She stood, untying the fringed wrap around her waist to reveal skimpy black bikini bottoms. In fact, the scrap of material hardly qualified as a bikini. More like a rectangular patch in front. As she turned to walk to the pool, he sucked in an appreciative breath at the thin string separating the perfect globes of her ass.

He shot to his feet, ready to follow, then frowned at himself. "Hey, I don't have a bathing suit."

"You certainly didn't need one last night," she reminded him with a grin, wading into the water. "I've already seen the package."

So she had. His erection wanted free. "That's not fair. You're covered. Mostly."

"Wear your underwear if you want."

He was wearing boxers, but those would look pretty ridiculous. Once they got wet, he might as well be naked. Nudity had never been one of his hang-ups, so whatever.

Shrugging, he undressed, leaving his shoes and clothing in a pile on his chair. Slowly, he strode to the pool's steps, aware of her hungry eyes devouring him. Letting her look at leisure. Serving the pleasure of others was a skill he'd learned well.

He joined her, the cool water swirling about his hips. Kept his hands at his sides, his submissive sexual nature so ingrained in his bone marrow that he was helpless to fight it.

Lips curving upward, she reached behind her back, untied the strings of the bikini top. Repeated the process at the nape of her neck. Peeling the wet fabric away, she revealed a pair of lush breasts, just full enough to fill his palms. Her rosy nipples were taut, begging for his hands. His mouth. He stared, unable to speak.

"You may touch me, Jason," she said hoarsely, tossing the top onto the pool's edge. "If you'd like."

It was the second part that shook him. He'd rarely been given the option of doing what *he'd* enjoy, and certainly not in the past year. She welcomed his attentions, but wouldn't force him.

Desire coursed through his blood, hot and thick. But caution stayed his hand. "Only if you're sure I won't open my door to find myself looking down the barrel of Alex's gun."

"If you're suddenly staring down the barrel of anything belonging to Alex, I assure you it won't be his gun."

Oh, shit!

Olivia clasped her arms around his neck, toyed with his hair. Her nipples brushed his chest, branding him. With a groan, he cupped her face in his hands and brought his mouth down on hers. Kissed her with all the pent-up hunger he normally held in reserve.

His tongue twined with hers as she pressed against him, slick and wet. He licked the roof of her mouth, behind her teeth. Sucked her tongue, holding her closer, backing her toward the side of the pool until she was against the wall.

His hands slid below the water to her waist and on to her slick, bare ass cheeks. He palmed them, lifting her, nestling her sex against his aching cock. Even through the thin fabric of her thong, he could feel her heat enveloping his dick. Making a sweet whimpering sound, she wrapped her legs around his waist, grinding into his cock.

He broke the kiss, panting, and slid his right hand between them. His fingers rubbed her tight little nub through the suit and she arched toward him, gasping.

"Please, Jason! I need . . ."

"Tell me," he rasped. Many had wanted him. Had taken him.

But nobody had ever *needed* him, much less said it as though he were their lifeline.

"I need you to fuck me! *Please.*"

"Ah, God."

Jason pushed aside the material, unable to wait even the few seconds it would take to remove her bottoms. Deftly, he parted her slit, bringing the head of his cock to her opening. Still, he paused. Gave her the opportunity to regain her senses. "Olivia, are you sure?"

"Fuck me, Jase," she whispered.

Grabbing her hips, he impaled her on his cock. Began to move in her scorching heat, marveling in the joy of being with someone who wanted him. Whom he wanted in return. The freedom to act on his desires, to please her—both of them—because he chose to do so.

"Ahh, God, yes! Liv . . . so goddamned good. So hot and tight."

He fucked her hard and deep, angling his thrusts so his cock brushed her clit with every stroke. Never, ever anything like this. A completion, like coming home. She had no idea what a great gift she'd given him, and the least he could do was make sure she received the best he had to give at the moment.

Faster, faster he pumped. Pounded into her until she tightened her legs around him, clutched at his hair. She cried out, her channel convulsing around his cock. The rippling sensation, proof of her wild pleasure, sent him over the edge. He stiffened, and with a shout released himself inside her. Pulsed on and on until they were both spent, clinging to one another, dripping wet.

Jason stayed buried inside her as they came down to earth

again. Placed gentle kisses on her lips, her nose. Christ, what a lady. Why did he feel so whole with her? Who knew he could enjoy sex with a woman so much?

Maybe it was just *this* woman.

"I've never been with anyone except my husband, until now."

Jason's heart plummeted to his toes. "I-I'm sorry. I didn't use protection, but I'm clean, I swear. I shouldn't have—"

Shaking her head, she pressed her fingers over his lips. "No. I'm just saying this is a special occasion to me, that's all. I don't believe I could've taken the plunge with just anyone, Jason. But when we met yesterday, I felt this . . . connection to you. That probably sounds stupid."

"No, it doesn't," he said, thrilling to her words. "I felt it, too." Didn't make sense, but there was the truth all the same.

She let out a deep breath, untangling her legs from his waist. Reluctantly, he withdrew, but didn't let her go.

Gazing at him in question, she ran her fingers down his cheek. "All of that stuff about my problems with Alex and our bargain . . . you're under no obligation to involve yourself with anything. This ends here if you want, no strings."

"What I want is to please you. Again and again."

"What if I told you I wanted you to stick around? To be a part of our bargain, see where it leads us?"

"Are you kidding? I can't wrap my brain around ending anything after a mind-blowing experience like this. Here. With *you*." He stroked her raven hair and looked helplessly into her lovely face, hardly able to comprehend the import of what he was saying.

Idiot! What the fuck are you doing? Hadn't he taken on enough trouble to last a lifetime?

"That's wonderful," she said, giving him a smile. "But I want you to think about this, okay? There's no rush."

But as Jason followed his lover from the pool, his lonely soul won the argument over his head. Hands down.

He'd already made his decision.

And he prayed it wouldn't be one that destroyed them all.

Four

✦

Alone in his big corner office, Alex stared out at the city of St. Louis. Darkness had descended, peppering the landscape with a trillion lights. The Arch, a masterpiece of architecture, beautifully lit beside the river a mile or so away, dominated the striking view.

Tonight he failed to muster his usual enthusiasm. The past few days had been sheer hell. Ken's verbal cheap shots were becoming downright nasty, and their colleagues were starting to notice. God knows he'd made a mistake in overlooking Brock, but he had to stand by his decision. As the boss, he couldn't second-guess himself or tolerate disrespect. Ken's behavior certainly qualified as unprofessional.

You should know, buddy.

To add to his misery, both of the women in his life had all but ignored him since Monday.

Liv had a brand-new sparkle in her eyes, a spring in her step. She was keeping a secret, and he wasn't stupid. The truth remained unspoken between them, but it was there just the same. She'd taken a lover, and the younger man obviously made her happy.

Last night as they ate dinner together at their special private table at her restaurant, he'd tried to broach the subject, but she'd cut him off. She'd give him details when she was ready. Not one second before.

Part of his agonizing punishment.

Yeah, it was working.

Two savvy women had his cock in a vise. Who was he to complain? Most guys would give their left nut to be in his position.

Behind him, the door to his office opened, closed. The lock turned with a soft snick. He swiveled in his chair, not surprised to see one of the objects of his lustful musings saunter toward him. Rising, he rounded his desk to meet Jenna.

Cool topaz fire seared him as she twined a hand behind his neck, toyed with a lock of hair. "Most everyone on the floor is gone."

"Is that right?"

She pulled him down, and he captured her mouth with his. He kissed her fiercely, with all the bottled-up passion of several frustrating days. He swept his tongue inside her moist heat, rasping behind her perfect teeth, the roof of her mouth. She tasted sweet, as though she'd recently eaten fruit. He longed for her to eat him instead, and to return the favor.

"God, Jenna, I've missed you," he whispered, going for the buttons on her green blouse. "I need you."

"Ooh, bad boy." She took over, tossing her shirt and bra in the direction of his plush sofa. Her breasts, high and firm, beckoned. "What will your lovely wife have to say?"

"Not much, I suspect, with her own bad boy's cock between her lips."

Jenna's gaze widened in amazement—and delight. "How juicy, and how convenient for all of us. Are you both operating on the sly?"

Reaching around her waist, he unzipped her dark skirt, peeled the material down. He shook his head. "No. We have no secrets. Olivia and I have a new arrangement. Short story, we can fuck whoever we wish."

"An open marriage." She stepped out of the skirt, kicked off her black heels. "Your idea?"

"Hers. She saw us together at the pool party and realized I'd been miserable for a long time." He cupped her breasts, pinched the sweet little nipples to tight peaks. "Seeing us kissing turned her on, sweetheart. Besides, like you, she was smart enough to know I was going to cave soon. You were both right."

"Everybody wins. Mmm, I like that."

He wouldn't tell Jenna about the rest of the bargain. She'd gotten what she wanted—him—so what did it matter?

Moving around behind her, he gestured to his desk. "Brace your hands on the edge and spread your legs for me." She did, and his hard-on twitched at the sight of wild red curls tumbling down her back. "Lean over more; stick that pretty ass out. Feet farther apart. That's it."

He knelt between her spread thighs, parted her ass. Wetting one finger, he began to massage the tiny, puckered entrance. A low, feminine moan greeted his attentions as he circled, worked the finger into her anus, slow and easy.

"Relax, open for me. Let me make you feel good, baby."

Angling his head, he nuzzled her damp sex. Flicked her slit with his tongue, loving that she kept the folds shaved bare, only a neat triangle at the apex of her thighs. Her luscious mound was slick and ready, the contact of his tongue on her naked pussy electric, shooting to his cock.

"Oooh, Alex!"

He plunged his finger into her hole, working her as he began to nibble and lick. Slowly, he laved her clit, circling the nub, then between the lips of her sex. Plunged his tongue into her as deeply as possible, fucking both entrances.

She spread her legs even more, arching into him, the helpless mewling noises in her throat making him chuckle darkly. His controlling, self-assured Jenna, coming undone. Fastening his mouth to her clit, he ate her. Without mercy. Deep and hard, until she writhed above his mouth, cream flowing down his throat.

"Oh, shit, Alex! Yes!"

Standing, he unzipped his pants, freed his straining cock. This wasn't going to last long. Christ, he needed to be inside her. Placing one hand between her shoulder blades, he gave her a gentle push toward his desk. Obeying the silent order, she bent at the waist and laid her upper body atop the surface. Totally exposed and ready to receive him.

"Fuck me!" she cried.

He nudged with the head of his cock, parting her soaking pussy lips. "You want this, sweetheart?"

"Now, please!"

He slammed into Jenna so hard and fast, they gasped together. He stayed buried to the hilt for a moment, reveling in her sheath hugging his rod, locking him in her very core. Amazing. Erotic. How had he lived without this?

Gripping her slim hips, he began to shaft her. "You wanted

my cock? Now you own it. Every inch, yours whenever and however you desire, baby."

"Damned right." She rocked back into him, meeting his thrusts.

How did he get so goddamned lucky? *Liv.*

Thank God for Liv. His wife and their new lovers would receive all the attention they needed. The best of both worlds for everyone. He'd make sure of it.

To know Liv was experiencing this high with her young stud gave him untold satisfaction. Made him hot as freaking hell.

He fucked Jenna faster, loving the slap of their bodies, his balls bouncing against her sex. Driving them toward the pinnacle, spinning out of control.

Alex's body spasmed. He exploded with a hoarse shout, coming deep inside her. She screamed and her channel began to clench, warm honey flooding his cock, bathing him. She milked him dry and still he remained there, never wanting to leave.

Finally he had to, and pulled out with regret. Jenna turned into his arms and he pressed his lips to hers in a brief kiss.

"Christ, I love fucking you," he murmured.

"Becoming addicted?"

"Oh yeah."

"You ain't seen nothing yet, tiger." She smiled, the strange gleam back in her eyes. "Whoops, the Boardman file is at home again."

His rampant libido drowned out whatever warning his brain might've latched on to. "Who are we to let our work slide?"

"Let me fix myself and grab something from my office." Quickly, she dressed, then sent him a seductive smile. "Be right back."

Yanking up his pants, he watched her sashay from his office. Confident. Cool. She was a viper, and he knew it.

But the danger only added to the allure.

The call of the forbidden.

A ghost of a whisper chilled his skin, a sudden foreboding curling through his gut. Stabbing him with unreasonable fear.

Annoyed, he shoved the ominous feeling aside. Residual guilt, nothing more. He and Liv deserved to find themselves—and each other—again. To share in their sexual reawakening.

Tonight, he'd give his second confession.

But it was his punishment he anticipated most of all.

. . .

The watcher quickly slipped into an empty office and closed the door, crossing to the phone on the desk. His dick still throbbed from listening, imagining Alex's big cock working Jenna the bitch until she screamed. They made an extraordinary couple, and Alex was an okay guy. It almost made him regret the call he had to make.

Almost.

At the first ring, Palmer picked up. "I'm in a bad fucking mood, so make it good. Have you found Seraph?"

He braced himself. "No, we don't have anything new. It's like the goddamned earth swallowed him."

"Not what I want to hear." His even tone belied his ruthlessness. "I don't appreciate loose ends."

He was glad the bastard was several states away. Not that Palmer couldn't reach him if he wanted. His network was extensive and deadly. "We'll find him. Soon."

"What about Quinn? Do you finally have him by his obviously delectable cock?"

"He's ours now. All is going according to plan ... except for one minor problem," he said, nervously wiping a bead of sweat from his temple. "We can't blackmail him anymore. Not for infidelity."

His boss's reply was lethally quiet. "Why not?"

"Quinn and his wife now have an open marriage. I heard it with my own ears."

"Fine, revert to plan B. Kill him."

His blood ran cold. Sure, he was an opportunist. But murder?

"We can't do him too quickly or everyone will suspect. Most of them figure he's been checking his little slut's temperature since the pool party. They might wonder—"

"Need I remind you we're working against the clock? Quinn is a genius in the courtroom. He has to be out of the way before the trial. Make it happen."

Pompous son of a bitch. Boardman would go to prison and Alex would die so Palmer's hands could remain clean and he would be free to ply his evil trade.

"I understand. But it can't happen overnight," he said, stomach curdling in dread. "We need time to make it look like a tragic accident or suicide. He and his wife are struggling, and now that he's strayed, open marriage or not, it shouldn't be too hard."

The monster chuckled, apparently pleased. "Poor bastard caves under the pressure, takes his own life. Or becomes so distraught, his car plummets into the Mississippi." He paused, the silence heavy. Measuring. "Or perhaps his own wife has him murdered in a fit of jealous rage, and *soon*. No jury alive will buy her claim of condoning his affair after he's been brutally slain. Understand?"

"Yes. The possibilities are endless," he agreed coldly, masking the sickness assaulting him in waves.

"Excellent. You have two weeks to conclude this unpleasantness. Don't disappoint me."

Palmer disconnected, and the watcher replaced the phone with a trembling hand. Resolved, he steeled himself against feeling anything for their unsuspecting victim. To save their own hides, they'd do this. They had no choice.

In a few short days, Alexander Quinn would die.

. . .

Olivia paced, waiting for the sound of Alex's Jag in the driveway. Caught in the exquisite hell of wondering what tale he'd have to tell tonight, and whether he was still as excited as she about the sharing.

What if he began to leave out details? To keep secrets? If so, this plan would fail right along with their marriage.

Don't think like that, or you're sunk.

Their communication and mutual pleasure would remain intact. The alternative didn't bear considering.

Headlights cutting through the living room, the hum of the garage door ended the agonizing wait. Thank God.

She steeled herself as the door leading into the kitchen from the garage opened and clicked shut. In a moment, Alex appeared in the living room and paused, meeting her gaze. He looked beautifully disheveled, and not quite as unsure as before.

Giving her a tentative smile, he laid his tie, jacket, and briefcase on a wingback chair. "Did you . . . enjoy yourself tonight, as well?"

"These are your confessions, not mine," she admonished softly. In truth, despite her sly teasing, she hadn't seen Jason since their rather steamy lunch encounter, had no idea what he'd been up to. Alex didn't know that. She saw no reason why he should.

"True," he agreed easily, though his green eyes flashed with dangerous emotion. Desire? Jealousy?

"You're much earlier tonight," she remarked, waving a hand at the wall clock as she led him upstairs. "It's barely past ten thirty."

"I learned my lesson about excessive tardiness the first time." Wry humor colored his voice.

"You're more at ease with our arrangement, I see."

"I'm not sure *at ease* is the right way to put it," he mused. "Maybe less nervous, less . . . trapped. Isn't that how I'm supposed to feel?"

Trapped. That was never a word she'd heard Alex use before, and it made her shudder. "Don't hedge your answer. Tell me."

In their bedroom, she turned to face him. He stood staring at her, unwavering, and she knew by his expression he was searching for the most honest response.

"For the first time in years, I'm free to be my own man. I'm someone in my own right again, outside of these four walls. Outside of *us*," he said quietly.

Why did the most necessary self-realizations have to be so god-damned painful? Her expression must've exposed her turmoil, because he closed the distance between them, cupped her face in his hands.

"That doesn't mean I'm excluding you now, or loving you less." Trailing a finger down her throat, he nudged aside the silk of her robe, brushed the swell of her breast. "No, I love you more than ever. She'll never hear confidences from my lips; that right belongs only to you. I might slide my cock deep inside her, fuck her for hours, but that's all she'll ever have of me."

Her womb clenched, moisture gathering in her pussy. "I think she has a stronger hold on you than you realize, Alex."

"You believe I'm obsessed?"

Interesting word choice. "Perhaps. Are you?" She waited, holding her breath as he struggled with his truth. Glanced away.

"She takes me somewhere I never thought I'd dare to go. Someplace dark. Dangerous."

"And you want to go there, don't you?"

"Yes," he admitted, closing his eyes. "God, Liv, you're right. It's more than sex when I'm with her."

"But not love?" she pressed. *Anything except that.*

Opening his eyes, he shook his head, expression firm. "No. It's a game of power. Control. One I'm not sure I want to win. I've never allowed myself to be led astray, and I like it. I'm tired of being a fucking saint."

"Thank goodness you don't have to be, then. However, there is the matter of your confession," she reminded him with a small smile.

"And punishment." He perked up in anticipation.

She laughed at his eagerness. "That, too. All right, get naked; then let's relax on the bed while you talk."

"No cuffs or whips tonight?" He began to undress.

"You sound disappointed."

"Hmm, I think I am."

"Good. Keeps you guessing. Lie down on your back." Slipping off her robe, she joined Alex in bed. His head was propped on his pillows, his muscled body sprawled next to her. "You smell like sex."

His jaw clenched, and he kept his gaze straight ahead. "I'm sorry, Mistress. I can shower before—"

"No. Hiding behind niceties would only defeat the purpose." She studied him, pleased he was already into his role. "You may begin."

He inhaled a deep breath. "Well, I hadn't seen her since Monday. We've been busy on the Boardman defense, not to mention several other pressing cases. It's been crazy."

"Wait a minute." Liv frowned. "Jenna's working with you on Henry Boardman's trial?" Had Alex ever told her that specifically? If so, she didn't recall, but she didn't think he had.

"Yes, she is. Why?" His expression was pinched, voice tight. A bit defensive.

"That's a huge, high-profile criminal case, Alex. Not something you'd normally allow a junior partner to be involved in, especially one who's been at Quinn and Quinn only a few months."

Red flags tinged his cheekbones. "Jenna came highly recommended, and she's proven herself a valuable asset to the firm in a short period of time."

I'll just bet she has. Wasn't the first time the boss's little head had done the thinking.

"And everyone is *okay* with this?"

"Other than Ken, who's ready to punch my lights out?" He gave a self-deprecating laugh. "Sure, everyone's peachy."

She winced. "I guess that explains why Ken didn't show at our pool party."

"I'd say so."

Well, that was understandable. Ken had been with the firm for many years, had won many important trials. Still, something about this whole thing bothered her a great deal. Unease itched under her skin, more than Alex simply being a vulnerable man who'd given in to the luscious new employee.

Shaking her head, she brushed the shadow aside.

"Never mind work for now. Go on with your confession."

"Okay." He sighed, made a visible effort to relax. Her questioning had obviously put him on edge. "Anyway, Jenna came to my office after most everyone was gone. I had her face my desk and spread her legs. Then I knelt behind her and ate her while I used a finger to work her little hole."

"Did you make her come?"

"Yeah. Afterward, I bent her over my desk and fucked her pussy from behind. Cliché, I know, but I've always wanted to do that—take a lover in my office."

The portrait he painted sent tiny shivers of arousal skittering to her sex. "You and I have made love in your office," she reminded him. "But I know what you mean. So, did you take her home?"

"She had her own car back from her sister, but I followed. God, I'd just had her and I was already hard again."

"Tell me, honey," she whispered, stroking his chest. His cock stirred at the order. "Take me there."

"I made the drive to Jenna's place in half the time it had taken before...."

Liv's desire matched her husband's, his hushed confession winding a strange bond between them as his tale unfolded.

• • •

Their hastily discarded clothing trailed to her bedroom. Jenna had instructed him to relax while she fixed them something cool to drink. He reclined on her bed, his erection rapidly recovering from their office tryst.

In less than five minutes, she returned with two glasses. "Wine for me, Jack and cola for you."

"My favorite. How did you know?"

"I pay attention to the details, love. You're a man who prefers his alcohol with more . . . kick."

"Thanks." Taking the glass, he gave her a kiss, then downed several swallows. "Oh, that's damned good."

"Glad you approve. Have another sip, then close your eyes. Let me help you get rid of the tension of the day, my darling."

"Sounds like a fine idea." He took another draw of his drink and set the half-empty glass on the nightstand. Lying back, he closed his eyes. Felt his bones melt into the mattress.

Absent were the guilt and inhibitions of just days before. His brain had fuzzed pleasantly from the drink, limbs relaxed, his soul lighter than it had been in years.

"Comfortable, Alex?"

"God, yes." His lips tilted up. His brain processed her words, but he felt as though he were floating. Drifting in a sea of erotic desire. Eager for whatever dark plans she had for him, unable to prevent whatever was about to happen even if he wanted to. Strange.

"Look at me, Alex," she commanded.

With an effort, he pried his eyes open, but couldn't focus on her face. He raised a hand to touch her cheek, his arm heavy. He had little control over his body, had become nothing but the white-hot cock jutting between his legs. A blaze of need.

Jenna smiled, satisfied. Knowing. "Good. You're ready."

Comprehension stunned him. "What did you put in my drink?"

"Why, nothing! Don't you feel well?"

She seemed sincere. Concerned. "Yes, but Jenna . . ." Fear warred with the fire sweeping his body.

"Perhaps you're tired, and the alcohol didn't help."

"Maybe."

She traced his lips with one finger, her voice seductive. "You said I own your cock now. Every inch, however and whenever I desire . . . unless you lied to me."

He blinked up at her, the declaration he'd made in a moment of passion haunting him. Getting in deeper, no way out. Because he'd meant every word.

"No, I wasn't lying."

"Tell me again." Jenna leaned over, breasts crushing against his chest. Flicking her little pink tongue, she licked the path her fingers had traced over his lips, slowly.

"When we're together, I'm yours to use whenever and however you wish," he whispered, erection straining.

"*When we're together?* I'm not sure I like the qualifier."

"I love my wife, and I won't leave her. I've made that clear." Thank God his brain was still working well enough to remind Jenna, and himself.

"You also claimed we wouldn't be together after the first time, yet here you are." Gaze feral, she licked a taut male nipple. "Fine, for now. During our trysts, your body is my toy. I have your full consent to do anything I want." A demand, not a question.

"Yes, anything."

Smug, she tossed her glorious hair. "Could get dangerous for you. Make absolutely certain you understand what *anything* means."

Dangerous. Christ, the temptation of the unknown was too great to resist.

"I could hurt you." Reaching between them, she rubbed his cock. "Or worse. You can walk away."

"You know damned well I won't." For months, he'd longed to place himself in Jenna's capable hands. Tread the razor's edge.

"Excellent." Sitting up, she retrieved his glass from the nightstand, held the rim to his mouth. "Drink the rest."

Shaking in anticipation, he complied. The bittersweet drink poured down his throat, cool and soothing. He wondered whether she'd lied, if it contained an aphrodisiac, and shuddered. Did it matter?

He was at her mercy, right where he wanted to be.

Jenna took the glass and pushed him onto his back. His brain whirled, his entire body throbbed as she opened a drawer beside the bed and removed three black scarves. Quickly, she spread his arms, bound his wrists tightly to the bedposts. Next, she grabbed a spare pillow.

"Raise your hips."

He did, and she slid the pillow underneath, raising him into a vulnerable position. "What are you doing?"

"Looks like I'll have to make use of this." With brisk efficiency, she placed the third scarf between his teeth and knotted it behind his head. "My God, you look delicious all tied up, ready for whatever I want to do to you."

Breathing hard around the gag, he trembled in anticipation, his dick pointed at the ceiling. She bent over his chest, grazed one brown nipple to a peak with her teeth, teased it with her tongue. Then the other, making him squirm.

She reached over to the nightstand and opened a drawer. He turned his head to see her remove two small clamps. Realizing her intent, his eyes widened. He shook his head, a sound of distress emerging from his throat. She smiled.

"You're mine. Yell all you want; nobody will hear you."

With that, she took a clamp, opened the serrated jaws, and sprung one onto his right nipple.

"Ahhh!" The wicked little device hurt like a bastard. From the pain, however, came the rush similar to what he'd felt when Liv had flogged his balls and cock. The need.

"Why, Alex Quinn," she breathed in approval, arching one slender eyebrow, "you're a pain slut. Who knew?"

Certainly not him, until a few days ago. Helpless, he watched her clamp the second one onto his other tit, and yelled again. She was right; no one could hear his muffled distress, and the fact ramped up his arousal to unbearable levels. His cock was flushed, the slit dripping pre-cum.

"Don't you dare go off. I'm not anywhere near finished."

She fished in the drawer again and emerged with a monstrous rubber cock that made his butt cheeks clench in self-defense. Holy shit! He'd never seen anything like it. If she put that thing all the way inside him, she'd probably stab his heart.

A bottle of oil came from the drawer next. Jenna crawled between his spread thighs with her treasures, grinning. Flipping open the cap, she squirted some of the clear liquid into her palm. The scent of vanilla reached his nose, and for some reason, the tension left his body.

Maybe it was the scent. Or the sensual glide of her hands as they manipulated his balls, squeezing, caressing. Or perhaps it was her softly spoken command to raise his legs and bend his knees, thus opening himself fully to her, which he did.

Suddenly, he felt completely wanton. Filled with lust, overwhelmed by the desire to submit to her. To give his body to another as he never had before, even to Liv. To enjoy dark pleasures with an illicit lover.

With Jenna.

"You're mine."

Yes. He could only affirm her words by letting his legs fall open. He raised his hips, affirming her total control. Giving himself over to her.

"That's it, baby," she crooned, rimming his hole. Coating the entrance in slick lube, she slid one finger past the taut ring. Pushed in, nice and slow.

His channel stung a bit, felt strange at first. The weirdness fast gave way to wondrous sensation. It felt good, and he wanted more.

His moan resulted in a husky laugh from his lover. She added a second finger, stretching him. The extra width burned, snaking tendrils of heat around his groin. *Jesus, yes!*

After a few strokes, she removed her fingers. Dazed, he looked to see her still kneeling between his legs, slicking the big phallus with oil. The intensity of how badly he wanted what she had planned shocked him.

He didn't have long to wait. Parting his cheeks, she nudged the broad head against his opening. Began to push. Slow and steady, she inched the phallus past his resisting muscles. Christ, it hurt. Sweat trickled down his face, and he began to shake.

"Easy. I wish you could see how hot you look with this cock impaling your ass, my love. You're doing fine. Just let it happen."

He embraced the agony. Breathed through it, concentrated on the eroticism of her owning his body. Gradually, as the phallus slid deeper, the pain dissipated. Pleasure unfurled in his abdomen, bled to his limbs, his cock. Became unbelievable, indescribable ecstasy.

"There, it's all the way in. You took it like a champ," she declared, smiling. Tipping the bottle, she dribbled some of the oil over his aching cock. She closed her fingers around his shaft, coating him. "This is mine, love. *You're* mine. Do you understand?"

He nodded, knowing he'd agree to anything at this point.

"Good, because I'm going to fuck you. I'm going to use you like I promised, and there isn't a damned thing you can do to stop me. Know what will happen when I do?"

He hesitated.

"While I ride you, that big dildo in your ass is going to set off fireworks, that's what. When it rubs your sweet spot, you'll explode like the Fourth of July."

All it would take was one stroke, he knew. He was already so close, his resistance in tatters.

Straddling his hips, she brought the flared head of his penis to her sex and lowered herself onto his lap. The dual stimulation of her hot pussy squeezing his cock and the phallus rubbing his channel rolled his eyes clear back in his head.

Bracing her palms on his chest, she began to fuck him in earnest. He closed his eyes, dimly aware of the hoarse groans erupting from his throat. Oh, this was so goddamned good. He was drowning in pure bliss. Never wanted it to end.

Then the cock buried in his ass hit a magic button.

With a strangled cry, he bucked, his entire body detonating like an atom bomb. Helpless, he thrust into his lover, swept away on a red tide. His hips undulated wildly, bright colors bursting behind his eyelids, cum spurting in a glorious fountain. On and on, until he lay panting, trembling like a racehorse. After a couple of minutes, she removed the gag and flung it aside.

"Holy freaking shit," he gasped, opening his eyes. Jenna lay spent, draped over his chest. And, apparently, quite satisfied.

"Jesus, Alex. I do believe the heart of a very naughty boy beats in that nice chest of yours."

"I aim to please." He wiggled his hips for emphasis, making her laugh.

"You could've had quite a rosy future as a sex slave, you know."

Her matter-of-fact tone gave him pause. "What makes you say that?"

Jenna slid off him, giving him an amused look. "Hel-loo. Teasing here. We're working on the defense in a sex slavery case, remember?"

"Oh. Sure."

"I can see we need to work on relaxing you more often. Get rid of all the stress you're toting around." She eased the phallus out of him, chuckling when he grimaced in discomfort.

"You're right," he said, as she untied his wrists.

"You work too hard."

"And you're my self-appointed therapist?"

"That's right . . . and don't you forget it."

. . .

"I got dressed and came home right afterward," Alex said, ending his recounting.

Liv's clit pulsed in the aftermath of her husband's erotic tale. She should be upset—no, enraged—to hear of Alex's scorching evening with his lover. To learn this woman had met a need Liv never knew Alex had hidden, even from himself.

She wasn't.

Their sharing was working. Performing CPR on a sex life gasping for its last breath. Alex's erection lay against one thigh, irrefutable proof of her theory, along with the smoldering desire in his jewel green eyes.

"Are you going to punish me, Mistress?"

"Oh yes. I've given this careful consideration." She went on, carefully gauging his reaction. "I want you to know my lover's name is Jason. He's young and extremely hot, and he fucks like a dream. That's all you're going to get from me, dear Alex. I dare you to try and sleep tonight knowing only that much and nothing more."

His pupils dilated, cock twitching. "Jesus Christ, Liv."

"One last thing—no matter how badly you need to come while lying there picturing my sexy Jason sinking his cock into me, you're not allowed. Not tonight."

Clearly in pain, he swiped a hand down his face. "I signed up for this, didn't I?"

Leaning over him, she brushed his lips in a gentle kiss.

"Yes, my adventurous husband. You certainly did."

Five

✦

On Friday, Alex dragged his exhausted, sore ass into work. Tired as he'd been after coming home from Jenna's, he'd hardly slept a wink. Imagining Liv with this Jason guy had almost driven him insane with lust. And yeah, the hard bite of jealousy. Once, he'd attempted to catch his wife off guard after she drifted off to sleep, his roaming hand creeping around her to tease her nipples. Lower, rubbing her mound through the silky panties.

At first she'd responded, turning into him to kiss the curve of his neck the way he loved. Once she'd come fully awake, however, she pulled away, declaring the punishment for his next confession would be doubled. Feeling bereft, he'd rolled over and let her be. He'd only wanted to love his wife.

No complaints, though. He was a lucky man.

"Hey, buddy, what's up? I haven't seen much of you this week."

Swiveling in his office chair, Alex shot a wan smile to Kyle Murphy, his colleague and good friend of the past several years. "Impeccable timing, as usual."

"Damn, Alex. You look like something the cat hawked up. What gives?"

"And charming, as always."

"You're not paying me to be charming . . . well, actually, you are. Scratch that."

Kyle sprawled his lean frame in a chair across from Alex's desk, steepling his fingers. His brown eyes pinned Alex with his best Do Not Bullshit Me look, his thin, attractive mug pulled into a frown. "In all the years I've known you, I've never seen our fearless leader slouch in here looking like a used crash-test dummy. Spill." His friend knew him well.

Not well enough to see through his lie, he hoped. "I've got the caseload and client list from hell right now. You know how it is. Maybe I ought to delegate more, huh?"

"Uh-huh. And I suppose your ragged state has nothing to do with Jenna Shaw stalking you like a starving lioness on the Serengeti?"

Belatedly, Alex glanced toward the door, relieved to see his friend had closed it. "No, it doesn't."

Kyle snorted. "Come on, man, this is *me*. I saw you guys groping each other at your pool party. Stumbled on you purely by accident, of course. Now Ken's storming around here, snarling at everybody who looks at him cross-eyed, and considering how the three of you have been acting the last few days? The conclusion ain't such a stretch, ya think?"

Alex opened his mouth. Closed it. Kyle hooted with laughter, getting a kick out of his predicament. Goddammit, he'd hesitated too long and blown it!

"Ho, boy! You're a real piece of work, you know that? A knock-out wife and some hot pussy on the side. Better pray Olivia doesn't find out. Your finances—or worse, your balls—will be toast by the time she's done with you."

There was his opening. The opportunity to set his friend straight, and sure, maybe brag a bit about the arrangement of every man's dreams. Something stilled his tongue, though. This wasn't any of Kyle's biz, friend or not.

"Good advice. I'll keep that in mind."

Kyle stood, shaking his head. "Fuckin' A. Sucks to be you, huh? Call me if you need an alibi. Or a place to nurse your wounds when the wife throws you out. It's the least I can do to repay the loan you gave me."

"Thanks. Kyle . . . do you need any more money?"

He paused, hand on the knob. For one split second, his friend's expression was stricken. Then the impression vanished as though Alex had imagined it. "No, no. I'm good."

"All right. And buddy?"

"Yeah?"

"Let's keep this thing with Jenna between us, okay?"

Kyle stared back at him. When he answered, his voice was quiet. "When have I ever given up your secrets, Alex?"

Alex's troubled gaze remained on the open door long after his friend left.

Kyle's comment hung over him like a shroud for the rest of the day.

.   .   .

"What the hell are you doing up there?"

The irritated male bark nearly sent Olivia tumbling from her perch. Twisting her position awkwardly to peer under her raised arms, she spied Jason standing at the foot of her ladder, a worried scowl on his face.

And scrumptious enough to eat, too. He wore a pair of swim trunks and nothing else.

"Honestly, you scared the crap out of me! What does it look like I'm doing?"

"Trying to break your neck?"

"I'm going to fill this bird feeder, thank you very much. It's empty, and I enjoy watching them." She turned to study the problem again. Alex usually filled it and the feeder was hung on the tree branch within his reach, not hers. Drat it, she couldn't quite get it off the hook.

"The vast majority of accidents occur in the home," Jason informed her.

"I'm not in the home, I'm outside."

"Smart-ass, you know what I mean. Get down from there *now*."

"Ooh, have a bossy side, do we?"

"When I need to, yes. Olivia—"

"All right, keep your shorts on." Starting down the ladder, she waggled her eyebrows at him over her shoulder. "Or perhaps not."

His amused rumble tickled every female hormone in her body as he took her arm, helping her down. He waved a hand at his lower half. "What, you don't like my new threads?"

"Depends," she said, wiping her hands on her khaki shorts. "Does this mean you've given up skinny-dipping?"

He grinned. "Of course not, but a guy can't walk around naked *all* the time."

"Pity." Damn, the man was adorable. All male, and maybe a bit older than she'd first believed.

"Let me get that," he said, indicating the feeder.

In two minutes, Jason had the thing down, filled with seed and hung in place again. She took advantage of ogling his fine backside. The way his trunks were slung low on his hips, the material hugging his tight ass. The muscles in his lean back flexing and bunching . . . exactly the way they would when he drove into his lover.

Finished, he stowed the bag of seed and the ladder in the garage and returned, his gaze devouring her from head to toe.

"I finally made it to the store. Thought I'd come over and ask if you'd like to sit on my patio and share a bottle of wine," he said, his voice low and sensual.

The invitation, both spoken and implied, enveloped her in a fog of need. Not just sexual, but for closeness. Companionship. As necessary as it had seemed, turning down Alex last night had left her feeling out of sorts. Lonely.

Well, Alex sure wasn't lonely these days, and she saw no reason why she should be, either.

"I'd like that very much."

Jason held out his hand, and she took it. His grip was warm and strong, and he smelled fantastic. Spicy with a hint of manly aftershave, a scent that never failed to drive her wild.

Next door, he led her to a pair of loungers. In between, on a small, round glass table were two wineglasses. "Get comfortable, and I'll be right back."

"Pretty sure of my answer, were you?" she teased.

"Hopeful," he corrected, ducking his head with a shy smile. He disappeared, returning in moments with a bottle and opener. "Is Merlot okay with you?"

"Wonderful." He wriggled out the cork and poured, handing

her a glass. She took a sip, enjoying the rich, dark flavor. "Mmm, that's great."

"And much needed after the week I've had." He settled in his lounger with his own glass, taking a deep draw of wine, then resting it on his thigh. "I'm done with the lawyers, thank God. Talk about an exercise in frustration!"

"Tell me about it," she commiserated, trying to keep a straight face. "Alex is a lawyer."

"Well, shit. Stuck my foot right in it, didn't I?" He made a face.

She giggled. "I couldn't resist. Believe me, Alex has heard all the jokes. He's a damned fine criminal defense attorney, but sometimes when he tells people, by the way they react, you'd think he told them he's a drug lord instead."

"I didn't mean to sound like that. It's been a tough week dealing with my uncle's estate, cleaning his stuff out of the house. God, listen to me—I'm whining."

"You're entitled. It's an awful, sad task for one person to face," she said softly. "If you'd like help with the rest, I'd be glad to lend a hand."

"You have no idea how much the offer means to me," he replied, lips curving upward. "I've about got it licked, but thanks. Now I can simply bask in my lovely neighbor's company. Did you think I'd changed my mind about participating in you and your husband's . . . adventure?"

She took another sip of wine, eyeing him over the top of her glass. "The thought occurred to me. Change of heart?"

"No. You?"

"Absolutely not. I can't wait for you to meet Alex." She bit her lip, wondering how delicate to be in broaching the particulars. "Why don't you tell me your preferences? I don't want there to be any misunderstandings about what gives you pleasure."

He grinned, her concern seeming to make him happy. "I've always preferred men. Though recently, I've discovered the joy to be found in being with a gorgeous, passionate woman. I'm a natural submissive, and there isn't much I won't do."

"Wow, you're almost too perfect. What's the catch? Are you a wanted criminal or something?"

His humor slipped, face paling. "Sorry?"

"Kidding, Jase." Wary, she noted the fear in his brown eyes. "Jeez, you're not on the run, are you?"

He paused, looked away. "From a rather bad breakup, Olivia, but not from the law," he whispered. "I swear it to you."

His statement held the ring of truth. Reaching over, she patted his bare shoulder in sympathy. "I'm sorry. Want to talk about it?"

"I can't yet. I hope you understand."

"Of course I do. I'm here whenever you need me."

"Thanks, I—"

Whatever he'd been about to say was interrupted by the sound of a car pulling into the driveway next door. Alex's car! She couldn't recall when he'd last come home early on a Friday afternoon, and said so to Jason, who sent her a mischievous smile.

"Looks like the day just got more intriguing. Good thing I have plenty of wine."

.   .   .

Alex climbed out of the car, tired and annoyed. Liv had left the three-car garage wide open, an invite for burglars to help themselves. Dammit to hell.

He almost turned back for his briefcase before remembering he'd left it at the office, on purpose for a rare change. He'd canceled his last two appointments on the way out the door and given his delighted secretary the rest of the afternoon off, as well.

He had no idea whether Jenna was in her office, and hadn't sought her out. For some reason, getting out of there without seeing her was important to him. Oh, he wasn't afraid of raising eyebrows. He was fucking her, and that was his and Jenna's business.

Rather, he needed Jenna to know he wasn't sitting around like a lapdog, waiting obediently for her to pat him on the head. So to speak.

Whatever. His mood bordered on homicidal as he strode inside, yelling for Liv. Silence answered, so he jogged upstairs. Their bedroom stood empty, as well, and he frowned in puzzlement. Her car was here, the garage open. Where else could she be?

Ordering himself not to panic, he pushed outside, onto the balcony. . . . And spotted her. Next door, on Bill's patio. Relaxing and drinking wine with a nearly naked man who, he had a sneaking suspicion, was Jason the Superstud.

Fan-fucking-tastic.

In his current foul mood, he was sorely tempted to head back inside and sulk. Alone. But he found himself drawn to the cozy scene below. Liv and the man appeared completely at ease. They must've heard his car, too. If they'd wanted to exclude him, they'd have gone into the house.

On impulse, he called out, "Hello! Is that a private party, or can anyone join?"

They turned as one, smiling up at the balcony as if they'd been waiting for him to make a move.

"Hey, sweetie!" Liv called back. "Put on something comfortable and come on down!"

"All right, give me a minute." Noting the other man's tanned, toned body clad in nothing except swim trunks, Alex didn't have to debate too much about what to wear.

He donned his own trunks, forgoing a shirt or shoes. He wasn't twenty-something anymore, but he kept himself in shape. He couldn't avoid getting older, but at least his wife didn't have to be ashamed of his physical appearance.

Energized now, he hurried downstairs and outside, across his back lawn and through the gate. At the new neighbor's gate, he hesitated, battling an unwanted case of nerves. What the fuck did he have to be nervous about?

Unlatching the gate, he pushed inside. Liv turned, obviously glad to see him, a sight for sore eyes in a pair of cute khaki shorts and a black tank top matching her loose hair. The man rose from his lounger, setting his glass of wine on the table. He started toward Alex, beaming a genuine, welcoming smile. . . . And the world stopped.

Alex's breath caught in his throat. The guy was young, fit, all tawny skin and lean muscle. Shoulder-length brown hair streaked from the sun, huge brown eyes. A walking wet dream for anybody's fantasies, man or woman.

He was, by far, the most striking man Alex had ever seen.

The kid stuck out his hand, which Alex automatically shook. "Jason Strickland," he said. "Bill's nephew."

"Alex Quinn, Liv's husband. I, um, took off a bit early today." Duh.

Jason nodded in understanding. "Had all you could take for one week, huh?"

"And then some." The young man still hadn't let go of his hand. A jolt of sexual awareness hit him in the center of the chest and shot straight to his groin. Jesus, he'd never had such a strong reaction to another man before! He shifted and gently tugged his hand from Jason's grip, hoping his burgeoning erection hadn't been noticed.

If it had, no one let on. Instead, Jason played the gracious host, fetching another wineglass from the kitchen, pouring a healthy amount for Alex, and then dragging over another lounger. They rearranged themselves in a semicircle so they wouldn't have to lean over and talk across one another. Alex was glad, because it gave him the chance to study Jason and Liv at the same time.

"So, Jason, what do you do?"

The question was a typical, harmless icebreaker, but it clearly took his new neighbor by surprise. From the way Liv's curious gaze snapped to the younger man, she was interested in the answer, too.

"I . . . nothing much, at the moment," he hedged. "I was telling Olivia that I'm here recouping from a bad breakup. I'm planning to take it easy for a while, get my bearings. Decide whether I'll stay in St. Louis or not."

Evasive, Alex thought. *Nothing much* could mean Jason was either a typical bored, unemployed underachiever, or a serial felon.

Or he could be what he seemed: a perfectly nice, educated young man at loose ends.

Alex had a feeling the truth lay somewhere in the middle.

Deciding to play a little hardball, he pinned the young man with a steely look. "Find anything yet that might keep you here, Jason?"

To his credit, the kid remained cool under pressure. Didn't

budge an inch. Jason swirled the wine in his glass, lips tilted up, catlike. "I believe I have, Alex."

Liv's blue eyes rounded, darting back and forth between the two men. Alex gave Jason a feral grin, his dick swelling in his trunks. This was like the adrenaline flooding his veins in the courtroom while cross-examining a witness. But way better.

"St. Louis has a lot to offer."

"Oh, I'm discovering new delights every single day." Jason lowered his lashes, sending Alex a sultry look. "You know, the Arch, Busch Stadium, the casino boats . . ."

"You're a gambler, are you?" he asked. No way could his dual meaning be misinterpreted.

"Sometimes, when I feel lucky." Jason took a sip of wine, watching him closely.

Christ, his cock ached. "And do you feel lucky?"

"Let's just say I'm due for a change in fortune, and it can't come soon enough." The younger man let that statement ride for a moment, and then, as though sensing they were headed for deep water, changed the subject. "So, Olivia tells me you're a defense lawyer? I'll bet you have some great stories to tell."

The strange sexual tension broken, Alex launched into recollections of some of his most memorable cases. Afternoon melted into evening, and two more bottles of Merlot bit the dust. Alex was drifting in a mellow sea of contentment. So much that it took his brain a second to catch up with Jason's question.

"So, how's Henry Boardman's defense coming?"

"Wh-what did you say?"

"You are Boardman's lawyer, right? Damn, what a creep. Deserves to go to prison, if you ask me." Jason shuddered for emphasis.

"Where the fuck did you hear about my defending Board-man?"

Jason's dark eyes narrowed. It was probably Alex's overactive, alcohol-soaked mind that conjured the cold rage on the younger man's handsome face.

"Must've read it in the paper, Alex." He picked up a bottle, poured another Merlot. Saluted Alex with his glass.

"Oh. Right." He wasn't surprised that Jason had read about the upcoming trial so much as the abrupt way he brought up the subject. What was that about?

"Here's to freedom of information. Life's a bitch, ain't it?"

. . .

Alex lay in the darkness, listening to Liv's even breathing. Too much wine had put her out like a light, but the alcohol had left him aroused, cock aching, tension coiling every muscle. Sleep was elusive as his thoughts churned, his mind replaying every nuance of his conversation with Jason.

To be honest, it wasn't just the wine playing havoc with his libido. Sure, he'd found men attractive. But never before had he thought a man could be so alluring, so sexy he wanted to taste and explore. To push the man to his back, spread him, and have his way.

Never before had he imagined such a scenario within his reach.

Restless, Alex slipped from the bed quietly, careful not to awaken Liv. Groping at the foot of the bed, he found a pair of shorts and pulled them on, then headed downstairs. For a few seconds, he considered turning on the television, but discarded that idea. A late-night rerun wasn't going to come close to satis-fying the burn between his legs.

Lured by some force he didn't take time to understand, he went out onto the patio and stood, letting the cool evening breeze waft over him, enjoying the night sounds, the stars. There was something very seductive about stealing out here, wearing nothing but shorts, the air licking his half-naked body like a tongue. Knowing he could indulge in a fantasy to quench the lust consuming him and nobody would know.

Smiling to himself, he padded to his favorite lounger and moved it to face his neighbor's house. He sat down and sprawled out, not caring that his view of Jason's patio was mostly blocked by the fence. He could still picture the way Jason had looked earlier—young and lean with too-long brown hair, dark, seductive eyes. Verbally parrying with Alex, his comments ripe with innuendo.

"Jesus, I want him," Alex whispered to no one. He wanted his wife's lover.

And if he couldn't have him right now . . .

Alex unzipped his shorts and pushed them down on his hips, freeing his erection. His fist closed around the throbbing shaft and he sucked in a breath as he gave it a slow stroke from the head to the base. Up again.

God, that felt so wicked. Especially as he imagined Jason walking over here to kneel at his side, stroke his belly, run those capable hands over his thighs. The younger man would take Alex's cock between his sensual lips and suckle, taking him deeper.

Alex groaned, pumped his cock harder, his dream lover bobbing on over his lap. Eating him, taking him deep down that beautiful throat—

At that moment, Alex caught a movement from next door.

Saw a lean figure standing half in the shadows of the neighboring patio, moonlight glinting off his brown hair. Jason.

Sweet Christ, he's watching!

"Please, don't let me stop you," drifted from the darkness, so quiet the voice barely carried.

Alex went up like a flamethrower. Just like that. The object of his fantasy was nearby, enjoying the show, and even if Jason didn't know this was about him before, he was part of it now.

Spreading his legs wider, he thrust his hips upward with a helpless moan, gaze trained on the spot where Jason stood immobile. No phantom lover but flesh-and-blood man, connected with him in the moment, a coconspirator of sorts in this naughty, wanton act.

Faster and faster, Alex worked his cock in steady rhythm, until his body quickened, balls tightening. The familiar rush enveloped him, swept him over the edge.

"Yes! Oh, shit!"

He came hard, splashing his bare stomach with liquid heat, shuddering again and again until he was spent. Panting, cock in hand, he wondered when the embarrassment would hit. The guilt at being caught like this, perving over Jason whether the man realized it or not.

Neither happened. His desire wasn't wrong, not when all parties were on the same page, and he couldn't feel bad about it. He wouldn't.

Still, he wasn't sure what to say to Jason, how to smooth over a potentially awkward second meeting. Did a man simply say "I beg your pardon" for jacking off in his own backyard? While thinking dirty thoughts about the neighbor in question, no less?

"Damn," he said, tucking himself into his shorts once more. He needed to go inside and get washed off, but first . . . "Jason?"

He peered into the darkness, but the figure was no longer there. Like a ghost, he'd vanished, leaving Alex to wonder whether he'd been real at all.

. . .

Another Mad Monday.

A quiet, relatively normal weekend at home had succumbed to the craziness of a new week. Even so, Alex had managed to steal a few minutes alone here and there to reflect on Liv and Jason.

Friday evening had been awesome. Sitting by Jason's pool, drinking wine, shooting the breeze and watching the world go by. Sexual heat had stretched taut between the three of them, but they'd chosen not to act on it. Well, except for the stolen few moments when Jason had watched Alex pleasuring himself. In the long run, he knew their restraint would make their eventual encounters all the sweeter.

He could hardly wait. This was different from the combustive—almost destructive—obsession he'd developed for Jenna. He couldn't have articulated how; it just was.

"Jesus, you're a frickin' mess," he muttered to himself, stepping into the men's room down the hall from his office.

"I'll say."

A little jolt of adrenaline zapped his system and he jumped as though he'd been goosed. Casting a glare at Kyle over his shoulder, he unzipped to take care of business. "Damn, don't sneak up on me like that."

His friend merely looked amused as he did the same. "I was right behind you. Said your name twice."

"Oh. Sorry." He finished and zipped up, hoping he sounded apologetic. "It's been a hectic day."

"Sure. So . . ." Kyle lowered his voice, but it still echoed off the tiles, way too loud for comfort. "How's it going, burning the candle at both ends? Has Olivia thrown your ass out yet?"

Alex smiled and shook his head, turning on the faucet to wash his hands. "You just don't quit, do you?"

"Of course not! You've got a story, and your bored, undersexed friend wants to hear it. Come on, have mercy." Kyle waggled his brows. "Hey, I know a good divorce lawyer."

"So do I, but I don't need one," he said, drying his hands. "And I won't, either." He tossed his paper towel into the wastebasket, and his dubious friend followed suit. Rather than ending the matter, his cryptic claim only stoked Kyle's curiosity.

"Oh, right. You won't need a lawyer because she'll kill your sorry butt when she finds out."

"Not if she already knows."

Kyle's mouth fell open and he leaned against the wall. "Okay, now you *have* to explain. If you don't, I'm going to be your frickin' shadow all afternoon until you tell."

Kyle would, too. Annoying shit.

"Listen, it's not that big a deal." Liar. "Liv and I reached a crisis point and we, uh . . . agreed to an open marriage."

Kyle whistled between his teeth, eyes wide. "Damn, boy. What a deal. You're either the luckiest or the dumbest bastard I know."

"That remains to be—"

"I think you're the sickest bastard I know," Ken sneered, stepping from a stall. "And I bet it will only take me one guess as to who you're screwing around with."

Alex swore and wished he'd kept his fucking mouth shut. Of

all the rotten goddamned timing. Ken stopped next to Alex, giving him a look of disgust, voice filled with anger.

"Despite our differences, I never imagined you'd let your dick rule your brain where business is concerned. Now I know what it takes to get ahead in the firm, huh? Your daddy must be rolling in his grave, man."

He stormed out, yanking the door so hard it slammed against the wall and chipped the paint.

Kyle clapped him on the shoulder. "Jeez, I'm sorry. I had no idea he was in here."

"Not your fault."

Yes, he owned this one. In spades.

Much later, around eight, Alex closed his office with a sigh of gratitude. He rode the elevator down to the parking garage, thankful for the time alone. Jenna had left a couple of hours ago, but not before attempting to lure him into "working" at her place tonight. He'd put her off for the honest reason of being dog tired. She'd pouted prettily, and he'd promised a rendezvous tomorrow night.

Soul willing, body drained. Or something along those lines.

Stepping off the elevator, he fretted over the Boardman case. He knew he could get the man acquitted, with little effort, due to lack of evidence.

The problem was, his client wasn't cooperating. *Was* Henry Boardman the boss daddy of the sex-slave ring, or were there more players in this game than he knew?

Alex wasn't sure.

His footsteps echoed in the near-empty parking garage. The underground area seemed cooler than normal, the atmosphere menacing. He walked quicker, his flesh prickling. The Jag crouched alone in a darkened corner about forty yards away, a safe haven waiting to carry him home.

Fishing in his pants, he brought out his key ring and punched the unlock button. The lights flashed, and the car emitted a cheery double blip. Moving his thumb, he depressed the button he'd encoded to automatically start the engine.

An odd *click, click* sounded from the vehicle. Two seconds of hesitation as he closed the distance, the starter failing to catch.

"Well, shi—"

The Jag erupted in a fiery ball, the deafening explosion lifting him off his feet. Blowing him backward with the force of a runaway jet. Through the air, his body twisting like a rag doll.

His flight ended abruptly as he slammed into unforgiving concrete, his skull striking the surface like a bullet shot from a gun. His vision shattered, went white.

He rolled to a stop, vaguely aware of the roar of fire, heat licking over his skin. Acute, agonizing pain, a serrated knife stabbing deep. Obliterating all else.

He struggled to hold on to consciousness, and lost.

Amid shouts, the crackle and heat of flame, his world went black.

Six

✳

Olivia ran into the lobby of the emergency room and skidded to a halt at the check-in counter, slapping a hand on the pristine surface and startling the receptionist who was seated behind it, talking on the phone.

"I need to see my husband! He was—"

The lady held up a finger and took another thirty maddening seconds to conclude her business. Endless seconds, while Alex was hurt. Needing her. He could be dying. Unless he'd already— *Oh, please, no!*

"How may I help you?" the lady asked, hanging up the phone.

"A police officer phoned and said my husband had been brought in," Olivia said, panting in fear. God, her heart was about to hammer through her sternum. She couldn't breathe.

The receptionist's face softened in sympathy. "Your husband's name, honey?"

"Alexander Quinn. Do you know how he's doing? Can I see him?"

The woman nodded. "Through those double doors and down

on your right. He's in room number six, and I believe the police are still in there with him. The doctor will fill you in on his condition."

"Th-thank you."

Liv hurried past the desk, mind whirling. In an ER cubby, not in surgery. That had to be a good sign, right?

Sweet heaven, not forty minutes ago she and Jason had been snuggled on her sofa, sharing a glass of wine and anticipating their first real stolen evening. Her head had been resting on his shoulder, hand exploring his flat belly, when the phone rang. She almost hadn't answered.

He'd insisted on driving and had dropped her off at the ER entrance before going to park the car. She hadn't wanted to impose, but was extraordinarily glad to have him along, however selfish that might be.

The ER didn't appear too busy tonight, but the quiet murmurs of nurses and doctors, the sterile environment and antiseptic odor, got to her all the same. Alex didn't belong in this place. In all their years together, he'd never been seriously ill or injured.

Pausing in the doorway to room six, she gaped at the sight of three police officers standing around Alex's bed. Two were in uniform, one in plain clothes with his badge and gun clipped to his belt. A detective? What in God's name . . .

Then her gaze found Alex. Her breath hitched and her hand went over her mouth.

The right side of his face was scraped and bruised, the eye swollen and blackening. His right arm was in a sling, preventing her from seeing its condition, but the left was scraped raw like his face. His eyes were closed, his breathing even. The officers were speaking in low voices, faces solemn.

She stepped inside and three pairs of eyes swung to her, curious. "I-I'm Olivia Quinn. Alex is my husband."

"Mrs. Quinn, I'm Detective Steve Lambert," the plainclothes officer said, extending his hand. He was a small, skinny man with dark salt-and-pepper hair and friendly blue eyes that crinkled in the corners.

The hammering in Liv's chest calmed, but only a little.

"Detective Lambert." She shook his hand, and got right to the point. "Tell me what happened to my husband."

Lambert, the obvious spokesman of the group, studied her carefully. "Ma'am, there's no easy way to tell you something like this, but there was an explosion. Your husband took the brunt of it, but the good news is he's going to be fine. Banged up and sore as hell, but fine."

"An . . . explosion? Did you say *explosion?*" She stared at the three policemen, trying to assimilate the word. "How? Where?"

Now she saw it. Alex's reddened, slightly blistered skin. The ends of his blond hair singed. *Oh, God!*

"According to your husband, he closed his office and left work around eight this evening. As he approached his car, he used the automatic unlock and starter on his key ring. The engine glitched, but when it took hold, the vehicle blew."

In that moment, the entire universe stopped. Reversed. Tilted on its axis.

"C-cars don't just blow up for no reason."

"No, ma'am." Lambert waited for her to put the pieces in place.

"If Alex had been inside, h-he'd be dead."

"Yes, ma'am."

"Someone rigged Alex's car to blow up?" Inconceivable. Liv started to tremble. All over. As if the mechanism in her brain that controlled her nerves had shorted out.

"I'm afraid that's the reality we're facing. Our experts are going over the vehicle now, but what we expect based on your husband's account is a simple device attached to the starter."

On watery legs, Liv moved close to Alex's side and closed her fingers around his good hand. Took comfort in the fact that he was warm and alive. "Who would do this to him? Why?"

"Your husband lost consciousness again before we got that far. We're hoping you might be able to shed some light on a motive for us. Mr. Quinn is a highly visible presence in the city, both professionally and socially. In his position, I'm sure he's stepped on a few toes. Has he received any threats lately? Phone calls, e-mails or letters?"

"This is so unreal." She tried to think straight, but the shock was too great. "No. Not that I'm aware of."

"What about the trial he's working on at the present? There's something in the newspaper about the case almost daily."

She thought. "No, nothing."

"Disgruntled employee?"

"I . . ."

And everyone is okay with this?

Other than Ken, who's ready to punch my lights out?

"Mrs. Quinn?"

Shaking herself, she met the detective's gaze squarely. She wasn't about to open that Pandora's box without speaking to Alex first. "No, I can't think of anyone."

"All right," he said slowly, as though he sensed her hesitation on the last question and perhaps didn't quite believe her answer. "Let me give you my card. I'll be in touch tomorrow to speak with your husband again about the incident, when he's feeling a bit better."

The *incident*. What a clinical word for *attempted murder*.

"Thank you, Detective. Gentlemen," she said, including the other two officers. She took the card he offered, shoving it in her purse. Her attention was already on Alex as they filed out.

Pulling up a chair, she sat by his side, stroking his soft hair. She watched his chest rise and fall, thanking the angel who'd been sitting on his shoulder tonight.

Someone tried to kill my Alex.

Her soul mate.

By lying to the police to protect their reputations, she might have placed him in even greater danger.

Liv bent her head and let the tears fall.

. . .

With awareness came the pain.

Every single molecule in his body throbbed like a son of a bitch. Especially his head. Deep in his brain, Agony Central pulsed fiery shit to every limb. *Lucky to be alive*, a paramedic had commented as Alex was rushed into the ER.

Well, strike up the band and let's throw a fucking party.

Then he heard the sniffles. And a low, masculine voice speaking in a soothing tone.

". . . be all right, Olivia. You heard the doctor."

"I know, it's just . . . a car bomb? My God, Jase, what if they try again?"

Car bomb.

The two words floated in his head, disconnected from reality. For about five seconds.

Until he remembered the Jag blowing up in his face.

With effort, he pried open his eyes—crap, make that *one* eye—and squinted. His vision was gritty and blurry, but he could just make out Liv and Jason parked at his bedside. Their neighbor had come with her? Huh. He didn't have the energy to sort through what that meant.

Liv leaned forward, and though he couldn't focus on her features, he heard the tremulous smile in her voice. "Hello, sweetie. You're going to be all right. Do you remember what happened, or talking to the police?"

He nodded, managing a croak. "Yeah. Car . . . blew up."

"Someone meant to kill you, Alex. Why?" she whispered, tears threatening.

"Don't know, baby." And that was the truth. He was a defender, not a prosecutor. He worked to keep people out of jail, not incarcerate them. So what enemies could he possibly have?

"Hey, man." Jason scooted closer, trying to sound upbeat. "They're going to spring you soon. I'll help Olivia get you home and settled in."

"Thanks, Jason."

"No prob."

"So . . . it's not bad?" Alex tried to tilt his chin down to examine his injuries, but succeeded only in making himself dizzy.

Liv squeezed his hand. "The doctor came in while you were sleeping. You've got quite a goose egg on the back of your head, but just a mild concussion."

"This is mild? Jesus." He focused on his wife, relieved when some of the fuzziness cleared. Thank God he wasn't blind.

Her expressive blue eyes warmed with love and concern, but he read the underlying terror in their depths, as well. The very real knowledge that whoever was responsible for the explosion meant business—and wouldn't quit.

"I know you're hurting. Your head, shoulder and wrist took the brunt of the impact," she told him. "Your shoulder is wrenched and the wrist is sprained, but nothing's broken. The doctor is sending you home with a prescription for a good painkiller. It'll help you sleep later."

Sounded good to him. *Let's hear it for drugs.*

"I want to go home. Now."

"Honey—"

"I'll go see if I can hurry them along," Jason offered with a smile. He stood and left the room.

Alex stared after him, thinking he ought to feel odd sharing such an intimate, horrible ordeal with his wife's lover, and wondering why he didn't. Sharing wine and trading innuendo by the pool was one thing, but this?

He liked Jason, plain and simple. Enjoyed having him around.

Really enjoyed imagining the young stud pleasuring his Liv.

And just like that, his cock hardened enough to cut glass. Despite his aching body. Despite everything.

He shifted, hoping the sheet provided sufficient cover for his problem. But he couldn't hide his reaction from Liv. Spying his discomfort, one corner of her luscious mouth lifted, the shadows temporarily banished.

"Beautiful, isn't he? I remember when you used to have the same reaction from looking at *me.*"

"I still do," he said firmly. "Don't ever suggest otherwise. I was imagining the two of you together, and see where it got me? In a fix I can't do anything about."

"At the moment."

"God, I love you."

"And I love you back." Leaning over, she kissed his unmarred cheek. "We're going to be fine, and so will you. The police are going to find out who did this."

"I know, sweetheart."

He wasn't sure he believed the last part. But for Liv, he'd try.

Jason returned, and within fifteen minutes Alex was lectured, released, dressed and wheeled out to the curb. As Jason pulled up in a Jeep Wrangler, Alex wondered what the younger man said to get him sprung in record time. Whatever; he was damned grateful.

Jason helped ease him into the vehicle, then drove them straight home. The pharmacy wasn't open this late, but the doctor had given him a couple of pills to hold him over until morning. He wanted one of those and his bed, in that order.

He must've dozed off, because it seemed only a minute later someone was tugging gently on his arm.

"Alex? Sweetie, we're here. Come on, let's get you inside and into bed."

"Hang on a sec," Jason said. "Olivia, give me your house keys and I'll check things out first."

Alex peered at the two of them with his good eye, his alarm matching Liv's.

"A precaution," Jason added, face grim.

Everything had happened so fast, he hadn't even considered being attacked in his own home. Or, God forbid, Liv. She'd been spending so many hours of her day at home . . . Christ, what if his would-be killer tried to get to her?

More than his injuries, that possibility made him sick as they waited for Jason to return with the all clear. He'd rather die than let anyone harm his wife.

He could very well get his wish.

And on the heels of that thought, it occurred to him to mull over what a young, slender guy like Jason thought he could do against a professional assassin. He'd get his ass kicked.

Yet he'd taken charge, here and at the hospital, like a man who knew what he was doing.

Jason trotted out the front door, giving them a thumbs-up. Alex slid from the Jeep with a groan, trying not to lean too hard on Liv. He felt like an elderly man shuffling up the walk, just the way he'd dreamed of feeling next to Studly Do-Right.

Ditto being tucked into bed like a drooling infant, which was exactly the way it played out. Jason hovered, ready to jump in as Liv stripped him to his boxer briefs and helped him lie down, then smoothed the covers over his chest. He'd be embarrassed if he wasn't in so goddamned much pain.

Liv sat at his side, stroking his hair. Nice. The younger man disappeared into the bathroom, then came back holding a glass of water.

"Why don't you two rest? I'll take the sofa downstairs," he said, holding out the glass to Liv and dropping a pill into her palm.

Liv looked up at him in surprise. "You're staying?"

"Yes. Alex is going to be passed out, and I'd feel better keeping an eye on your house." He paused, raking a hand through his shaggy, sun-streaked hair. "I doubt there will be another attempt tonight, but still."

"Good idea." Liv gave him a shaky smile. "You're welcome to a guest room."

"Downstairs is better. I can hear if someone attempts to break in."

Even in the dim lamplight, Alex saw the color drain from Liv's face.

"I-I suppose that's a good idea. Thank you, Jason."

"No biggie."

Christ. Had he ever been that young and bulletproof?

Alex took the pill and glass, downing the painkiller in one swallow. Liv took the glass from him and he settled into the pillows, waiting for the stuff to kick in and knock his ass out. Liv brushed his lips with a soft kiss, and he closed his eyes in pleasure.

But he couldn't open them again.

The last thing he heard was his wife saying something about fetching their self-appointed protector a pillow and blanket.

With his last wisp of consciousness, he imagined what it would be like to have Jason curled up in their bed instead.

.   .   .

He answered the phone, hand trembling, uncertain which was the greater hell—trying to kill Alex or the failure to accomplish it.

"Hello?"

"He's terminated?"

Goddamn. "No."

A telling pause. "Why the fuck not?"

"He wasn't in the car. He uses a starter on his key ring—"

"I pay you well to circumvent these problems. Fail me again and I'll be forced to cut you loose."

Cut your throat, he meant.

"I understand."

The phone went dead. As dead as Alex would be soon. He lowered his face into his hands.

"Sorry, man. Better you than me."

.   .   .

At ten, Detective Lambert came to call. Much too early, considering Alex's restless night. Two doses of pain medication barely kept him comfortable enough to sleep, and Liv doubted he'd be up for questions right now.

Frowning, Liv answered the door, a mug of steaming coffee in hand. Jason stood right behind her, prepared to intervene again if their visitor wasn't welcome, like he had when the news crews arrived at the crack of dawn. Forcing the reporters to retreat while keeping his face off camera had been a challenge he'd gladly accepted. He'd been so good to her and Alex, and his protective side was really sweet.

"Detective, please come in." Quickly, she let him inside and shut the door on prying eyes.

"Quite a circus out there," he commented, fishing in his shirt pocket for a notepad and pen.

Lambert's observation didn't require an answer, and Liv refrained from venting her frustration on the subject as she ushered him into the living room. The detective took a seat in Alex's favorite chair while she and Jason settled on the sofa. Though Jase kept an appropriate distance, the detective glanced at him in curiosity before addressing Olivia in a kind tone.

"Mrs. Quinn, how is your husband this morning?"

The inflection in his voice made the question sound more like he was really asking *where* Alex was rather than how he was doing. A cop-to-interviewee psych-out that was probably as natural to him as breathing. Liv set her mug on the coffee table as she answered. "In bed. He had a restless night, but I'm sure he'll be up soon."

"A hell of a thing, what you two are dealing with. Well, let's get started, and hopefully he'll join us later." Leaning forward, elbows on his knees, he gazed at her, expression unreadable. "I'll start by confirming what we pretty much already knew. The starter on your husband's Jaguar was rigged with a simple explosive device. Quick, clean and professional."

Liv was extremely glad to be sitting, or she would've fallen. She'd been expecting this, but hearing the horrible truth was a blow. Perhaps she'd been clinging to some stupid notion that the car had been . . . defective. Right. A strange, forlorn sound like a whimper escaped and she stared at her clasped hands, the knuckles white.

Jason scooted closer on the sofa, squeezing her shoulder. "It's going to be okay, I promise."

"Will it? Someone obviously knew what they were doing, Jase."

"Not enough to know that Alex uses the starter on his key ring," he pointed out. "Which means the culprit hasn't been watching very closely. Sloppy. He's *not* a pro."

Detective Lambert's brows lifted and he inspected Jason as though attempting to look inside his soul. After a pregnant moment of silence, he clicked his pen. "Didn't catch your name, son."

"I didn't give it." He smiled, taking the sting out of his terse reply. "I'm Jason, their next-door neighbor."

Lambert nodded, began to write. "Last name?"

Was it her imagination, or had Jason tensed? He appeared relaxed, except for his tight mouth and a hard glint in his brown eyes she'd never seen before.

"Strickland, sir."

"Jason Strickland," the detective murmured, almost to himself. "How long have you known the Quinns?"

"A few days."

The detective lifted a brow, glancing between Jason and Liv. "You seem very comfortable together for having known one another a short time."

"Yes, sir. We hit it off right away." To his credit, Jason didn't appear the least bit uncomfortable about that, nor did he look away from the detective's penetrating stare.

"I see. What brings you to St. Louis, Mr. Strickland?"

"My uncle passed away and I'm here to settle his estate."

"Thinking of staying on?" His pen scratched on the pad.

"Maybe."

Liv didn't miss how Jason volunteered only the information he was asked directly, nothing more. Lambert didn't miss it, either.

"What's your occupation?"

"I'm between jobs at the moment." Jason broke eye contact for a fleeting instant before locking gazes with Lambert again. "Times are tough. You know how it is."

"Not exactly, Mr. Strickland. There's always somebody breaking the law. Job security." He gave Jason a toothy smile. "You know how it is."

A corner of Jason's mouth quirked upward. "Not exactly, Detective."

The tense undercurrent between the two men was so strong, Liv felt compelled to dispel it somehow. She latched on to the first idea that came to mind. "Coffee, Detective Lambert?"

"No, thank you."

"I'll take his cup," Alex said, groaning as he inched slowly down the stairs, holding on to the rail with his good hand.

Liv shot to her feet and hurried to help him. "Oh, honey, should you be up walking around?"

He gave her a sound good morning kiss on the lips and a rueful grin. "Seemed like a good idea before I got vertical."

"Too stubborn for your own good. Here, put your arm around me." She hugged his waist and he did as told, letting her guide him to a big, soft recliner. Lowering himself into the chair, he gritted his teeth in pain. Only then did she notice his free right arm. "Where is your sling?"

"Took it off. Damned thing was driving me crazy. But I'm still wearing the wrist brace, see?" He held it up briefly, then nodded at the younger man. "Good morning, Jason."

"Mornin'. Man, you look like shit."

Alex's lips twitched. "Why, thanks. Don't worry about my self-image. It's fine." He turned his head toward their visitor. "Hello, Detective . . . "

"Lambert," the man reminded him. "You were conscious very briefly when we spoke last night."

"Detective, I'd say it's nice to see you, but under the circumstances I'd be lying. No offense."

"Occupational hazard. None taken." The detective glanced at each of them before continuing. "Since you're here, let me get right down to business. First, in the interest of privacy and the fact that we're dealing with an attempted homicide, not to mention your acquaintance with Mr. Strickland being recent, I'll have to ask that he go elsewhere for this part of the discussion."

"Sure, if you think it's best, but I don't think—"

Jason stood and held up a palm, cutting off Alex's protest. "Hey, it's cool. I'll be right next door if anyone needs me." He grabbed his keys from the coffee table.

"I'll walk you out," Liv said.

"No need. I'll catch up with you guys later, yeah?"

She gave him a smile. "All right. Thank you for everything."

His gaze heated, straying from her to Alex. "What are neighbors for?"

Liv watched him go, hoping Lambert hadn't caught his subtle meaning. But from the interested expression on his face, he likely had. Alex provided a distraction by grumbling for his coffee, and she gratefully excused herself to get him a mug.

Nerves assailed her as she poured the steaming brew. What did the detective have to say that couldn't be said in front of a third party? God, she hated this.

No, she hated whoever had tried to kill her husband.

Padding into the living room once more, she handed Alex his mug. Jason was right; he did look terrible. The swelling around his eye was better—at least the pupil was visible—but the bruise was an angry purplish-black. The scrapes on his face and arms were raw, and though his sweatpants and T-shirt hid them from view, she knew his torso and legs sported bruises, as well.

She'd like to snuggle next to Alex, but there wasn't room in the chair and she didn't want to jostle him. So she returned to the sofa and waited for Lambert to continue as Alex gingerly sipped his coffee.

"Mrs. Quinn, last night you stated that you couldn't think of any reason someone might want to kill your husband, is that correct?"

Lambert kept his voice neutral, conversational. But Liv sensed a slight change in his demeanor. A wolf on the scent. She shivered and nodded.

"Yes. I mean, Alex is a well-known social figure in St. Louis, and he's defended several high-profile clients. He's had his share of sensational cases, but for someone to want him—"

She couldn't say the word. It stuck in her throat along with the rising bile.

Lambert paused, flipped a couple of pages in his notebook. "Do you know an attorney at your husband's firm by the name Ken Brock?"

"Not very well, but we're acquainted," she said slowly. Where had he gotten Ken's name?

"And are you aware that Mr. Brock is having difficulty accepting your husband's decision to appoint a junior partner, Jenna Shaw, as second counsel on the Henry Boardman trial?"

The blood drained from Liv's face. Obviously, Detective Lambert had been a busy man this morning. She should've realized he'd pay a visit to Quinn and Quinn to speak to Alex's employees, and she'd been stupid to lie last night when he'd asked about disgruntled employees. Scrambling, she attempted to salvage where this was heading.

"Office politics, detective. Alex is the boss and as such can assign cases and duties as he sees fit. If we named every employee who'd been angry with him for some reason or another, however petty, we'd have quite a list."

"Jesus, I'm not that bad," Alex muttered, mostly to himself.

Lambert ignored him. "One of them might lead to the person who wants your husband dead. Or not, but it's my job to follow all possible leads. And you didn't answer my question."

"I was aware of Ken's feelings on the subject, but I didn't think it was important. He hasn't made any threats against Alex," she stressed.

"That may be," he mused. "However, I'm more interested in a claim Mr. Brock made regarding your husband's relationship with Jenna Shaw."

The bottom dropped out of Liv's stomach. Speech deserted her. She had no idea how to respond without mucking things up even more.

Alex came to her rescue. "What claim is he making, Detective?"

Lambert turned his attention to Alex. "Mr. Brock says he overheard you and your friend, Kyle Murphy, speaking of the open sexual arrangement you have with your wife. He claims you and Miss Shaw are having an affair."

Liv stared at Alex, stunned. Hurt. He'd been bragging about his sexual conquests to Kyle?

Alex pressed his lips into a thin line, rubbing his temple and staring into his coffee. For several seconds there was complete silence, except for a lawnmower starting across the street. The tick of the wall clock.

"I don't know I'd classify it as an affair," he said quietly. "I've had sex with Jenna. I might again, or I might not. Yes, Liv and I recently agreed to an open marriage, but it's nobody else's business. *Nobody's.*"

Lambert's eyes widened the merest fraction, a hint that Alex managed to surprise a cop who'd heard most everything. "It's mine when someone tries to roast you like a wiener at a Fourth of July campout, Mr. Quinn. The emotions provoked by extramarital relations are highly volatile at best, dangerous at the worst. I've seen the results before, and statistically, the spurned spouse or significant other is almost always the culprit in a crime of passion such as murder, or attempted murder."

"Are you accusing me of blowing up Alex's car?" Liv asked, voice rising. "Of—of trying to kill my husband?"

Alex's eyes flashed with anger. "That's absurd."

"I'm not accusing anyone, folks, just trying to get at the facts." He flipped to a clean page in his pad and addressed Liv. "Can you account for your whereabouts yesterday between ten a.m. and eight p.m.?"

"Of course I can!" Couldn't she? "I was home until shortly after two, then I ran by my restaurant, Giancarlo's. I stayed there about an hour and a half; then I picked up my dry cleaning, went to the grocery store and came home. I think it was close to five thirty when I got back."

"You were home for the rest of the evening, until you were called to the hospital?"

"Yes."

"Can anyone verify your being here?"

Her cheeks warmed. "Our neighbor, Jason, came over at six and was with me until I received word about Alex."

"Is Mr. Strickland part of your *open arrangement,* Mrs. Quinn?"

God, the man was relentless. Alex looked ready to tear his throat out. "Yes."

"Hmm. Explains a few things. Did you and Mr. Strickland have sex last night?"

"No, we didn't." She forced herself to look him square in the eye, chin up. "But Alex is aware of our relationship. We're both being open about everything."

And then some. She prayed they'd get out of this conversation before Lambert learned the rest. While she stood by their arrangement, the details were for their knowledge alone.

"Detective, my wife had *nothing* to do with the explosion," Alex said, his tone uncompromising. Absolute. "We love one another very much, which is why we're taking steps to spice up our marriage. You're going down the wrong path while someone is plotting to finish what they've started."

"I wonder, Mr. Quinn."

"About what?"

"The timing. You stated the agreement with your wife is recent. Then someone tries to kill you. It's a logical path to tread."

Alex shook his head. "Not in our case, I assure you."

Lambert clicked his pen, closed his notebook and shoved both into his front shirt pocket as he stood. "Loose threads all lead somewhere; it's just a matter of tugging the right one. I'll leave you two alone for now. Call me if you think of something, no matter how insignificant it seems."

"Will do."

Alex struggled to rise, but Liv waved him down. "I'll see him out."

Lambert walked out with a polite good-bye. Liv closed and locked the door after him, worrying over his logic.

A bargain of mutual sexual pleasure.

Followed by a murder attempt.

Could the two be tied somehow?

She couldn't see how. Her thoughts turned to Alex.

Oh yes. She had a bone to pick with her sexy, bigmouthed husband.

Seven

✳

Oh, boy. He was being stalked. And not by a car bomber, but a gorgeous, black-haired, extremely pissed wife.

Liv returned from seeing out the detective and stood over Alex, fists on her hips. The position pulled her breasts snug against her tank top and caused her shorts to ride high, hugging her sex. His cock perked up at the sight.

"So, you and Kyle have been discussing our sex life, yucking it up like a pair of horny teenage boys?"

"No!" He tried to sit up straighter and winced at the pull on his sore muscles. "It wasn't hard for him to guess what was going on with me and Jenna, and he's been riding my ass ever since. Kept teasing me about how you were going to throw me out and offered me a place to crash when you did."

"And naturally, you couldn't resist regaling him with the naughty details." Blue eyes flashed, frying him more effectively than any bomb could have.

"Not true. I wanted him off my back, so I told him you weren't going to give me the boot. I said we have an arrangement. That's *all*." He saw her expression soften, the anger draining away. "I'd never gossip about our private lives, sweetheart. My confessions are for your ears alone."

She hesitated, unsure. "This is still my show?"

"All the way." He should've known she was afraid of losing control of their game. Frankly, so was he.

For the time being, however, worry fled in the wake of new awareness. Mollified, she knelt in front of his chair, between his legs, resting her hands on his thighs. Her fingers branded him through the soft, cottony fabric and his hips rolled in reflexive response to her nearness. Amusement colored her voice as her gaze fixed on his lap.

"Problem, dear husband?"

"God, yes. Liv . . ."

"Hmm?" The little tease ran a finger along the stiff ridge of his erection.

He almost whimpered. "You're going to make me beg, aren't you?"

"Tell me what you want." She licked her lips, giving away her anticipation.

"Touch me, please," he whispered. "I need to feel you licking and sucking my cock. It's been so long."

"You'll have to promise not to move too much. I don't want to hurt you."

"I promise! Please, baby, before I have a heart attack."

"Can't have that, can we?" Reaching for his waistband, she tugged his sweats and boxer briefs down together.

Cool air caressed his sex and he sucked in a deep breath, loving the sensation of being spread before her, a banquet for her feast. She held the power and he trembled beneath her, eager and ready.

Frowning, she brushed her fingers over his right hip and thigh. "Those bruises look worse than I thought."

"They're not nearly as agonizing as a certain part of me."

With a satisfied hum, she lifted his balls, manipulating them with clever fingers. She lowered her head, lifted her veil of hair to one side so he could see, and began to place sweet, gentle kisses on his sac. His penis. His cock. Up, and down again. Driving him crazy with those lips.

Prickles of delight shimmered along his skin, but when she took one of his testicles in her mouth, he thought he might die. Hot, wet suction spread fire through his limbs, melted his bones. She lavished attention on one, then the other, before releasing it to lave his rigid cock to the leaking tip.

She captured the pearly drop with her tongue, then suckled the head of his penis with such care and skill he wanted to weep.

"God, yes," he moaned, arching his hips. "Deeper, baby."

Those blue eyes flashed to his; then she returned her attention to his cock. She did as he begged, but not quickly. No, she made him suffer, swallowing him bit by bit, keeping the pressure tight, tormenting him with the scrape of teeth. The teasing of tongue.

Deeper, deeper, until her nose met his groin.

His aching cock. Shoved all the way down his wife's lovely throat.

Intense. Electrifying.

"Oh, shit . . . Liv, please . . . have to fuck your sweet mouth."

He couldn't have stopped at gunpoint, his promise not to move blown to dust. Ignoring the twinge in his wrist, he fisted her silky hair in his hand and held her firmly in place as he began to thrust. Faster, harder. Fucking that talented mouth for all he was worth, hips snapping.

She gave as good as she got, too, working his dick like a pro. Sucking and licking, hanging on for the ride. He would feel bad for being so rough if he didn't know she loved doing him, always had. Loved driving him higher, fraying his control.

His balls drew taut and the familiar tingle gathered at the base of his spine. He fucked her without mercy, out of his mind with the need to come—

And then he yelled, shooting, lost to the spasms as she drank every drop of him. He shuddered on and on, until at last he went limp. Blind and wrung out. Exhaustion weighed him down in a heavy, fuzzy blanket as she licked him clean.

She pulled up his sweats, restoring him to order. He cracked an eye open and managed a tired smile at her disheveled state and the glow in her cheeks. Yeah, he'd done that and was damned glad.

"You broke your promise," she scolded, trying to appear stern. And failing.

"Couldn't help myself. Jesus, what you do to me. Allow me to return the favor?" Reaching out, he fingered a wild strand of black hair.

"Later. You need to rest."

"More punishment?"

"No, just me being concerned about you."

Leaning into him, she took his mouth in a slow, sensual kiss. He tasted himself on her tongue, and it turned him on. Made him want to start all over again, this time with him as her tormentor.

But she stood, shaking her head. "Sleep. I'll wake you in a bit for some breakfast before I run and get your prescription filled. Come on."

Carefully, she helped him over to his favorite chair, the one Lambert had vacated earlier, and cranked it back to recline with his feet up. He grumbled a protest, but Liv was right. He *was* tired. In moments, his eyes drifted closed.

Rest, not punishment.

If he kept telling himself that, maybe he'd believe it.

. . .

He was bored as freaking shit.

Forty-eight hours limping from his chair to the bed and back again, eyes glazed, thumb wearing out the remote control in a fruitless endeavor to find something interesting. Anything to occupy his mind for more than two minutes.

On *Oprah*, a family cry-fest was in session, a group of women sniveling all over each other about God-knows-what.

Click.

On the Discovery Channel, a male seahorse was having babies. Gross.

Click.

The History Channel touted the Americans' march to victory during World War II. For the millionth time.

Shutting off the TV, Alex tossed aside the remote in frustration. After the constant, insane rush of daily life at the firm, this inactivity was driving him bonkers. At least Danielle was keeping him updated, and Kyle had phoned a couple of times to check on him. And last night, Jenna left a naughty voice mail on his cell phone that left him hard for hours afterward.

Glad you're in one piece, sexy. Give me a call when you're feeling better and we'll make plans to speed your recovery. Shall I tie you to my bed again? Or perhaps something even more wicked. Sweet dreams.

More wicked than being bound, at her mercy? Hell. He'd promised Liv he'd take the rest of the week off to rest his body, but one tormented part of him hadn't received the message.

Where the hell *was* Liv?

Worried, he pushed from his chair and stretched for a minute, working out the stiffness. Then he went in search of his wife and mounted the stairs, glad the scream of his abused muscles had become muted to a bearable ache.

In their bedroom, he paused. "Liv?"

"In here."

He headed for their spacious bathroom, relieved and trying not to act paranoid. Poor Liv had to be tired of his overprotective attitude and feeling as cooped up as he was.

In the doorway, he stopped and drooled. His wife made a beautiful sight, perched on the edge of her vanity seat, fooling with her hair, wearing a scrap of silky peach material posing as a robe.

She glanced at him in the mirror. "Going stir crazy?"

"Yeah. Wherever *you're* going, it must be better."

"Jason's dropping me off at the restaurant for a while, remember?"

"Oh." Damn, how could he have forgotten? "I could take you. I'm not helpless, you know."

"But you *are* on pain meds and aren't supposed to drive yet. Anyway, Jason doesn't mind."

"What if *I* mind?"

Her hands stilled. "It's a little late in the game for jealousy now, Alex."

"This isn't about my ego," he muttered, annoyed. That earned him The Look. "Okay, maybe a little. But the problem isn't Jason; it's being unable to protect my own wife, dammit."

"Just for a couple more days, until you're off the heavy drugs." Pushing up from the vanity, she stood and turned, opening her arms to him. "Come here."

He met her halfway, folding her into his arms. Tucking her head against his heart, where she should be. God, they didn't do this much anymore. Simply drink in each other, taking strength in the contact between man and wife.

She felt good, too. Warm and soft, smelling like raspberry shampoo, her breasts snuggled against his chest. His cock hardened against her tummy and he tipped her face up with one finger.

"I need you, baby. No games, no punishment. Just us, making love."

Her uncertainty showed, and he resented it. Hated the awful possibility that, in spite of their efforts, they may have reached a sexual and emotional impasse, adrift and unsure where they stood. That maybe love really wasn't enough. He had to erase the doubts, kiss them away, and he started by fusing their mouths together with gentle pressure.

He drew her into their room, not breaking the kiss. Pushed her onto her back and parted the robe. Bared her to him. Completely. Dusky-tipped nipples and slim hips. Dark curls between her thighs, falling open for him. The pink slit of her pussy, inviting.

She helped him off with his T-shirt and he stood for a second, slipping out of his sweats and yanking off his wrist brace to join the pile. He wasted no time crawling to her, up her body, covering her smaller form with his. He framed her face with his hands, the tip of his hungry cock nudging into her folds, seeking home.

He took her mouth again as he slid inside, deep into her welcoming heat. They moaned together, hips thrusting, busy hands touching everywhere they could reach.

They both knew this wasn't about sex.

"Tell me there's still an us," he breathed into her lips. Desperate. Aching inside. He couldn't lose her now.

Ever.

"Yes, Alex. Yes."

"I love you. Oh, God . . ."

They made love slowly, the passion spiraling them upward. Sweet, familiar. Flying higher until they plummeted over the edge, clinging to one another, cries mingling, hearts pounding.

Alex came hard, pumping into Liv, giving her all of him. At last, he lay draped over her, shaking and spent. He never wanted to move, but his muscles were complaining. So he rolled to his back and pulled her into his arms, where she seemed content to remain—if only for a while.

"There's still *us*," she whispered, stroking his chest. "We're altered, that's all."

"I know, baby." He kissed her temple and thought for a long while. Long after she'd resumed getting ready and departed with Jason.

He replayed their lovemaking. Sweet, conventional, comforting. The truth was inescapable. Sometimes they had to reconnect, enjoy the fuzzy, warm-security-blanket sort of loving they'd shared earlier.

But they also needed the fire, the sizzle that Liv's bargain had put back into their sexuality. Needed the decadence as much as air to breathe.

Alex needed to be bad now and then, and he absolutely loved having Liv's permission to play. Anticipating his confession and his wife's punishment—not to mention what she and Jason might be cooking up—even more so.

The change between him and Liv was permanent. There was no going back to what they'd been. And yeah, it made him a little sad.

Mostly, it make his cock iron-hard to wonder what escapades were next for them all.

. . .

From the kitchen, Olivia sneaked a peek at Alex prowling the living room like a caged beast. Day three of his incarceration and the more he healed, the more he growled. Terminal boredom.

Thank goodness she knew a cure. In light of the attempt on Alex, she and Jason had at first disagreed over how to proceed with the plan, but they'd worked out the details.

Tonight was for herself, Alex . . . and Jason.

Drying her hands, she padded into the living room. Alex stood looking out the glass patio doors into the night, spirit troubled. A little down.

Olivia to the rescue.

"Hey, sexy." She slid her arms around his waist and pressed her cheek against his broad back.

"Baby."

His arms hugged hers and they remained that way for a few moments, Liv basking in the solid heat of her husband. She'd nearly lost him. Would have if not for a small auto device anyone could buy for their key ring, for less than the price of a burger and fries.

"It's time for another punishment," she said calmly.

At that, Alex turned in her arms without letting go, brows raised. "What for? I haven't done anything—well, lately."

"Haven't you?"

Hesitating, he studied her knowing expression. Finally, he gave her a faint smile. "You've been talking to Jason. He told you, didn't he?"

"Suppose *you* tell me."

"Oh, boy. Am I in trouble? I didn't think beating off on my own patio would count as worthy of a confession, since I didn't know Jason was watching!"

"At first," she emphasized, raising her brows. "But once you did notice, to hear him tell it, you gave him quite a show."

"Liv—"

"Spill it."

Chuckling, he shook his head. "All right, you win. It was the night I met him, when we drank wine on his patio. Later, I couldn't sleep, so I went outside, reclined in the lounger and indulged in a little fantasy about him. When I realized he was watching me . . . God, I exploded."

"I can imagine, and I don't blame you. But since you chose not to mention it to me, I have no choice except to dole out your consequences," she said cheerfully.

The prospect brought him right out of his funk.

"Mmm." His vibrant green eyes darkened. Became . . . ravenous. Feral. "Lady, you're just what the doctor ordered."

"Oh, you might want to wait before you sing my praises. I have something painfully tantalizing in mind for a very naughty boy."

His erection rubbed her belly through the denim of his jeans. The sharp intake of breath, the dilation of his pupils, gave away his willing surrender. Excitement quickened her blood as she led him upstairs to their bedroom and glanced at the digital clock on the nightstand. Jason would be waiting by now, watching for her signal.

"Take off all your clothes," she ordered. "Every stitch, then go stand by the window next to the bed."

Alex threw her a puzzled look, but did as he was told. When he pushed down his jeans, his cock, ruddy and highly aroused, arched to kiss his stomach. He walked over to the window and waited in eager silence.

"Open the blinds and tell me what you see."

He did, and shrugged. "I see Jason's house next door."

"What else?"

"I—I can see right into a bedroom on the second floor, and the lighting is low."

"Like mood lighting?"

"Yes."

"Good. Now, turn out the lights so it's completely dark in here," she said in a soft, seductive voice. "So that you can see without being seen very well. Then come back and stand in front of the window, facing out."

"Liv, what—"

"Do it."

After switching off the lamps on either side of the bed, he returned to his spot—and gasped.

On cue, Jason stepped in front of his own window. A very naked, lean-muscled Jason with his legs spread, erect, shiny cock in hand. Fisting it, stroking at leisure. Up the considerable length and down to his balls.

Jason's head tipped back in obvious rapture as he worked his cock, sun-streaked brown hair falling away from his face and to his shoulders.

"My God," Alex breathed. "He's—he's—"

"Gorgeous? A young man you'd like to sample for yourself?"

Alex swallowed hard. "Yes, Liv. You know I would."

"I do know. He's one of your fantasies come true," she mused. "Mine, too. Unfortunately for you, your punishment tonight is only being allowed to watch."

Taking advantage of his temporary loss of speech, she removed a pair of binoculars from where she'd stashed them in the nightstand drawer. "Every good voyeur has one of these," she said, handing them over. "You're all set. Enjoy the show, and don't move until I get back."

Trembling, pussy hot and needy, she turned to go.

"Wait! You're not staying to watch?"

Looking over her shoulder, she smiled. Lord, her pair of guys made a luscious sight. "No, sweetie. I'm part of the show. See you soon."

She hurried out, eager to give them all a night to remember.

. . .

As soon as Liv cleared the door, Alex returned his stunned gaze to Jason. The younger man fisted his cock as if he hadn't a care in the world, his stance catlike, those eyes staring across the distance between them as though Alex could hide nothing from him.

Don't move? His brain had packed its bags and left for Aruba. A one-way ticket. His own cock was hot as a solar flare between his legs and he didn't dare touch it. Not yet. He wanted to shoot off, but not this early.

He nearly did, anyway, as Liv entered the room and crossed to Jason. She made a production of stripping, first the powder blue T-shirt, baring her braless breasts, nipples peaked. Next her jeans and panties.

Naked. His wife was naked with another man.

About to play with her gorgeous young stud, do anything she wanted with him. While her husband watched every scintillating detail.

He was so fucking aroused right now, it wouldn't take a bomb to kill him. The impending orgasm would finish him.

Jason and Liv faced each other, giving Alex a perfect view in profile. Liv went down on her knees, dark head bent to her lover's cock. She bobbed on the tip and Alex jerked the binoculars to his face so fast he almost broke his nose.

"Jesus Christ."

Wickedness in wide-screen.

His wife laved the younger man's slick, veined cock. Swirled the tip a few times, then wrapped her lips around it. Inched his impressive shaft farther into her mouth, swallowing him by degrees.

Alex felt it snap into place. An invisible cord stretched between all three of them. Decadent, delicious, undeniable. They fed off this connection, and so did he. The bond they'd formed in that instant seemed as vital as his heartbeat, thrumming in tempo to Jason's hips thrusting into Liv's sweet mouth.

She sucked a bit more before pulling off him, leaving him erect. With a flick of her hand, they switched positions, angling their bodies so Alex could see her front. She spread her legs, bracing one hand on Jason's shoulder as he nuzzled her curls, flicked her nub with his tongue.

He began to eat her, alternating between sucking and licking, his tongue plunging between the lips of her sex. Gathering her juices. Alex groaned, palming himself with his free hand. He knew how damned good Liv tasted, how rich and dewy, and a sudden image of him and Jason licking her together, two tongues feasting on her flesh, seared itself into his mind.

Alex's cock jerked and he cupped his balls, staving off his orgasm with difficulty. *Don't want to come! Make it last!* Another gesture from Liv, and her lover stood, following her to the bed. His wife owned both men, had them hanging on her every move, her every wish.

She lay on her back, the top of her head toward Alex. Jason crawled between her legs, scooped his hand underneath her rear, and lifted her bottom half clear off the bed. Hooking her knees over his shoulders, he pulled her toward him, impaling that lovely pussy on his cock.

"Oh, God! Shit . . . "

Alex pumped his own shaft harder, mesmerized by the scene in front of him. He could see where they joined, the younger man fucking his wife with deep, sure strokes. Burying himself to the balls again and again. Plunging faster and harder as Liv's hands fisted in the bedcovers.

Wild. Wanton.

So fucking sexy.

Jason thrust one last time, lips parted in an obvious cry of ecstasy. Pumping his cum deep into Liv, marking her. Branding all three of them. Alex's hoarse shout pierced the silence of the room as his own orgasm slammed him, hard. The binoculars tumbled from his grasp and he worked his cock for all he was worth, riding the waves, semen splattering the window. As the shudders subsided, it occurred to him to wonder whether the cop parked on the street had seen any of this, and decided he didn't care.

God, had he ever come so hard he thought he might shake apart?

Panting, he leaned against the edge of the window, transfixed as Jason withdrew from Liv. Very deliberately, the younger man dipped his fingers into her sex, brought them to his lips, and sucked away their combined juices—while lifting his head to stare in Alex's direction.

A challenge? Or a simple acknowledgment of their connection?

Hardly mattered. Not with his cum streaking down the glass and his body trembling like he'd touched a live wire.

He only knew he already craved much, much more. Didn't want to be kept at a distance next time, unable to touch them or participate. And that had been his brilliant wife's plan all along, hadn't it?

Well, it worked.

Liv slid off Jason's bed and gave the man a lingering kiss. Hand in hand, the pair disappeared from view. Alex stayed put like she'd told him to, but as the minutes crept past and she didn't return, he began to suspect they weren't quite done torturing him.

Twenty minutes later, his sore muscles were starting to bitch a little. He couldn't stand here much longer and decided to give her five more minutes before he parked his ass on the bed.

Just then, Liv strolled in, dressed, hair damp, sporting the glow of a well-fucked woman. Her step, however, was hesitant, her expression revealing worry that she'd gone too far.

Smiling, he met his wife halfway and pulled her close. "Baby, you sure know how to make it hurt so good."

There. Her blue eyes sparkled in satisfaction, concern vanished. "I try. Did you . . . enjoy?"

He laughed. "I don't think there's a word strong enough for how thoroughly the two of you blew my mind. I doubt poor Alex Junior will ever function properly again."

Her giggle warmed his soul, and it struck him how much good this had done them both. Make that the three of them.

Wrapping her arms around his neck, she looked up at him, face shining with love. "It's working, isn't it? Our deal, all of it."

"Yes, it is." He kissed her nose. "And tonight was incredible, Liv. You and Jason . . . God, I can't describe how turned on I was seeing you swallow his cock, watching him fuck you."

"Oh, Alex." She hugged him tightly.

"You were beautiful together. I can't wait for more, and I mean that."

Christ, yes. This was damned near perfect.

And it would be, the second the police caught the man who wanted him dead.

Eight

✳

Jason wasn't getting old yet, so the sex must have been making him stupid.

He should've noticed before now. Alex bent over in his front flower bed. Damn, what a fine ass. The man radiated untapped sexuality from every pore of his skin, and Jason was willing to bet his inheritance Alex was a natural sensualist.

In fact, he couldn't wait to find out for himself.

Peering out the dining room window, Jason figured the guy had been at it a while, what with the piles of weeds dotting the yard. Didn't a rich dude like Alex hire a lawn service? Could be he was a practical man who enjoyed doing things himself. *Like me.*

The idea pleased Jason, though he wasn't sure why.

Whatever. He had a great excuse to venture out and talk to Alex, not that he needed one. He just hadn't been sure how to approach the man after the other night.

Hey, you handsome bastard! Did you get off when I fucked your wife? Can I do you next? Nice day, huh?

Alex hadn't rung his doorbell either, but Jason guessed now was as good an opportunity as any to move things along.

In the front hallway, he checked his appearance in the mirror with a sober stare. Snug black T-shirt emphasizing his flat stomach, worn jeans hanging off his hipbones just so. Looking hot as fuck had never been his problem.

On the surface, anyway. On bad days he fantasized about taking a knife to his pretty mug and—

"Suck it up, shithead," he told himself. "Own your mistakes."

His cell phone vibrated on the hall table, belting out, "Boulevard of Broken Dreams."

Next step on the road to self-enlightenment: download a ringtone that didn't make him want to dive for his unopened bottle of Prozac.

Reaching for the phone, he sighed. Reginald was the only person from his other life who knew where he was, or gave a shit. "Yeah?"

"Why the fuck haven't I heard from you all week?"

Well, giving a shit might be a bit optimistic.

"Been busy, Reginald." *Banging Quinn's wife like the sun ain't gonna come up tomorrow. Gonna nail him next. Go me.*

"Don't be flip with me, kid. I've had to pull everyone so far back on this thing, we're watching from goddamned Mars."

"But you are watching. I'm on the bench."

Silence. Jason could practically see the big vein pounding in the big jerk's temple.

"Someone needs Quinn dead," the man enunciated. "If not Palmer Hodge, then who? The wife?"

"Wrong tree." A person couldn't fake the terror he'd seen on Olivia's face when she learned about Alex being hurt. Nobody was that good. "With Alex dead, his caseload gets redistributed, and the Boardman trial is the most important of them."

"But he's defending the asshole."

"Whom the D.A. is prosecuting as the head honcho, when we know it's Hodge. Only Hodge doesn't *know* we know." *And when he finds out how, I'm a dead man.*

"Hodge wants Boardman to go down, and Quinn is in the way. Which means . . . Hodge has people inside. *Shit.*"

"Yep."

"Find out who the players are. And Jason?"

"Yes, sir?"

"Don't let me down this time."

Click. "Fucker." Aggravated, he tossed down his phone, knowing his boss wasn't to blame.

You won't fail again, Jase. Believe that. On bad days, the pep talk usually worked. Today, having Alex as a distraction helped a ton. He strolled out his front door, taking in a lungful of crisp spring air. Getting warmer, summer on the way. Best to enjoy the last of these mild days before the heat fried them all like eggs in a skillet.

Stepping off his porch, he heard birds chirping in the trees, a dog barking, a car cruising down the street. His gaze found Alex, the man busy stuffing the weeds into a black garbage bag, and he halted his trek across his own lawn to admire the view again, close-up.

Jesus, Alex was one gorgeous sonofabitch. Feet bare, wearing cutoffs and an old St. Louis Cardinals T-shirt, dark sunglasses, blond hair shining in the sun, he looked good enough to eat. *I've got the whipped cream; you be the cherry.*

Grinning, he started forward again, a cheerful greeting on his lips. The car approaching from down the street slowed as it drew near. "Alex! Need a hand? I—"

Instinct made him break off and glance toward the car.

The driver's window began to lower and Jason saw the man inside looking toward Alex. Saw the arm extending.

He ran, screaming, reaching for his gun that—*fucking hell*—was in the house.

"Alex, get down! Get down!"

Alex straightened and turned his head, eyes wide and questioning, lips parted. Held up a hand as if to ward off Jason's flying tackle.

Jason hit him like a linebacker, wrapping his arms around Alex's torso, taking him right off his feet. They crashed through the bushes, Alex's "Oomph!" grunting in his ear as they landed hard in the dirt, Jason on top of him.

Jason stared down into Alex's green eyes, protecting him with his own body and panting with the surge of adrenaline, waiting for the bullets to rip through their scant cover. Rip into his flesh.

Better him than Alex.

Seconds ticked as they stared at one another, the whine of the retreating car giving way to the normal sounds of a spring day. Alex had stilled and was staring back at him, confusion and something much more combustible in his gaze.

"Well," Jason began, mouth hitching in a half smile. "No bullets. Must've scared him off, appearing the way I did. Some rescue, huh?"

One eloquent, dark blond eyebrow lifted. "A truly amazing feat of heroics. Now I know who to call next time I need to be rescued from my frickin' *paper boy*."

Jason blinked. "What?"

A flush crept up his neck. He looked, though he didn't want to. Sure enough, the daily newspaper lay on the lawn—right where the delivery guy had tossed it.

"I'll be goddamned," he muttered. The body underneath him began to shake. Alex's face split into a wide, breathtaking smile, the absurdity of the situation obviously getting to him. "Don't you laugh at me, you shithead. I thought you were about to be peppered full of holes."

Which, of course, made Alex laugh harder. "L-local attorney killed by rogue newspaper boy! Story at t-ten."

"Shut up, nimrod. You shouldn't be waltzing around out here with a target on your fucking chest."

Alex sobered some, laughter fading, the reality of what *could've* happened sinking in. "I know, but I was about to lose my mind haunting the house, and with Liv at the restaurant today . . ." He paused, voice going quiet. "Anyway, thanks, man."

Jason made no move to roll off him just yet. Awareness crackled between them, sharp and electric. Sizzled the length of their bodies from chest to groin, every inch of where they were pressed together. Jason shifted, settled himself more firmly between Alex's spread thighs, testing the waters. To his satisfaction, if not surprise, Alex was rock-hard just like himself. And blazing hot.

"Jason," he whispered. Those striking eyes were wide again, for a totally different reason.

"Yeah." Reaching up, he plucked a few leaves out of Alex's hair, then let his fingers trace the other man's strong jaw, his full lips.

"You can get off me now."

"I could." Dipping his head, he brought his mouth to hover over Alex's. So close, making him want. And Alex did want this. The proof was in the muscled body vibrating underneath him, the dilation of his pupils, the quickening of his heartbeat.

"Jase, get off me."

"Why?"

"Because Irma Finklestein is probably plastered to her front window with *her* binoculars, that's why."

The weird tension broke and Jason laughed, pushing off Alex and getting to his feet. "Good reason," he said, offering his hand. Grinning, Alex took it. Jason helped him up, thinking maybe he should retreat. Give the man time to process.

"Want to come in for a beer?"

Or maybe not. "Sure, sounds great."

Yeah, a nice, manly beer to equalize the testosterone level in the atmosphere.

Subduing his smile, Jason trailed Alex into the house. In the kitchen, his friend fished a couple of Coronas from the fridge, twisted the top off and handed him one.

"Thanks." They took a long draw of their beers, studying each other and pretending not to. Well, that was bullshit. "How long have you known you were attracted to men?"

"Jesus, you don't pull any punches." Alex set his bottle on the counter and raked a hand through his hair. "Always."

Jason waited, letting Alex relax into the conversation, tell things his way. He seemed a little hesitant at first, warming to the subject as he went.

"With my folks, there was never a big meltdown or a lot of drama over my sexual curiosity. When I was in high school, my mom walked into my room, caught me and a buddy kissing when we were supposed to be studying, excused herself and walked right out again. I mean, sure, they weren't happy, but I was their son and they loved me. Dad sat me down later and advised me to think on it hard, said if I was just as attracted to women, why bring a load of difficulty on myself? Made sense to me."

"So you suppressed your desires and lived the status quo."

"I didn't see it that way. I dated plenty, had a great time. Then I met Liv during my last year of law school, and she knocked my socks off." He gave a wistful smile. "She became my best friend, and the sex was incredible. What more did I need?"

"At the time."

"Yes."

"And now?"

Alex wandered into the living room, quiet. Thoughtful. Jason followed, keeping his distance. This was Alex's show and he wouldn't make the first move. No, it was important for his friend to take that step alone.

"What if . . ." Alex shored up his nerve and looked Jason in the eye. "What if you were given permission to have your fill of any sexual indulgence you wanted? To give in to your passion and take whatever you desired, with whomever, however and whenever you desired it? No taboos, free of guilt or consequences—and I don't mean the sort of punishments Liv makes up, but the messy, life-altering kind. Would you do it?"

God, those eyes. They ensnared him completely and he had no will to get away, no inclination to run, though it would be best. A fist closed around his throat, making speech difficult. "I *have* indulged, Alex. I've done things you can't imagine, have had those things done to me, and reveled in them all. But there's always a consequence," he whispered. "Always. No one escapes, and you're a fool if you don't understand that."

No way in hell did he want to drive Alex away, but he owed the man at least part of the truth about himself. Alex had to go into this with his eyes open, or any relationship between them would fail miserably.

"What price have you paid?"

"You really don't want to know." Even though, to be fair, Alex should. "Just run, fast and far."

God, please don't run.

Alex took a step closer. And another. "What if I don't want to escape, Jase?"

His heart hammered, a wild beast in his chest. "You should."

"I don't." He closed the remaining couple of feet, his gaze feral. Hot. "If I'm going to pay, I'd better make sure my sins are worth the price."

Cupping the back of Jason's head, Alex brought his mouth down hard. This was no gentle kiss, but one of possession. Hungry, brutal. His tongue speared the seam of Jason's lips, explored and stroked. Jason melted into him with a groan, seeking his heat, desperate to crawl inside the man and never come out.

"Tell me," Jason gasped between kisses. "Tell me what you want."

"You. On your knees."

"Thought you'd never ask."

"I'm not asking."

Oh, God, yes! The man was a dominant. A beautiful, natural dom who'd never seized the reins before—at least not with a man.

Lucky, lucky Jason.

Sinking to his knees, he reached for Alex's cutoffs. Flicked open the button and lowered the zipper. The shorts were loose and slid down easily, the man's long, thick erection springing free and leaking from the flared tip. Alex kicked away the shorts and yanked the Cardinals T-shirt over his head, tossing it. Jason let his eyes roam up that magnificent body. Naked, tanned and muscled, ready to take what it wanted from him. Jason's own cock ached for relief, but would have to wait.

He'd never been as grateful for his training as he was now.

"Suck me," Alex ordered, vibrating with excitement, burying a hand in Jason's hair. "Do it now."

"Damn." Hell, yes. He'd make the man's eyeballs cross or die in the attempt. "This beats the shit out of watching you from a distance, wanting you inside me."

Leaning in, he nuzzled Alex's balls, encouraged by the tightening of his sac, the soft intake of breath. He loved the silky skin on his lips, the brush of fine hair on his cheeks, the musky male scent. He rolled one in his mouth, suckling, the salty taste delighting his tongue. So different from a woman, yet no less wonderful.

"Fuck, yes," Alex rasped.

And Jason fed on the power a submissive held over his master.

Jason laved Alex's cock from base to head, manipulating those taut balls with his fingers. Alex spread his legs wider in invitation, moaning, already incoherent. Just like Jason wanted.

He sucked the flushed head oh so gently, driving the other man out of his mind. Dipping his tongue into the little slit, tasting the pre-cum that evidenced pleasure Jason hoped he'd be the only man to ever give.

No, don't set yourself up for another fall. Just fly.

And crash later.

He drew the delicious cock deeper, keeping the pressure tight, drawing it down, down into his throat until his airway was blocked. To the place of true nirvana, sacrificing himself to serve another.

This was what made a sub tick. Not so much the physical act, but the joy to be found in subservience. And this was Jason's strength as well as his one unfulfilled desire—until now.

To give his total trust, and have it *returned*. To achieve a bond with his partner beyond sex. No posturing, no lies.

Closing his eyes, he let himself go. Allowed himself to *feel*.

Alex's fingers clutching his hair.

Alex's cock slamming down his throat.

Strong thighs spread, hips pistoning.

The man's body claiming his. Owning him.

Can't breathe.

And it was good. So goddamned good.

Why couldn't Alex have been his first? Why?

No more thinking. His lungs screamed and his vision grayed as his own cock began to pulse. He poured out his release, giving Alex everything he had, everything he was.

Alex cried out, plummeted over the edge after him, seed pulsing, thick and hot.

Jason wished he could express his immense happiness, but could only swallow, throat working.

And swallow.

And swallow.

Home. Alex and Liv are home and nothing else matters.

Nothing else.

Jason slipped away and the world disappeared.

· · ·

Alex's cock pulsed in tempo to his heartbeat.

He pressed Jason's face into his groin, held him there, not quite believing how fantastic it was to possess such control over another man. *This* man. To have Jason willingly give himself over, making it clear he belonged to Alex, was his to use however he wished.

"Ah, fuck! Yes!"

The rich scent of sex teased his nose, and he knew the other man had achieved his release. He pumped with abandon as Jason swallowed—until the younger man went limp and began to slump sideways.

"Jason? Shit!"

Alex hit his knees, catching Jason by the shoulders and easing him to the carpet. Anxious, he peered into the other man's pale face, caressing his jaw. Jason's chest heaved and he began to breathe heavily, color once again flooding his cheeks.

"Jesus. God. Thank God."

Warm, dazed brown eyes met his. "Holy freaking shit, that was amazing."

Laughing nervously, Alex popped his arm. "You scared the hell out of me, dammit. Are you all right?"

"Hey, don't curse the one that pleases you," he said, sitting up. "I'm fine, just a little breath play, you know?"

"No, and don't do it again." Alex took his lips in another kiss, this one slow. Easy. It was so good, better than he'd ever expected, and he was torn between marveling that he'd waited so long to experience this and being awfully glad he had.

"Christ, you make love with your mouth," Jason said. "Ought to have those lips insured."

The compliment pleased Alex. "Liv says they're my sexiest feature."

Jason's eyes glinted with mischief. "Oh, I don't know about that."

"Jase, I'm not gay," he blurted. Smooth, real smooth.

"Oh. I see." Jason's handsome face went blank and he started to rise.

Alex caught his arm. "No, wait. All I mean is I don't care for labels. Sex is what it is and I've always believed people should be with whomever they choose without everyone making a huge deal."

"Sure," he said, studying Alex intently. "I agree. Now what?"

Alex wanted Jase again. So swiftly and with such force it shook him. "Now I take you upstairs."

Standing, he headed for the stairs, self-conscious about being buck naked and Jason still dressed. What if the man didn't follow? A glance behind him soothed his concern—Jase was grinning, the telltale bulge pushing at his zipper once more.

"Nice view, Quinn."

"Shut up."

"Make me—"

He yanked Jason into the bedroom and spun him around, kissing him hard while backing him up until his legs hit the mattress. "You're overdressed. Fix it."

Jason complied quickly, pulling off his black T-shirt and toeing off his shoes. His hands trembled a bit as he unbuttoned and unzipped his jeans, pushed them down. Excitement and arousal rolled off him in waves, along with the musky scent of his earlier release.

"You like to be told what to do," Alex mused aloud, recalling their conversation the evening by the pool. Not to mention his response downstairs. "Dominated."

"Only in the bedroom." Jase lifted his chin.

"Works for me."

Unable to resist, Alex buried a hand in the kid's hair. He loved the wild, sun-streaked waves falling to his shoulders. He smoothed a palm over his chest, thumb flicking a hard brown nipple. Skimmed downward over the flat, almost concave, abdomen, brushed the smattering of dark brown curls surrounding the burgeoning sex.

"Get on the bed and lie on your back."

Jason hurried to obey and spread out for him, totally wanton, lids half closed, expression needy, cock stiff against his lean thigh.

Alex crawled between his knees, as eager as he'd been when he'd had his first woman. "My turn to taste you."

He ran his hands up the insides of Jason's thighs, liking how the younger man whimpered in anticipation. Throaty, happy noises that increased when he rolled the man's balls in his fingers. God, they were soft and pliable, in contrast to the steely rod jutting above them. Testing one, he rolled it in his mouth, suckling as Jason had done to him.

"Oh . . . oh, Alex . . . "

Hell, yeah. He loved how Jason went liquid, giving all of himself. Trusting. With one finger, he swirled a drop of pearly cum over the head of Jason's cock while lavishing attention on his balls. Laving until the man writhed, lost to whatever he wanted to do.

And he wanted to taste more. Grabbing the base of Jason's cock, he brought the head to his lips. Began to suck.

"Mmm, yes." Earthy, salty. "Good."

Dipping his head, he sucked in earnest, tongue stroking the ridge underneath. Driving his prey mad.

"Alex . . . shit, yeah. Please . . . "

He pulled off. "Please what?"

"I n-need you. Inside me."

"Beg me."

"P-please, fuck me. I'm begging you," he whispered.

Something fierce and primal rose in him at the younger man's plea. His cock ached and throbbed. He had to claim what was his, or go insane.

"Mine," he heard himself snarl.

"Yes, yours."

That did it. With no effort, he flipped Jason onto his stomach, then pulled at his waist, guiding him to kneel, thighs spread. Alex got into position behind his lover, aching so badly to slam home he had to remind himself to prepare the kid. Although he'd only taken Liv this way, he figured the process wasn't so very different. He didn't want to hurt Jason. Much.

Wetting two fingers, he parted Jason's cheeks and slipped them inside. Stretching as quickly as he dared, using his saliva for lube.

"Don't wait. Just fuck me, please," Jason moaned.

Replacing his fingers with the head of his dripping cock, he issued a warning. "I won't be gentle. I can't, not this time."

"Hurt me—I don't care!"

The last of his resistance crumbled and he grabbed Jason's hips, pushing firmly past the tight ring of muscle. The sight of the sweet flesh parting to admit him, knowing the willing body underneath him was his to use as he wished, set him on fire.

Burying himself deep, he held for a moment, a guttural moan escaping his lips. So snug and hot around his prick, ass to groin, their balls rubbing. Delicious.

He pulled out slowly, then rammed inside again, ripping a harsh cry from his boy's throat. "That's right, my slut. Let me hear how much you love it."

"Oh, God! Fuck me hard!"

He did. Drove into that beautiful ass fast, hard and deep. Fucked his lovely toy right into the mattress, the slapping sounds of rough sex echoing through the room.

Angling to find Jason's magic gland, he pegged it without mercy, fucking them both into oblivion. The man's body went taut as a bowstring underneath him as he cried out, and Alex lunged even faster, reaching around and pumping Jason's cock.

Jason shouted, bucking, spilling liquid heat over Alex's hand. Alex went over, as well, erupting like a megaton bomb, pumping Jason full.

The younger man collapsed and Alex went with him, sprawled across his back. They lay in a panting, quivering heap for God knows how long, neither of them game to move for a while.

Reason returned, with none of the guilt or self-recrimination Alex might've expected. No way around the truth. He'd enjoyed the hell out of being with Jason, looked forward to being with him again, and he wasn't going to feel bad about it.

But how would Liv feel now that the deed was done?

He hoped she'd be pleased. In every way.

Nine

✺

Well, that was oodles of fun.

Soothing her irate head chef's ruffled feathers, spending another hour on the books and filling in as hostess for the girl who called in sick. An afternoon of madness that didn't quite hold the appeal it once had, all while waiting for her ride. And waiting.

Neither Alex nor Jason ever showed, or bothered to phone.

"Thank you, Chrissy," she said, shouldering her purse and fishing out her keys. The cute waitress pulled the VW Bug to a stop in front of Liv's house and grinned, snapping her gum in tempo to some god-awful screeching dubbed new-wave rock. All of this combined with the girl's purple-streaked red hair made Liv feel as though she'd fallen into a weird time warp and emerged about a hundred years old.

"Gotcha covered, Miz Q. Go give Mr. Q. hell, huh?"

"Fabulous idea," she muttered, stepping out. "See you next week."

As the little car sputtered and coughed its retreat, Liv stalked up the sidewalk, fuming. Black trash bags and weeds dotted the yard, and a pair of hedge trimmers lay in the flower bed. Alex had been the one to insist she not go about unescorted for a while, and he'd gotten so busy playing in the dirt she'd slipped his mind?

Wonderful.

Letting herself in, she closed and locked the door, then cut through the formal dining room into the kitchen. "Alex?"

No answer. Grr.

A half-consumed bottle of Corona sat abandoned on the counter, and Liv frowned. Obviously, he'd come inside for a re-freshment break from the yard work, so where had he gone? Walk-ing over, she wrapped her fingers around the bottle. Warm. It wasn't like Alex to leave a perfectly good beer to ruin.

Fear skittered along her spine. "Alex, honey?"

What if he'd been surprised by whoever rigged his Jag . . . oh, God.

She jogged to the back patio doors. No sign of him in the back-yard or in the pool. Hand over her pounding heart, she turned and scanned the living room, looking for signs of a struggle. Any-thing out of place.

What she found was a pair of cutoffs and a T-shirt on the floor. Alex's clothing. And another deserted beer.

Oh.

Of all the terrible scenarios she'd imagined as to why her hus-band had forgotten her this afternoon, Alex inviting a woman here wasn't one of them.

Jenna. Had he given her a call, asked her to drop by with an *important file?* Had she stayed, enticed Alex upstairs for some af-ternoon delight?

Here. Another woman. *In our bed.*

Oh, no. That, she could not handle.

Like you have a choice?

She mounted the stairs, numb. Mind spinning. She didn't want to see but had to, like a rubbernecker passing a fatal accident. Her hands shook and her stomach lurched. Because Alex would never violate the sanctity of their personal haven with someone he didn't truly care for.

That's what frightened her more than anything—to think he'd fallen for the object of his lust. A female third, she couldn't do. Or worse, what if her plan had backfired and she'd lost Alex to Jenna altogether?

On wobbly legs, she entered their bedroom—and her mouth fell open. The air whooshed from her lungs, the profound relief not unlike what she'd experienced in the ER upon learning Alex would be fine.

Her husband had gotten busy playing all right. Just not in the dirt.

And not with Jenna.

"Thank God," she whispered, moving forward.

Intrigued, Liv studied the sleeping pair. They lay in a tangle of sleek, golden limbs, with Alex sprawled on his back, Jason draped across his chest, legs entwined. Two gorgeous lions basking in the sun. The decadent sight and unmistakable scent of male musk called to the core of her as a woman.

Yes, this she could do. More, she desired it. Against all odds, this felt good and right.

Because these men were *hers.*

She perched lightly on the edge of the bed, drinking them in.

Both were dead to the world, one of Alex's arms draped around Jason's waist as though making sure he wouldn't get away. There was something so sweet about that, so damned innocent for men who were anything but, the irony made Liv smile.

Reaching out, she pushed a lock of blond hair out of Alex's eyes. He shifted, a low, satisfied hum rumbling in his chest, and blinked at her.

"Liv? What . . . "

"Hello, Casanova," she said, trailing a finger over his lips. "I see why you forgot me, though you'll have to grovel to get back in my good graces."

"Forgot you? I don't— oh. Oh, shit!"

Alex bolted upright, dumping Jason, who grouched a muffled complaint as he buried his face in the covers.

Alex blinked at Jason, eyes widening, then back at Liv, face leaching of color. "Liv, baby, I'm so sorry."

She cocked her head, enjoying this perhaps more than she should. "For dooming me to catch a ride with Chrissy in her asthmatic Bug? Or for fucking Jason?"

Despite his obvious discomfort, he held her gaze steadily. "The first, not the second."

At his admission, a spark flared to life between them. Passion, now so close to the surface where there used to be emptiness, cold and dead.

She covered his hand with hers. "What do you think this means?"

He didn't pretend not to understand. "I don't know," he said, looking down at their sleeping lover with unmistakable affection. And no small amount of desire. "But it feels right."

"You sound surprised."

"I am. I thought I'd feel ... different. You know, afterward. More confused. A little sleazy."

"Hell-o, awake here." Jason rolled to his back and stretched, muscles flexing over his ribs and hard abdomen. His cock lay in repose against one lean thigh, round balls nestled underneath. "If this is where you two play True Confessions, Dirty Neighbor Edition, I'm gone."

Alex grimaced. "Sorry, Jase. I didn't mean it as an insult."

"No sweat. Just wait until I ghost out of here before you go all Dr. Ruth and shit." He pushed up, his expression a mixture of amusement and annoyance.

"Please don't go." Liv placed a palm in the center of the younger man's chest, halting his departure. "Don't you want to participate in my husband's punishment?"

He paused, glancing between her and Alex with renewed interest. "Yeah? Dishing out the discipline isn't normally my thing, but for you? I'm glad to make an exception. And I have to say, Olivia, your man doesn't look particularly worried about the prospect."

Indeed he didn't, if his rising erection was any indication. He looked gloriously debauched and ready for round two. "Good. I want him aroused and pleading for release, not anxious. Stress kills the libido."

"Not a problem at the moment," Alex said with a wry grin.

Jason slid from the bed and stood, comfortable in his naked skin. "Well, you're the boss lady. Where do you want us?"

What a mouthwatering, loaded question.

"Somewhere a bit more stimulating. Come with me, gentlemen."

Walking out, she glanced over her shoulder. They trailed her like a pair of eager puppies—or more appropriately, drooling frat brothers, from their good-natured ribbing and the lewd stares fixed on her bottom.

Predictable, but cute. She'd have to yank their leashes and bring them to heel, that much was plain.

Downstairs, Liv led them into the media-turned-playroom and switched the light on dim. The windowless space was a wicked cave with her toys spread around, inviting its occupants to partake in a feast of sensual delights.

Jason whistled. "Damn. I didn't figure you guys as being into the scene."

Liv studied his rapt perusal of the setup. "The scene?"

"Leather, BDSM."

Good lord. "We're not, really, other than spanking and tying each other to the bed once in a while. The equipment is new. This is where my darling hubby receives his punishment, and it can also serve when we're in the mood for something edgier."

"I'd say you're on the right track." Jason winked at her. "What's your pleasure?"

Liv gestured to the set of bondage poles Alex had become acquainted with on the night of his first indiscretion. "I want Alex bound, but we've sampled that one already. We need something with more bite. Something to drive him crazy."

Jason padded to a table loaded with all sorts of scary tools. Inspecting a leather harness, he lifted it, mischief dancing in those brown eyes. "Like this?"

"What is that thing?" Alex managed, tone doubtful.

"Butt-plug harness," Jason supplied with an evil grin. "Complete with cock ring. Gets you coming and going, if you'll pardon the pun."

Liv nodded, beaming. "Perfect! He'll look beautiful in the leather, stretched taut and tortured beyond endurance, don't you think?"

Jason eyed the object of their discussion as though he was a steak on a platter. "Hell, yeah."

Alex backed up a step. "Uh, I don't think—"

"You aren't required to think, only to obey. Get over there and Jason will help strap you in."

Harness in hand, Jason searched the table. "Lube?"

"Top drawer in the chest next to you."

"Jesus," Alex muttered, but did as he was told. He wasn't staring at either of them but at the contraption that would serve as his prison for the next hour or more. And gracious, his cock had hardened enough to penetrate steel, the hunger on his face surpassing his misgivings.

Oh, this would be fun.

Jason slipped the harness over his head while Alex stood, spine rigid. "We're going to leave the neck strap loose until we get the plug and ring in place. Kneel on those pillows." Alex complied. "Good, now spread your legs."

Squatting next to Alex, Jason grabbed the dangling front piece and ripped apart the Velcro enclosing the soft fabric of the cock ring. Next, he lifted Liv's husband's balls and fastened the ring behind the sac, around the base of his cock. This pulled the front of the harness snug against Alex's chest and abdomen, and raised his flushed sex to a seemingly impossible height. Alex groaned and closed his eyes.

Jason checked the fit of the ring and nodded in satisfaction. "Tight enough to keep you from coming, but not cause physical damage. I'm going to pull this strap connected to the back of the ring between your legs, then insert the plug. But I'm going to get you slick first. I'll talk you through it, okay?"

Robbed of speech, Alex dipped his head once.

Their lover moved behind Alex and took the small tube of gel, slicking two fingers. Fascinated, Liv stepped forward, drawn by the sight of her beautiful men together. One submitting to the other.

Both carrying out her wishes.

Jason parted her husband's cheeks, teased his puckered entrance. Then gently began to push inside.

"Oh, God," Alex whispered, head falling back. His eyelids were at half-mast, dazed, lips parted.

Jason kissed his shoulder, working deeper. Opening him. "Easy, babe. Just let yourself relax. Let go."

Flames ignited in Liv's sex. The room was suddenly too hot, and she unbuttoned her blouse, never taking her attention from the decadent scene before her as the garment slid to the floor. Alex moaned, arching into Jason's hand, seeking more of the younger man's skillful caresses.

"You're ready now." Jason withdrew his fingers, chuckling at his captive's distressed whimper, and smeared the excess lube on the plug. "In we go. Breathe."

As Jason pushed the plug home, Liv had to remind herself to breathe, as well. That was . . . oh. Oh, sweet heaven, Alex was lovely this way. A sexual banquet, eager to be devoured. How could she have been blind to his needs—and her own—for so many years?

Liv removed her bra and kicked off her heels, vanquishing them to the growing pile. Jason hooked the back straps of the harness to the piece connected to the plug, effectively securing the entire unit.

"How does it feel?" Jason planted light kisses on her husband's neck, nibbling.

"Incredible," Alex rasped. "I can't move without . . . "

"Fucking yourself?"

"God, yes! I don't know if I can take this."

Liv stepped around to Alex's front and took his chin in one hand, raising his head to meet her gaze. "You can, and you will. Jason, take those fur-lined cuffs from the table and fasten his hands behind his back." She didn't glance at Jason as he hurried to do her bidding. "Confess, my love."

Aroused as he was, it took Alex's brain a moment to catch up to her demand. He sucked in a sharp breath as Jason cuffed his wrists behind his back.

"I was working in the front yard, and Jase thought our paper delivery guy was a hit man. He tackled me, and we ended up in the bushes with him on top of me."

The image was funny, but Liv didn't laugh. Alex's would-be killer could have easily caught him outside, unprotected, in spite of the frequent visits by the unmarked police cruiser. Shaking off what might've happened, she said, "Go on."

"I thought Jase was going to kiss me, but he didn't. I wanted him to, but didn't know what to say. I invited him in for a beer instead."

"Which neither of you finished," she prompted.

"We were talking and I kept watching his mouth, wondering how he'd taste," he said quietly, as though still amazed by this. "How he'd feel. Around and under me. I couldn't resist anymore, so I kissed him."

"Show me."

Alex blinked at her. "What?"

"Show me how you kissed him." Glancing at Jason, she waved a hand to indicate the floor.

Their lover responded swiftly, dropping to his knees, nose a scant inch from Alex's. Waiting. Looming over Jase, Alex took the younger man's lips in a blistering kiss. Ate his mouth, bending Jase backwards, very much the dominant despite being bound. At last, Alex pulled back, green eyes flashing with desire. Both of them were breathing hard.

Lord, they were combustible together. Her exposed nipples tingled, tightening. Wanting.

"That's how I kissed him, Mistress."

"And it didn't end there. What happened next?"

"He helped me undress, and I ordered him to suck my cock." Alex's pupils dilated. "He did, too. Right there in the living room. Just deep-throated me until I shot so hard I thought I'd pass out."

Liv moaned. She couldn't help herself. "I want to see his pretty mouth on you," she said, rolling her nipples between her fingers. "Jason, give me a demonstration, but keep him on the edge. No coming, either of you."

Not that Alex could, his cock and balls bound to prevent it. Which was good, because the instant Jason bent and swirled the pre-cum on the tip of the flared head with his tongue, her husband gasped, looking like he might have a coronary.

Their lover suckled the crown, stroking Alex's restrained balls with one finger. His sun-streaked head bobbed, each stroke pushing Alex deeper between his lips. Making his length wet and shiny.

"Oh yes," she said, unzipping her pants. Pushing them off her hips and stepping out of them. "That's so beautiful. My sexy men, so into each other."

"Jason . . . shit! Liv, *please*."

She didn't want Jason to stop, but knew he must or her husband would implode. He might, anyway, considering what she had planned next. "All right. Jason, release him and kneel beside me." Jason pulled off his quarry with a noisy slurp, and gave Alex a cocky grin. She'd deal with Jase in a minute and wipe the smirk away. She addressed her panting husband. "Then you took him to our room?"

"Y-yes."

"To our bed?"

"Jesus. Yes."

"And did exactly what to him there?"

"Fucked him, Liv. Hard and deep. I fucked him and I loved every second of it." A shaky laugh escaped his throat.

"This concludes your confession?"

"Yes, Mistress."

"We've already begun your punishment, so let's get on with it, shall we?" Reaching up, she grabbed a horizontal silver bar suspended from the ceiling by a length of chain on each end. She lowered it to shoulder level—just enough for a man to stretch himself a bit while holding on to it. Last, she gave the bar a firm tug like one would to a window shade, causing the chain to latch and hold it in place.

"Since you, dear hubby, enjoyed using our new friend as your personal toy this afternoon, it's only fair that I do the same. While you watch, tortured, unable to participate. All right, Jason?"

Jason smiled. "Yes, Mistress."

"Reach above you, hold on to the bar and spread your knees. Don't let go for any reason, until I say we're done."

"I can't touch you at all?" He stuck out his lower lip in an enticing pout. Adorable shit.

"My rules, my way." She arched a brow, inviting him to challenge her. But he didn't dare if he wanted to play, and he knew it. The power flooding her veins, mingled with raw lust, was a heady, intoxicating thing.

Jason lifted his arms, wrapped his fingers around the bar, the action stretching and bunching his muscles. The young man was all smooth lines and lean grace. A sensual delight.

All hers.

He waited, outwardly composed, but the pulse throbbing at the base of his throat belied his excitement. Crouching on all fours, Liv crawled between his spread knees and gave the head of his cock a slow lick. He shuddered, his need to touch her evident in every tense muscle, the soft intake of breath, but he kept hold of the bar.

She laved the silken underside of his length, then lower, tonguing the velvety sac. "Mmm, you taste so good."

"Olivia, please!"

"Please what?"

"Fuck me," he begged hoarsely. "Or shoot me. Just put me out of my misery."

"Since I don't have a weapon handy, I'll take the first choice."

In truth, she wasn't willing to keep any of them waiting a second longer. Spinning around, she presented Jase with her backside and reached behind her, steadying his cock. Positioning the crown between the slick lips of her sex. God, it was incredible, so naughty, doing this with Alex in the same room, trussed, helpless and stimulated beyond words.

Slowly, she backed up, inching Jason into her fiery channel. He was shaking, moaning with mindless arousal, and she loved those sounds.

"God, yes. Liv, take him," Alex gasped.

She loved that, too. Everything she'd ever dreamed of, mutual pleasure, the freedom of fulfillment, was right here in this room. With these two men.

At last, Jason was seated to the balls. Groin to ass, his sac rubbing her wet pussy, fanning the flames. She began to move, impaling herself on his long, sleek rod. In and out. Again and again with languid strokes.

"Olivia . . ." Jason matched her tempo, thrusting, his strong thighs cradling hers.

She'd told him not to let go of the bar, but hadn't said he couldn't move his hips. Now she was extremely glad. He was poetry in motion, a man born to please his lovers. Every gorgeous part of him made to submit.

Faster and faster she rode him until her body sizzled, flashing hot and cold from head to toe, signaling her impending orgasm. Driven over the edge, she had no thought of holding back, but let the ecstasy wash over and through her. She stiffened, her pussy walls rippling and squeezing his cock, triggering his release.

Jason poured into her with a shout, buried himself fully inside, pulsing. Trembling. Angling to get deeper still, wave after wave electrifying them, sweeping away all reason. Her entire being was centered where they were joined. One blazing point of unfettered joy.

As the throes subsided, Liv came to her senses enough to risk a peek at Alex. He was still on his knees, but leaning back, bouncing a little, bearing down on the plug in his ass. Desire shimmered in his green eyes. And something else.

Love . . . and approval.

In that instant, Liv was never more aware that sometimes a sexual escapade was just that—it could be all about tasting the forbidden, like Alex's liaisons with Jenna. But not always.

Sometimes sex was about reconnecting and embracing new possibilities. *Me, Alex and Jason. Could it really happen?*

Reluctantly, she parted from Jason, wincing as he slid from her body. The acute sense of loss took her by surprise even more than it had when Alex had watched from their bedroom next door. Because of the increased intimacy? Her growing fondness for Jason?

Turning to face the younger man, she cupped his cheeks and gave him a lingering kiss. "Thank you. That was amazing. You can let go now."

One corner of his sexy mouth quirked up as he released the bar. "The pleasure was all mine."

"Oh, I don't think so," she said, flicking a hand at a sweat-soaked Alex.

"Good God, he's purple! Should we have mercy on him before his balls fall off?"

"Bastard," Alex hissed.

Liv giggled. "I believe so. Otherwise he'll be hell to live with."

"Ladies first," Jason said, giving them both a wide smile.

They crawled to Alex and without a word, Liv dove for his straining erection while Jason fisted his hands in her husband's hair and yanked his head back. As their mouths fused, Liv closed her lips on Alex's feverish cock.

She sucked him in, heard his low, desperate moan into Jason's kisses and knew she couldn't make him wait for very long. He'd been acquiescent to the last, so giving him relief was only fair.

With a flourish, she tore open the ring binding his sex.

"Liv!" he cried, jacking his hips toward her. Driving his cock down to her toes. "Yes!"

Salty spray pumped over her tongue, down her throat. She drank his cum, something she hadn't done often in the last few years, but knew he loved. That alone telegraphed to Alex how she felt in the way longtime lovers communicate.

More than sex.

Connection. Giving.

Love.

Believe in us. We're worth the fight.

Heaving, they clung together, and the unease seeped in, unwelcome. What should she say to mark such a profound moment in their healing as a couple? Their developing relationship with Jason?

"Holy fuck, I'm starving," Alex said.

A beat of silence, then the three of them collapsed in a heap and a fit of laughter.

Happiness filled Liv to overflowing.

Guess she needn't have worried after all.

Ten

✳

"**J**enna, I *can't*. I was out for a week and I'm so far behind I'll never get caught up if we get together tonight."

Alex studied his junior partner's mutinous face and sighed, leaning back in his chair and running a hand through his hair in exasperation. God*damn*, having a lover on the side was supposed to have been fun. Uncomplicated.

More and more, Jenna weighed like a stone around his neck, plunging him to the ocean floor.

Guilt assailed him. Had he led her on? No. From the first, he'd held fast that he loved his wife. Made it plain their affair was hot, no strings sex. Nothing more.

So why the theatrics?

Jenna skirted his desk, standing over him, and dipped a manicured fingernail into the part of his shirt. He'd discarded his tie hours ago, after his last appointment, and she took advantage, scoring his chest.

"I was good, you know," she asserted. "I didn't call again, even though I wanted to. Even though you said your cock belongs to me."

Christ, she looked terrific with that wild red hair unbound the way he liked. Nipples poking at her sheer blouse, long toned legs stretching from her short skirt. And he'd bet his fortune she didn't have on underwear because, God, he could smell her musk. . . .

Yeah, his traitorous dick was willing, despite the rest of him. He cleared his throat.

"I said I belong to you whenever we're together, which we can't be tonight."

Anger flickered across her face. And . . . fear? Why would she be afraid?

"You're so full of shit," she said, retreating some. "You've had me and now you're done, is that it?"

Staring at her, groin stirring, he shook his head. "No, that's not true." Jesus help him, he wasn't ready to give up his sexual liberation so soon. No matter how great it had been with Liv and Jason. No matter how increasingly tangled the situation. Skimming her bare thigh, he ran his palm up, underneath her skirt.

Bare buttocks.

If only. He had far too much work to finish. And not nearly enough energy to survive Liv's punishment. Not to mention un-wittingly entertaining the bodyguard he'd hired, who lurked some-where nearby.

"Tomorrow night?" he asked.

"The night after." She gave him a feral smile. "Bring clothes to go out; I've got a surprise planned. One I know you'll enjoy."

"I can only imagine."

"Is that a yes?"

"All right. Yes." *Idiot.*

Leaning down, she caressed the bulge in his crotch, making it clear she knew he wasn't hiding his need. "See you tomorrow, handsome."

Jenna strutted out the door, and he expelled a breath he hadn't known he was holding. The woman was sex on a fucking stick, so to speak. Funny, but he hadn't thought of her much this past week. Out of sight, out of mind and all that. When she came on strong, however, he could use his cock to pole vault.

"Damn, Alex. Concentrate."

Somehow, he managed to focus on his most important client's case file. For hours, long after Danielle and everyone else had called it quits, poring over the same questions. To which Henry Boardman had pat answers.

Why had Boardman initially resisted Alex's plan to enter a plea of not guilty to the sex-trafficking charges? He'd later taken Alex's advice, but the oddity had stuck with him. Why hire a defense attorney to *defend* you, especially when that attorney was top dollar and possessed an impeccable track record in the courtroom, if you wanted to plead guilty? Well, it was Boardman's dime.

Or was it?

Alex stared at the transcript of their initial interview as attorney and client.

Mr. Boardman, why would you want to plead guilty to these charges when the FBI has such shaky evidence, most of which is circumstantial?

A pause, while Boardman fidgets with his cuff links.

I did wrong, Mr. Quinn. I deserve to be punished.

I'm your attorney, Mr. Boardman. Anything you say to me or my junior counsel is strictly confidential. Are you guilty of these charges?

Yes.

The eyes lied. Always.

And Boardman had been lying, at least by omission.

Oh, the man was involved in the dirty operation to his eye-balls. But if the frightened weasel of a man was the brains be-hind it all, he'd eat his briefcase.

In the end, he'd decided, *What the hell?* Every American was en-titled to a defense, and Boardman would get a good one. The case was weak, which left enough doubt to appease Alex's conscience.

Boardman would most likely get off. End of story and every-one's happy.

Right?

Alex tossed down his pen and raised his eyes to his computer screen—

Just as the entire floor went dark.

As in pitch-fucking-black. The dying computer monitor cast an eerie glow, like the eye of a weird monster crouching in a cave. Confused for a moment, he sat, anticipating a brief power glitch. Expecting the light to return any second.

It didn't. His heart thudded hard behind his sternum, but he wasn't afraid of the dark. No, what freaked him out was the drone of the air conditioner thinning to a whine, the hum of electrical power one never noticed until it stopped, fading to nothing.

To absolute silence.

And Thompson, his bodyguard? Didn't call out.

No movement. At all.

"Shit," he breathed.

He stood as quietly as possible, groping for the edge of his desk. Feeling his way around it as his vision adjusted to the dark-ness. Took longer because the blinds in his office were drawn, blocking out the lights of downtown and the moon on the river.

The fact that his closing them was likely a good thing gave

him a jolt. If they'd been open, he'd have been illuminated. Exposed.

A target.

Ah, fuck.

He checked the urge to yell for Thompson. Fought a wave of sickness upon realizing the man wouldn't hear if he did. Someone was on this floor, stalking him. Preparing to finish the job they'd failed to complete a week ago.

They're coming for me.

He had to get out of this office to have any prayer of escape. Terror threatened to freeze him in place, but that mistake would mean certain death. Forcing his legs to move, he crossed to the door, straining to see any sign of movement in the common area beyond.

Alex could barely make out the shape of Danielle's desk, and thanked heaven his secretary hadn't stayed late. If she had—*No, don't go there! Just get out.*

Staying close to the wall, he inched his way toward the hallway on the other side of the commons. The elevator was next to the hall, but he couldn't risk waiting in the open. He'd have to reach the door to the stairwell at the end, call 911, because, dammit, he should've done that before—

A shadow detached itself from the opposite wall, flying across the space toward him. Banged into a desk, gave a vicious curse, but kept coming. The intruder was so close, Alex knew he'd never be able to outrun him.

So he charged, met the bastard head-on. A flash caught him by surprise, and he heard a *pop, pop* in rapid succession.

Son of a bitch!

Alex ducked low, caught the guy in a flying tackle, his momentum greater, propelling his attacker backward. They crashed over a rolling chair, over a desk, scattering items in every direction, then slammed to the floor. Metal glinted in the man's hand and Alex rolled on top of him, pinning the gun arm as the guy attempted to buck him off. Each struggled to gain the upper hand, and Alex knew he couldn't lose.

Or he'd die, right here and now.

Not happening.

Alex fought to keep his attacker under control as he groped for something—anything—to clobber the man with. "Who . . . hired you?" he grunted, fingers closing around a heavy, smooth round object. A paperweight? "And why?"

"Fuck you!"

"Not even if you gift wrapped it, asshole."

And Alex bashed the guy in the skull, gratified when he went limp, hands releasing his shirt to fall away. With any luck, he'd scrambled the man's brains.

The urge to bolt was nearly overwhelming, but he resisted, taking a few seconds to search his attacker's pockets for a wallet. Came up empty. Not that he'd expected a nice, tidy ID, but he'd had to look.

Prying the pistol from the man's hand, Alex stuck the weapon in his waistband and pushed to his feet. The police probably wouldn't get any prints from it except his own, though it was worth a shot. The cops!

He stumbled for Danielle's desk, going for the phone, and snatched the hand set. Fumbling in the dark, he managed to punch 911. It rang one, twice—

"Hey, did ya ice him?"

Jesus, fuck, another one!

The phone slipped from his hand, hitting the desk with a clatter as he sprinted for the hallway. Thank God the second man wasn't between him and the exit. Where had he come from? He must've been prowling elsewhere, heard the gunshots, the struggle come to an end, and assumed his partner had succeeded.

No matter. He had to get out.

Alex hit the door to the stairwell, wondering how long it would take the police to respond. A shout and another bullet whizzing past his head answered the question—too goddamned long.

He slammed the door shut behind him, knowing that would buy him mere seconds. *Why, why, why* drummed in his brain to the echo of his footfalls, the hammering of his heart against his ribs. His breaths came in sharp, terrified bursts. He held on to the stair rail, the only thing keeping him from falling as he practically threw himself downward, heedless of the fact that he couldn't see at all.

At least the other bastard couldn't see, either.

Cold comfort as the door banged open and quick steps sounded one level, perhaps two, above him. Six more floors to go? Quinn and Quinn occupied the eighth floor, and the entrance to every level was locked from inside the stairwell. He had no choice but to go all the way down, get outside.

Another *pop*, the bullet ricocheting wildly in the close, metallic space. Missing him.

Please, God.

He made the next level, running so fast he missed the handrail on the sharp turn and hit the wall. Hard. Kept going. Found the first step down but found only air on the second, and plummeted to the bottom, bouncing like a beach ball.

"Fuck!" He staggered upright, reining in his panic to find the rail again. No time to spare, his pursuer gaining.

Wasn't he? Difficult to tell with the roaring in his ears, the pounding of feet.

Bottom level? Exit—there! Alex ran for the glowing sign, thinking *This could be it. A bullet to the back of the head, and it's all over.* Without ever understanding why.

And Liv . . . God, he couldn't leave her alone to face this.

His legs pumped faster as he covered the remaining distance and exploded out the door. He ran, disoriented, groping the waistband for the pistol that was no longer there. Must've lost it when he fell, and he spat a vicious curse at the rotten luck.

Until he rounded the corner of the building, finding himself racing down the front sidewalk, straight toward a police cruiser just pulling to a stop near the main entrance. The cop emerged from the vehicle and stepped from behind his driver's door, spotting Alex at the same instant.

The officer's left hand went up, the right finding the butt of his sidearm. "Hey, stop right there!"

Alex showed his empty hands, but kept coming, praying he didn't get shot by both parties. "Behind me! He's got a gun!"

The cop's eyes widened, fixing on a point over Alex's shoulder. Out of sheer reflex, Alex looked, too. His pursuer halted, bringing up his weapon in both hands. Heedless of the officer, prepared to take Alex down no matter what.

Alex swung around again to see the cop's gun clearing his holster. Saw him shouting *Get down*, and Alex wasted no time kissing the pavement, arms over his head as though that would save his ass.

A deafening volley of gunshots rang in his ears, and he waited for a bullet to tear into his flesh. Expected the searing heat, the pain.

Just as suddenly, the noise ceased. Footsteps moved away from him a few yards, then stopped. Next, they crunched toward where he lay prone on the asphalt, frozen in fear.

"Jesus, what the hell was that? You okay, mister?"

"Oh, thank God." If he'd been standing, his legs would've given out. "I-I think so."

Alex pushed to a sitting position and swiped a shaking hand down his face. Christ, his entire body was vibrating like he'd taken speed.

"I'm Officer Wylie. Looks like he clipped you," he said, squatting to peer at Alex.

"What?"

"You're bleeding right here." The stout cop on the back side of middle age pointed to the side of his neck, careful not to touch the wound. "But you'll do, unlike the other guy."

"He's dead?" Alex clapped a hand to his neck, surprised to find his skin slick with blood. He hadn't felt a thing.

"Yep, the fucker. Shot up my car. You hurt anywhere else?"

Wylie's tone was kind, and Alex's shakes began to ease some. "Bruised, maybe. I fell down a flight of stairs in the stairwell, and lost the other guy's gun—shit! There's another one, outside my office on the eighth floor! I coldcocked him with something, and then this one chased me—"

A firm hand landed on his shoulder. "Easy. Let me call for backup, and the paramedics to see about your injury. Once we've checked the premises, we'll get a statement. All right?"

"Yeah. Yeah, sure." His mind whirled. "Look for the muscle I hired for protection, too. Ryan Thompson. He should've been on watch. Oh, and call Detective Lambert. Someone blew up my Jag last week, and he's got the case."

The officer's bushy brows lifted to his hairline. "I heard about that. Quinn, right? Damn, son, you've really pissed somebody off." He shook his head. "Sit tight."

"Sure."

Wylie got on the radio, and Alex sort of drifted in a numb fog. Every so often, his gaze strayed to where the hit man lay nearby. Faceup, arms flung out at his sides, inky stain soaking his chest. Dead.

That could've been me.

Alex became violently ill, stomach roiling, bile burning the back of his throat. He swallowed several times, willing down the sickness before he finally succeeded, the need to stare into the face of a man who'd wanted him dead eclipsing all else.

He stood and limped to the stranger, amazed by his sudden calm. Shock, perhaps? The man's eyes were open, his expression vaguely surprised. His hair was brown, short and neat, his features square and average.

"Mr. Quinn, I'll have to ask you to step away from the body," Officer Wylie said. "Come on back over here, son."

"He looks like just any guy," Alex remarked quietly. "Someone who'd show at the neighborhood barbecue."

"The worst ones always do."

The scene got busy after that, bustling with a parade of cops, each asking that he recount tonight's events even though he'd told the story until he wanted to scream. Doing their jobs, but the repetition, knowing they were testing the consistency of his account, made him nuts.

The paramedics arrived and checked Alex over, pronouncing his bloody wound an ugly scratch, no stitches required. However, after learning of his tumble down the stairs, they offered to transport him to the hospital for X-rays. He declined. If he landed in that place again, it would be toes up.

The paramedics were summoned into the building, and Alex tried not to think what that meant. The crime-scene unit arrived last, along with the news vans and the normally composed Detective Lambert, who appeared none too happy.

Join the club, little fella.

Alex parked his butt on the sidewalk, frustrated. He wanted to get home before Liv caught this on the evening news, and he didn't dare tell her something like this on the phone. She'd rush down here, and he didn't want her anywhere near this evil. The thought of her on the killers' radar made his blood boil.

Lambert spoke with the uniforms, raised a finger at Alex indicating for him to wait, then went inside the building for a while. Twenty minutes later, he walked out the front door, making a beeline for Alex, and halted at his feet.

"Helluva fucking past week, huh, Quinn?"

He gave a humorless laugh. "I'm thinking early retirement sounds fine." He waved a hand at the main entrance. "How'd you guys get in? It's locked after hours."

"Night janitor doing his rounds let us in. There was no forced entry on the ground floor, which means our perps were inside before closing, blending in, waiting to pop you and then beat a silent retreat."

Fantastic. "The good news?"

"We've got the dead guy. May take a while, but we'll get an ID. When we do, maybe some answers."

Alex's stomach sank. "What about the man I left unconscious outside my office?"

"Disappeared. We've got signs of your struggle and a brass paperweight with presumably his blood on it, which we've taken into evidence. We've also got Ryan Thompson, who was discovered in the men's restroom, unconscious. He had a nasty knot on his head, and he's ticked as hell those bastards got the jump on him. Ought to count his lucky stars they didn't kill him outright. He's your bodyguard, right?"

"Yeah. I hired him through a friend who runs a private service. Ex-Navy SEAL." Alex buried his face in his hands, relieved Thompson was alive. The man was only thirty-three, with a wife and two kids.

"Former SEAL? Tough sons of bitches."

Shit, his head, his entire body, hurt. He rubbed his temples. "If you can ID the dead assailant, you might be able to trace his partner?"

"We hope so, along with who hired them. Could be a break."

"I wish I could believe that."

From his grim expression, the detective did, too. Whoever was calling the shots wanted Alex dead badly enough to cover his trail.

"I suggest you work from home tomorrow. No late nights at the office, either, until the asshole behind this is caught," Lambert said firmly.

Alex fingered the bandage at his neck. One centimeter, and the bullet would've taken out his jugular. "No argument there. What about my employees? Can they return in the morning as usual?"

"Don't foresee a problem with that. We'll be done shortly. Go on home; take a Valium or something." The detective offered a hand up, which Alex took.

Sounded good to him. "Let me know what you find."

"You bet."

They let Alex inside to retrieve his suit jacket, wallet and keys, then escorted him to his rental in the parking garage. A cramped, nerdy little Probe because that's all that was available, and shopping for a new car was sorta last on his to-do list at the moment.

Thompson—who had a bad headache, but insisted on finishing his shift—and one of St. Louis's finest followed him all the way home and waited until he unlocked the front door and stepped safely inside before driving away.

Leaving him to face his wife with bad news.

To face a very uncertain—and possibly very brief—future.

Eleven

✳

"He's not dead."

Christ. "They were pros. It's not my fault."

"I'm beginning to think you couldn't arrange to kill an elephant with a hand grenade."

"H-he'll die. You have my word."

A nasty laugh. "Which means nothing. And Seraph?"

"N-not yet. We'll find him soon."

"You'd better. If he talks to the authorities, we're all going down. Except prison won't be an option for some." Palmer's tone sharpened to a fine blade. "Your two weeks are rapidly coming to an end. Then so will you."

"I p-promise I'll—"

Click.

He hung up, replacing the receiver. Wondering how he'd come to this. Selling out for the color of green.

Committing murder.

And for the first time in his sorry life, he considered eating the barrel of a gun.

If he failed again, he might as well save Palmer the effort.

. . .

Jason tapped a pen on his notepad, staring at a painting of an ancient ship in a storm-tossed sea on the wall of his uncle's office. Bill had loved all that nautical shit, most of which Jason had donated or thrown out, but this painting captured his own emotions, his life, perfectly.

It reminded him how small and insignificant people are in the grand scheme. How vulnerable, despite the best of preparations, hopes or dreams. In the end, a man has to battle forces greater than himself, knowing that any moment he can be crushed by the hand of God or the wrath of the devil.

Or granted reprieve by the same.

"Wow, Jason needs a good therapist, boys and girls," he muttered, frowning at his blank paper. "Or some great drugs."

At his elbow lay a file of information and photographs. Some of the pictures had been snapped in the previous months, some since he'd arrived in St. Louis. Covert, watching Boardman and listening to the underground buzz, following orders, while his new neighbors probably believed he was lounging in lazy splendor all day.

"I frigging wish."

Focus. First, he drew a large triangle on the paper to represent a pyramid. Across the base, he wrote *Alex* and *Olivia*. Above their names, *Jenna Shaw*, *Ken Brock*, and *Kyle Murphy*. Just over Ken's name, in the middle of the pyramid, *me*. Where the top began to narrow, *Henry Boardman* and *Dmitri Baranov*.

He paused at Baranov's name—the dead hit man, previously sought for capture in twelve countries, taken out by a beat cop. How poetic was that? Yet a much more capable foe than whoever blew Alex's Jag. The stakes had been raised, the hunt for Alex's head taken to a new, terrifying level.

And at the apex he scribbled *Palmer Hodge.*

His hand shook, and he dropped the pen.

Still, he felt stronger now than when he'd first arrived in St. Louis. Not as raw or broken.

"Motherfucker," he hissed, gut churning. "I'll get you if it takes my last breath."

He didn't know how long he sat, drawing lines from one name to the other, creating a crazy-ass spiderweb, mulling over exactly how all of the names were connected. Scouring his brain to think whether any were missing, or if all the players were present and accounted for.

As an afterthought, he added *Danielle Forney* to the second tier from the bottom, the woman who'd replaced Alex's longtime secretary. A hot little blond number who looked like she'd be much more at home working at, say, *Penthouse.*

Man, Alex knew how to pick great eye candy. Not that he was a great judge of females, but he was learning.

"Note to self: pump Miss Forney." He smiled. "So to speak."

A man had to make certain his skills were well-rounded, after all.

"Jason?"

Startled, he scooped the pictures into the file, then grabbed the folder and the notepad. "Coming!" Crap, he'd let Olivia keep the spare house key Bill had given her years ago, told her to come over whenever, but he'd expected her to knock.

Quickly, he shoved the damning notes and file into his top desk drawer, ready to congratulate himself on his reflexes—then his gaze lit on his gun, resting on the corner of the desk. He barely had the thing stowed with the rest when Olivia appeared in the office doorway.

"Hey, stud muffin." She did her best to seem sunny, but the strain in her eyes and around her mouth gave her away. "What are you doing?"

"Working. I didn't hear you come in."

"I knocked and got a little worried when you didn't answer."

"Oh." Damn, like she needed more stress on those pretty shoulders. "Sorry. Guess I was really into it."

"Into what? Your desk is bare."

Casting about for a viable excuse, he vacated his chair, waving a hand. "I was on the computer. Job hunting."

Sauntering toward him, slim hips swaying, she arched a dubious brow. "Right. Because you're really strapped now that you're saddled with this little shack and all."

He gave her a tight smile. "I need to feel useful."

"Jason," she said, pressing against him and resting a palm on his chest. "Your computer isn't on."

"I turned it off. Just now."

"Uh-huh. You know what I think?"

"W-what?"

"I think you've been sitting over here, brooding about your uncle's passing."

If only she knew. "No, that's not it." He wrapped his arms around her small waist, kissed her forehead. "The truth is, I've been worried about Alex. About what's happening to him and why."

There. That wasn't a lie.

The subject disarmed Olivia and she sagged against him, suspicions forgotten. "I don't understand why anyone would want to kill Alex. He's too driven, a barracuda in the courtroom, but . . . Jason, he's a *good* man. People admire and respect him. Not the type of man at all who'd warrant this sort of vicious plot."

"Even though he's the type of man who'd agree to your bargain?"

She pulled back, her eyes flashing with anger. "You didn't resist your part in the arrangement, and nobody's out for *your* blood."

Oh, honey. How I wish that were true.

"Relax," he said, brushing his fingers down one creamy cheek. "I'm just wondering if it's all connected somehow. I mean, the timing is awfully convenient."

She stilled and he saw her assimilate, her expression reflecting growing alarm. "What could Alex's sexual choices have to do with anything?"

"I don't know, sweetie." *But I have an educated guess.* "I just have concerns about so much of his attention being diverted from his job and you."

"He's out again this evening," she whispered. "Only two days since the attempt in the office, and he's with *her.* Doing God knows what when he should be home, where it's safe. Oh, I know he's not really safe anywhere, but when he's home, I can cling to the illusion."

She was so afraid, this tough, successful lady. He wanted nothing more than to erase the fear from her lovely face, to immerse her in good, happy sensations.

"Ryan is with him, sticking to his ass like a burr," he soothed. "That brute won't make the mistake of letting someone get the jump on him again."

In truth, Palmer—if he was indeed behind all of this—would get to Alex. Sooner or later. Something Olivia didn't need to learn.

"Jase?"

"Yeah, sugar?"

"Make love to me."

There was a stress-reducer he could advocate. Olivia nibbled his throat, fingers rubbing his crotch in lazy circles. His cock awakened, filling, eager to have her. To burrow inside her, sheathed in her sweet heat.

He backed up a step, shed his T-shirt and cargo shorts in a couple of swift movements. His erection reached for her seemingly of its own will and she smiled, some of the shadows banished for the time being.

She undressed with quick efficiency, and he led her to the black leather sofa. He sat, pulling her into his lap, not caring whether they stained the material or not. The sacrifice was worth the cause.

She straddled his hips, using one hand to position the head of his cock between her pussy lips. Deep blue eyes held his as she sank without a word, sucking him into that hot, wet channel. Taking all of him. Until she sat, unmoving, just letting them connect.

Her mouth brushed his, then settled, tongue sweeping past the seam of his lips. Wine. Chardonnay with a hint of fruit and oak. The marvelous essence of her taste. Loving him. Kissing and licking.

Jason shifted his ass and closed his eyes, seeking deeper sanctuary, happiness warming his chest at simply being joined with Olivia. The heat swelled as she began to move, sliding up and down. Creating unbelievable friction that vibrated to his toenails. Not too fast or slow, not too rough.

Gentle. Lift and descend.

Two people. Making love.

Not fucking.

Making love.

Oh, God, never . . . he'd never . . .

The feelings were like free-falling with no parachute. Racing down the highway at 200 mph. Opening your very first Valentine.

First kiss.

First love.

Heart engaged and locked.

"Oh, Liv, yes." He blinked his eyes open, nearly beyond speech, to see what must be his own emotions mirrored in hers. "Good, baby. Look at me while I come inside you."

And he began to pulse, unable to hold off. Crying out his joy, he poured into her womb, gaze fixed on her blue eyes. She moaned, arms tightening around his neck, arching so that her nipples grazed his bare chest, and let go.

Her walls clenched, convulsed around his cock, milking the last of his cum. When they were spent, she stayed put, raining tiny kisses over his face and neck. Each one so special because they were little gifts from Olivia, freely given. Expecting nothing in return, only wishing for his pleasure and well-being.

He could get used to this.

A terrifying and awesome realization.

Jason Strickland was capable of fulfilling and being fulfilled. Without pain or degradation. With mutual respect.

"I told Alex, I've done many things I'm not proud of," he said. "But if anything could ever redeem me as a man, change my life, I'd say it was meeting you and Alex."

Tears welled in her eyes. "That's the nicest thing anyone's ever said to me. I know Alex would say the same."

Lips curving up, he thumbed away an escaped tear. "Now I can say I know what it means to make love."

Sniffing, she wiped at her cheeks. "Ironic that my husband has strayed in the opposite direction, isn't it?"

His heart broke for her. He knew firsthand the darkness that pulled at Alex now. The lure of the illicit games, of sampling forbidden flesh.

He'd played them all.

"Come upstairs tonight, Olivia. To my bed. Let me hold you."

She gave him a watery smile. "I'll accept that fine offer, my friend."

Yep, let Alex come looking for her when he got home. Let him see that she wasn't sitting around waiting.

Tonight belonged to Olivia.

And to himself.

.   .   .

The Paddle and Whip? Alex glanced at Ryan, who shook his head, lips pressed together. Clearly, the man shared his reservations. Alex tugged on Jenna's hand, halting their progress at the entrance.

"A private BDSM club is a bad idea, especially in the warehouse district," he protested.

"It's secluded, anonymous if you prefer, and the inside is quite nice."

He hitched a thumb toward the gutter. "I saw a rat bigger than a fucking Chihuahua down there."

"You're going to enjoy a sensory experience to remember."

"Nobody's going to paddle *or* whip me, including *you*." Allowing Jenna to tie him to her bed had been his limit. Only Liv or Jase would have flogging privileges. In fact, the idea of a total stranger pounding on him left him cold. Uneasy, he smoothed his silk shirt and plucked at his black leather pants. Leather felt weird without underwear.

"I can't believe I agreed to try this."

Jenna wrinkled her nose. "Don't be silly. I have a surprise for you. A present, if you will, one I know you'll find scrumptious."

"I get to paddle *you*?"

"Of course not. I'm merely . . . your hostess."

What on God's green earth was she up to? "Is my present gift wrapped?"

Jenna didn't comment, just smirked, motioning them inside. "Come on. Your shadow might have to leave his sidearm at the desk, though."

Ryan gave her a smile that didn't reach his eyes. "They can take it off my corpse, lady."

She eyed Thompson up and down, but refrained from comment. The chilly glint in her stare caused a ripple of disquiet to unfurl in Alex's belly. The bodyguard didn't seem affected, though he was often difficult to read. Alex supposed playing it close to the vest was necessary in his line of work.

Jenna turned to the plain red door set into the brick building. Rather than an intercom to buzz for admittance, there was a keypad on the wall. Jenna punched in the code, not bothering to hide the numbers from them, no doubt figuring Ryan wouldn't allow her to keep the combination secret. She'd be right.

"I don't like this, Mr. Quinn. You shouldn't be here, in the middle of a crowd where anyone can get at you."

"He won't be, Mr. Thompson. I've reserved a private booth," Jenna said crisply.

"It'll be all right. We're not staying long," he assured the other man, earning a frown from his lover. "One hour, no more, then we're taking Jenna home."

Surprise and annoyance marred her striking features before she smoothed them into a blank mask. Inside, he sensed her sulking and found it didn't move him in the least. He couldn't work up one iota of guilt for cutting the evening short. He was here . . . why?

To satisfy his curiosity. To forget the horror of two nights ago. And yes, despite his recent impatience about being with Jenna, to appease the rising lust that had been building all day. To learn what erotic scheme she had up her sleeve this time and what boundaries she'd push. But there were no illusions about their relationship, at least on his part—their affair had the shelf life of a tomato, and it wasn't as if she had no clue.

They stepped inside and his self-examination was interrupted by the steady throb of bass. Hard-driving club music, muffled because it came from the end of a narrow corridor. A big, dark man wearing jeans, a black T-shirt and a scowl stood sentry at the doorway to the club proper, arms crossed over his massive chest, glaring straight at Alex as though he scarfed middle-aged lawyers for appetizers.

Jenna strolled right up to the giant, and he smiled as she said something in his ear, nodding his head. To Alex's amazement, the man waved them inside, sparing them the third degree. Jenna fit the scenery well, being gorgeous and looking fine in her skimpy leather skirt and bustier. Hell, any man would welcome a hot babe like her anywhere, no matter what she wore. But for his part? He felt like a can of tuna in a room full of alley cats.

As they followed her into the throng, he shouted to be heard over the din. "How long have you been coming here?"

"A while," she called back. "Not very often, just when I'm in the mood for something naughtier."

Well, Jenna had the market cornered on naughty.

"Damn, get a load of this crowd," Ryan said.

He wasn't referring to the numbers, either. Alex's eyes widened. Jesus, he'd lived a sheltered life. Even in his wild early twenties before he met Liv, he'd never been to a place like this, had never seen so many nearly naked, black-clad and silver-studded people in one place. Ever.

Bare asses in cutaway pants. Bare breasts, crisscrossed by straps. Partial nudity. Everywhere. Some patrons were on the dance floor, grinding together to the beat, some in booths or dark corners, getting busy. He'd stepped into some strange alternate dimension where almost anything goes. Pick your poison, fetish, partner. Whatever.

At the bar, a man openly fondled a woman's bare ass. In a darkened corner, a man was on his knees, head bobbing at the lap of the man standing over him. Near them, two men laved a woman's breasts. Decadence everywhere.

And dammit, he was a *guy*, one who'd been fantasizing for two days, so all of the blatant sexuality around them headed south to his dick. Especially with the devilish inner voice reminding him that he had carte blanche. Common sense didn't stand a chance.

"Here we are." Jenna slid into the booth, settling herself behind the table. "Will this do?"

Ryan nodded. "It's semienclosed and mostly blocked from view of the other patrons, unless someone walks right up. I can stand here and see pretty much the whole room, so it'll pass. Mr. Quinn, let me know if you need anything."

The bodyguard positioned himself outside the booth with his back to them, affording him and Jenna some privacy. Alex joined her, more eager by the second to see what she had planned. Despite the dark atmosphere, he had no trouble appreciating the loose red curls draping over her shoulders and framing her breasts, which were pushing at the top of her bustier. One sneeze and they'd pop out.

She scooted next to him, running a hand up the inside of one leather-clad thigh to the bulge in his crotch. "You're not nearly as unaffected as you're trying to pretend."

"Guilty as charged. So give me a hint about who or what we're waiting on?"

"Patience, darling." She teased the ridge of his erection through the slick leather.

He hated when she called him that, but the twitch behind his zipper gave away how his body felt about her touching him. Just being touched, period. He stifled a groan as a busty woman with long, straight purple hair and too much eyeliner was stopped and questioned by Ryan before entering the booth.

The woman shot the bodyguard a curious once-over before addressing him and Jenna. "I'm Violet. What can I getcha to drink?"

"Gin and tonic for me," Jenna said. "Scotch on the rocks for my friend who's joining us shortly."

Alex held up a hand. "Nothing for me; I'm driving."

"Club soda or something, then?"

"No, thank you."

The woman left, and Jenna worked on the snap of his pants, popping them open. "Nothing to drink? You're not in such a big hurry, are you?"

"If I can't see it poured, I'm not taking the chance. Who's the friend we're waiting for?"

She opted to ignore his question. Clever fingers lowered the zipper, parted his fly. Peeled down the leather and lifted out his cock and balls. Exposed him, caressing his sac, the turgid length of him.

"Jenna," he hissed. He meant it as a protest but it emerged as a demand. Her tongue found his ear, and her breath tickled his skin.

"No one can see, especially with the table in the way. We're alone."

"Yeah, with a couple hundred people right outside these thin walls."

"Most of whom are occupied doing exactly what we are, too wrapped up enjoying each other to care. Besides," she mused, rubbing the pad of one finger over the wet tip of his penis, "you can't hide how much this turns you on."

Ah, God. She was right. Down and dirty sex in a public place was one fantasy the old, boring Alex had never seriously considered. Sure, there was that time on the beach—the *deserted* beach—with Liv during their honeymoon. Not quite the same. Yeah, that screaming noise was the last of his resistance going down in flames.

The bar chick returned with two highballs, glanced in their direction with a faint smile and vanished. Jenna pressed against his side, took a sip of her gin and tonic, then pushed her fingers through his hair and tilted back his head, taking his mouth in a passionate kiss. The alcohol tasted crisp on her tongue and he sucked it away, seeking more of her flavor. The other hand continued to manipulate his balls, the contact light, keeping him worked up yet ensuring he'd last.

She shifted, pulling something from her bustier. Silk brushed his cheek and he drew back to see a black scarf dangling in front of his face. "The last time I saw one of those, I walked funny for two days."

"The difference is you won't be restrained tonight, and the cloth isn't going between your teeth."

"Blindfold?"

"I promised you a sensory experience, didn't I? What better way than to remove the most relied-upon of the five senses?"

"I'm impressed, Jenna. I didn't have you figured for a sensualist."

"More of an opportunist?"

More of a shark, but he thought it wise to refrain from saying so. "No, you strike me as uninhibited, a woman who isn't afraid to take what she wants."

She gave him a saucy grin, obviously pleased. "You have that right. Now, stop thinking so much and give yourself to the moment."

Alex wondered briefly if Ryan could hear what they were saying, but decided he likely couldn't since he was outside the booth, facing the crowd and the booming music.

Then she placed the material over his eyes, tied it in a knot behind his head, and what Ryan or anyone else might hear or see faded in importance.

"Clear your mind and *feel*," she instructed, freeing the buttons on his shirt to the waist. Her hand crept inside to stroke his chest, his belly.

Denied his sight, he concentrated on the sounds and musky smells of the club. Jenna's hands mapping his torso and groin, lulling him into a state of relaxed euphoria.

Alex heard voices, and soon another body pressed against his other side. Warm and inviting. Were those . . . breasts? Bare, against his arm, the erect nipples grazing him through the sleeve of his shirt. Four sets of fingers explored him everywhere, the newcomer's cradling his balls, stroking his shaft, and he thought he might die, it felt so good.

"God, you're hung," the mystery lady murmured in his ear. She nibbled his jaw, down his neck. Farther, to his chest and belly. "Just like I knew you would be."

An acquaintance, then? He couldn't place her voice, though it was familiar. She moved lower, slipping under the table and crouching between his knees.

"Tell me what you want," she said, giving his cock a butterfly kiss. Her palms skimmed up the insides of his thighs.

An easy request.

"Suck me," he rasped. "Do it."

The moment her lips wrapped around his cock, enveloping him in her wet heat, he was lost. In reflex, his hips jerked upward, sending his rod farther into her mouth. He gave himself to the women taking his body. Completely.

Jenna grazed one of his nipples, then its twin, with her teeth, driving him mad, while his other tormentor feasted on his cock. Sucked and laved the underside, swallowing him to the base, her nose buried in his curls.

"I—you're going to make me come if you don't stop!" The woman released him with a husky laugh and practically crawled up his body to straddle his lap. His palms skimmed her slim, bare thighs and upward, over a tiny skirt, to the smooth skin of her waist. His fingers sought her breasts and he received a shock to find them naked, supported by some type of half-bra thing. They thrust proudly into his hands, full but not too large, the nipples pointed and tight.

He pinched them and she gave a soft sigh of pleasure, leaning forward until a pert nipple grazed his lips, offering it to his mouth. Capturing it between his teeth, he grazed it, encouraged by her shiver of delight as she pressed closer, fingers in his hair. He laved and suckled, first one, then the other, until she pulled away, voice breathless. Urgent.

"I'm going to fuck you, Alex." Rising a bit, she reached down, rustled with something and sheathed him. Then she took his rod, lining up the leaking head with her sex.

No underwear. Jesus, he loved the fact that his mystery lover had been craving this, had come prepared to take him. She sank onto him and began to ride.

"Shit, yes," he breathed. "You're so hot, baby. So wet. Feels so good."

She set the rhythm, languid at first, letting him feel every inch of her channel squeezing his length. He throbbed inside her, pumping his hips, lost to this. Nothing existed except his cock buried in her fiery pussy.

On the fringes of his awareness, he felt Jenna take his hand and move it between her spread legs where she knelt on the seat beside them. Answering her silent request, he rubbed her sex, smearing her juices, working her clit.

But his attention was centered on the woman bouncing on his lap. Riding him hard now, breasts tapping his chest. Hips snapping, he fucked her, driving as deeply as possible. The wonderful quickening tightening his belly, his balls.

"So close," he panted.

She cried out, walls spasming around his cock, and he erupted. Pulsed into her as she ground her sweet cunt against his rod, wringing every drop from him.

Jenna gave a hoarse shout, coming on his fingers, pressing his hand into her mound. The three of them writhed for a minute or two, floating back to earth. Common sense returned, and with it, the realization that he was sorry for the evening to end. It had to, though, if he was going to make it to the office in the morning.

Grinning, he reached for the blindfold. "Damn, that was awesome. Who—"

Fingers closed over his wrist, preventing him from removing the scarf. "More titillating if she remains a mystery for now. If you're a good boy, she might cross your path again soon."

"Very soon," the woman whispered, kissing the corner of his mouth. "Thanks, Alex."

As she slid off his lap and made her exit, Alex had to admit Jenna's plan for tonight was pretty mind-blowing. Sensual? Illicit? Hell, yeah. Mentally, he wrung his hands in wicked glee, trying to figure out who the other woman was—and hoping for a repeat, face-to-face.

Jenna removed his blindfold and Alex blinked, letting his vision adjust again. The woman was indeed gone. Ryan peered inside the dark booth, his raised eyebrows the only chink in his normally unflappable calm.

"Christ, man," he muttered. "Can I be you for one day? Minus the crazy-assholes-trying-to-kill-me part?"

"Easy. Just get your wife to agree to an open marriage," he said, zipping up his leather pants. He'd have to discard the condom in the restroom.

The big guy snorted. "Right. I sorta like my balls attached to my body, thanks."

Alex had to wonder whether his would be after this confession.

He couldn't wait to find out what Liv had in store.

Twelve

✦

Liv watched Jason sleep, admiring how his too-long, sun-streaked hair fell in waves around his face. He looked even younger with his expression relaxed, dreaming, worries vanquished. Tenderness stirred in her breast, emotions that were rapidly progressing toward something scary. She knew nothing about this man and what he was hiding. Or the broken relationship he was running from.

He didn't think she'd seen him scrambling to stuff something into his desk earlier. But she had, and frankly, it had niggled at the back of her mind ever since. If he were job hunting, there was no reason to act like he'd almost been caught with top-secret documents.

And the fact was, he'd lied. About something that wasn't her business, but it bothered her nonetheless.

Her thoughts were interrupted by the peal of Jason's doorbell. Followed immediately by an insistent pounding.

She shook Jason's shoulder and he grunted, trying to burrow into the covers. "Jase, wake up. There's someone at the door."

"Hmm?" He rolled toward her, blinking off heavy sleep. "What . . . what the hell is that racket?"

"Three guesses," she said wryly.

He sat up, shoving wayward locks out of his eyes. "Um, the fox has returned to the den?"

"Maybe. And *if* it's Alex, from the noise, I suspect he's mighty unhappy at finding his nest empty. Do you have a robe?" She cast about, searching for something to slip into.

"Huh. Should've thought of that before he left his cute little vixen lonely and unattended. Hang on." He pushed out of bed and padded into the bathroom, returning seconds later with a navy terry-cloth robe.

"Thanks," she said, taking it from him. She stood and slid her arms into the sleeves, then belted it around her waist. The garment was big on her, but not too huge.

By the time she was ready, Jason had yanked on a pair of shorts and started for the stairs. As he reached the front door, she could hear Alex yelling from the other side.

"Jason! Open the goddamned door!"

After disarming the alarm, he did just that, standing aside with a bemused expression as Alex blew right past him. He rushed straight to Liv and she braced herself for anger—until she saw the stark fear dissolve to relief in his eyes.

Wrapping her in a crushing bear hug, he whispered into her hair, body trembling, "My God, don't ever do that to me again! I came home and you weren't anywhere to be found."

Her arms went around him, comforting, but at the same time she couldn't resist throwing back, "Funny, neither were you."

"I called to let you know I'd be late, and Ryan was with me.

I didn't know where you were or if something had happened. I was scared, Liv."

He had a point, though the smidge of a double standard rankled some. "I'm sorry. I just figured you'd assume I was here," she said softly, kissing his chest through the V of his shirt. "In the future, I'll leave a note in the house or a message on your cell phone."

"Call my cell. No need to broadcast your whereabouts to an intruder."

Yikes. The idea made her shudder. "All right. I promise. Honey?"

"Hmm?"

"You smell like an ashtray."

He pulled back, hands massaging her shoulders gently. "I was at a club."

"With Jenna?"

Nodding, he stroked her cheek, expression guarded. "Do you want my confession now, or would you prefer to wait?"

"Now, I think. It's not very late."

"Well, folks, I'll say good night." Jason edged away from them, ready to beat a hasty retreat, regret on his face.

Liv held out a hand. "Wait! I thought you wanted to participate. You don't have to, of course, but I thought..."

"I'd love nothing more, but I assumed since his last confession was about me and this one isn't, that you two would prefer I butt out." He shrugged as though it made no difference to him, but was betrayed by the spark of hope in his brown eyes.

"You're wrong, Jase," Alex said, flashing him a grin. "Why don't you come over and help Liv think of a devious punishment for me?"

The younger man glanced between them, expression full of mischief. "Okay, cool."

Liv went hot as a furnace. Just thinking about the last session in the playroom made her instantly aroused. She never imagined being as addicted to these occasions as her husband, considering the sins that came before, but despite the shard of pain in her heart, she quickly found herself ensnared in his erotic tale every single time.

Jason reset the alarm and locked up; then they walked next door in silence fraught with anticipation. Comfortable with one another, yet the air between them was supercharged.

We complement each other, Liv thought. *Like pasta and my finest Ledson wine.*

If only her husband would appreciate the gifts awaiting him at home.

Or perhaps he did, and the allure of the forbidden was too much to resist. Especially after coming home to an empty house for so many years.

Relegating the old guilt to the past where it belonged, she ushered them inside, locked up and armed the alarm as Jason had done. The unmarked car was parked in its usual spot on the street, giving her a measure of comfort, since Ryan had gone home.

Alex stopped in the foyer, hands on his hips. Her breath caught at the sight of her sexy husband, almost two decades together be damned. In those painted-on black leather pants and white shirt half undone, he was still the best-looking man she'd ever seen.

Alex turned to her. "Where to?"

"Upstairs. The bed will be more comfy for what I have in mind."

"Which is?"

"You'll soon see."

In their bedroom, she removed Jason's robe—now, *that* must've been an interesting sight for the cop outside—and draped it across the foot of their bed. Both men sucked in a collective breath at her nakedness, both muttering their apparent approval.

She smiled at them. "Lose the clothes, boys. Then I want Alex lying on his back in the center of the bed. Jason, see those two candles in the glass jars?" She pointed them out, one on the dresser and one on the nightstand. "Light them both, please. There's a matchbook on the dresser."

"Mood lighting? Love it," Jason said, shimmying out of his shorts.

"Oh, you're going to love it even more, trust me."

Both men gave her a curious look as they followed her directions. Both were half-erect by the time Alex was in place and the candles lit.

She sat on one side of Alex and gestured for Jason to take the other side. Then she nodded at Alex. "Spread your arms and legs slightly. Good. Keep them flat, your palms down, until we're done."

"No moving at all?"

"None. As soon as you gather your thoughts, we're ready for your confession."

Alex took a deep breath, let it out. The stillness of the darkened room, illuminated only by the two candles, settled around them like a cloak. The atmosphere, set to put her husband at ease and heighten the eroticism, began to take effect. The tension visibly drained from his body, except for one part of him enjoying a very fond memory.

"After work, we changed clothes and drove to this BDSM

club in a shitty part of the warehouse district. Ryan and I got the creeps, but Jenna insisted the place was safe. I guess it was, but when we got there all I could think about was making the stay short and getting her home."

"She rode with you and Ryan?"

"Yeah. She said her sister needed to borrow her car again."

Liv frowned. "You've never met her sister, have you?"

"No, but why would I? I've got employees who've worked under me for years whose families I've never met."

"I know, but the car thing just seems like an awfully convenient excuse on Jenna's part."

"Probably. Anyway, we went inside and Jesus, Liv—Mistress—I've never seen so much nudity in one place. Kinky stuff going on in every corner. One guy blowing another guy; two men sucking a woman's breasts. God."

Sounded raunchy. Removed from her normal, white-bread life. And fun.

"Jenna had reserved this semiprivate booth, so she and I went and sat in there while Ryan stood watch over the crowd." His cock jerked, filled to full attention, dark and flushed. "She undid my pants and felt me up, right there in front of God and everybody. Well, no one could actually see, but there were tons of people around. Everyone knows what's going on."

"Did you like being exposed?"

"After I got over the surprise? Yes. Sitting there having my cock and balls stroked was . . . wicked."

"You wanted more." She glanced at Jason, who watched Alex in rapt fascination, hanging on every word.

"I did, and I got more. She blindfolded me, and the next thing

I knew, another woman came in. She crawled under the table between my legs and—"

"Uh-uh," she admonished, smacking his hand away from where it crept toward his erection. "Hands down, flat."

He grimaced, his need to touch himself plain. "She sucked me for a few minutes, then rolled on a condom and straddled my lap. I returned the favor on her nipples, but not for long. She took my prick into her hot pussy and we fucked like animals. God, it was so good because I could only hear the sounds of sex, feel our heated skin, sliding and rubbing. The intensity was electric times ten, because I was connected to someone in the most intimate way possible, just high on sensation."

"Christ," Jason whispered, leaning back to fist his own cock. "What was Jenna doing?"

"Getting off on my fingers working her clit. I shot and made two women come at the same moment—can you believe that?"

Liv absolutely could. Alex had almost made her come simply by telling the story. Her sex throbbed and the insides of her thighs were moist. "Who was the woman?"

"I don't know. Jenna stopped me from taking off the blindfold until after she'd left. But her voice seemed familiar, and she made a comment about how my cock was better than she'd imagined. Or something to that effect."

"Another lawyer from the office?"

"Crap, I hope not."

Jason snorted. "Well, that'll liven up the workplace."

"Shut up, jackass."

"I happen to know you like my ass—"

"Boys! Let's get back to business." She slid a hand up Alex's leg, rolling his delicate sac in her fingers, thinking of the implications for her husband at work. If Ken Brock had been pissed about his boss playing with Jenna, he'd be livid if the second woman was also someone in the office and word got around. How much, if anything, might he have to do with Alex's current trouble?

Would Ken resort to murder?

A movement reclaimed her attention. Jason knelt behind her, trailed sensual kisses along her shoulder, brushed her hair aside to nibble her neck. Sweet lord, he nearly made her forget Alex's punishment.

While Jason's kisses traveled lower and he stroked her back, she bent down and tasted Alex's seeping cock, trying to live the experience through another woman's eyes. Through Alex's. Desire washed through her with such force, envisioning his legs spread for this woman, shuddering under her attentions. His cock penetrating his lover, filling her deeply. Every one of Liv's erogenous zones pulsed with pleasure, with the ache to be pushed over the edge.

But not yet.

"Jason, come around here." She smiled as he complied without question. "My randy husband must suffer for his sins before I even think of allowing him release."

Jason laid a hand on Alex's chest, thumb absently rubbing a hard nipple. "What's the plan?"

"Pain. Since Alex is all about sensation this evening, I'll use a different sort of pain that's used to heighten arousal—or so I've read. Watch." Both men tracked her hand as she reached for the glass jar on the nightstand containing the candle. "Oh, perfect. The wax is melted, so I'll get started. Remember to keep your hands flat, and try to relax. Let the burn sink into your skin."

"Oh, man," Jason said with a laugh. "Hot-wax torture! Dude, this is going to tie your cock into a knot."

"Eyes open or closed?" Alex managed.

"After what you told me ... closed, for the full effect."

After he complied, Liv suspended the jar over his chest. "I'm going to start with your nipples and work my way south. I want you to tell me how this feels."

Careful not to pour too much, she first experimented with a pea-sized dot on one brown nipple.

He flinched, lips parted. "Stung a bit, but not bad. More, please."

She dribbled more of the liquid onto the taut nub of flesh, gratified by the growling noise in his throat. The sexy noise he made when he was into whatever she was doing to him. She treated the other nipple to the wax, and to her surprise, he seemed to melt into the bed rather than tensing.

"Damn," he hissed. "It's hot. Feels good."

"Does it?" Encouraged, she trailed a thin line of the fragrant stuff down his abdomen.

"Yes. It's like a hot tongue on my skin—God, Liv!"

His cock flexed as she drizzled the liquid over his delicate sac, like hot fudge on a sundae and twice as delicious. He was writhing now, so close to the edge he whimpered, erection stabbing the air in a wordless plea.

When she poured the heated wax down his shaft, he erupted with a hoarse cry, hips jacking upward.

"Fuck, yes! Oh ... "

Cum spurted onto his belly, pumped down his rod to pool at his groin. His ecstasy had Liv burning, and she plunked the jar on the nightstand in a hurry, crawled across Alex's legs to Jason.

She settled on her back and splayed her legs wide in invitation. Unashamed.

"Jason, I need—"

Before she completed the urgent request, their handsome young lover was there. Knowing exactly what she needed. Taking care of her. His talented tongue drove between the lips of her sex, fucking her in rapid strokes.

"Oh! Jason, yes!"

"Shit, yeah," she heard her husband rasp. "Eat her, my friend. Give the lady what she wants."

The approval in his thick voice sent her barreling over the edge with no brakes. Jason suckled her pulsing clit and she shattered, gripping his long hair. Fucking his mouth, riding out the storm.

The spasms subsided at last and she collapsed into a boneless pile of mush as Jase planted gentle kisses on the inside of her thigh. Then he sat up, grinning, pleased with himself.

"Score one for the magic tongue," he bragged, lewdly wiggling the appendage in question.

Alex, propped on his elbows, made a face. "No complaints about your skills or Liv's. I, on the other hand, will be picking this crap out of my nether regions for two days."

Sitting up, Liv giggled at the wax dried all over his front. "That's part of the reason it's called *punishment*."

"Sadist," he threw back, without any real rancor.

"Not even close." Jason climbed from the bed. "She's much too pretty and has way too big a heart."

Alex sat up and stretched, picking a fleck of wax off one nipple. "Know a lot about sadists, do you?"

"More than you'd ever believe," the younger man said quietly.

He shook himself, restoring the boyish grin. "Group shower, guys?"

Jason headed for the bathroom without waiting for an answer. Taking Alex's hand, Liv followed, chewing on Jase's strange comment. And her earlier worries about his history. That and several broken pieces of conversation were whirling around in her mind, trying to form a picture. A disjointed portrait of something very frightening.

Jason Strickland was not what he seemed.

Neither were all of the people surrounding her husband.

Puzzles weren't her forte, but then, Alex's life was at stake. She needed to turn everything over in her mind a bit more.

And talk to Alex. Soon.

.   .   .

The phone blasted Jason's nice dream all to hell, and he rolled over, trying to shut out the noise and return to the beach, where Olivia and Alex had been rubbing suntan oil into his muscles. And other happy places, too.

But the damned bleating persisted. He grumbled and sat up, disoriented, getting his bearings. Right. He'd eventually come home last night, despite his friends' protests.

More awake now, he grabbed the phone, having a really good frickin' idea about the identity of the masochist who was calling him so early. "Strickland."

"Your man's getting himself visited. This morning. Seems the Dmitri Baranov thing yanked the director's weenie. Gotta say, your new fuck buddy really knows how to shove a rainbow up the government's ass."

O-kay. So he wasn't quite as awake as he'd thought. *Assimilate, Jase.*

A visit from the FBI to his man. Alex? Yeah. Utter the name *Baranov* without sprinkling fucking holy water and crossing yourself, and it was only a matter of time before they made tracks to St. Louis like their dicks were on fire. And the other comment—

"What makes you think Quinn is my fuck buddy?" A prickle skittered down his spine, and he left the bed. Padded to the window and peered out the blinds, scanned the back of the property. Still and quiet.

Always was, before a man caught a bullet to the head.

Reginald barked a tired laugh. "I know you, Jason. I don't care where you dip your wick . . . until it becomes a liability, like before. Just don't force me to put in for your early retirement, kid."

Jason jerked away from the window, the blood draining from his face. His palm was suddenly cold and sweaty around the receiver.

The sonofabitch would do it, too.

"I'm not a naive kid anymore," he said, congratulating himself on sounding cool and detached rather than ready to vomit. "Haven't been for months. I'm doing my job, and I could do it better without my hands tied behind my back."

Shit. He winced at the inadvertent reference to what had landed him in hot water in the first place.

"Prove it. You got some names for me?"

"Yeah." He gave his boss the rundown of the names on his rough pyramid and what he knew about each one, which wasn't much.

"It's a start. Since Baranov's hotel room and belongings were clean, maybe one of your names will provide a link to who hired the bastard and his partner. Give this information to Campbell when he knocks on your door."

"He's the one visiting Quinn this morning?"

"The same."

"The cops might be out front, man."

"The *cops*." He spat the word like a foul curse. "They're the dickheads who moved on Boardman before we could stop them, putting the whipped cream on your clusterfuck cheesecake. For all they have the sense to figure, you're exactly what you appear to be instead of what you are."

"And what am I?"

A heavy silence.

"Remains to be seen, kid."

Reginald hung up, and Jason sat on the bed for a long while, sick to his stomach. Thinking about traitors. Liabilities.

And how the old-school regime, very much alive and well in the United States government, dealt with both.

Thirteen

❋

God, he'd have to stop indulging on a weeknight.

Alex exited the elevator with Ryan and made his way to his corner office, head up, trying not to appear as though he was so exhausted he might pass out on his desk. Not to mention sneaking glances at every woman in the building who'd ever given him a less-than-professional double take and wondering *Is she the one?*

He might be able to persuade Jenna to tell, but where was the fun in knowing?

Was she Feliz, the voluptuous receptionist on the ground floor? Perhaps there was more to her perky greeting each morning than met the eye.

Or perhaps Lauren, the willowy, beautiful black attorney who was next in line for senior partner, who'd made her attraction to him clear on more than one occasion?

Then again, maybe Jenna had enlisted the seductive skills of her sister. Another wild redhead bouncing on his lap?

Double trouble.

Danielle ended a call as he hurried past her desk. She shot

to her feet, jabbing a ballpoint pen in the air. "Mr. Quinn, you have—"

"Danielle," he interrupted. "Reschedule my two o'clock and set up Henry Boardman for a conference call."

"Yes, sir. But—"

"Then call Millie Foxx and decline my representation on her case. I don't consider insanity as a defense for pumping three bullets into her neighbor's barking pit bull."

"Of course, sir. If you'll—"

"And make sure the dry cleaners will have my suits ready by six. Is there any coffee?"

"Yes! *Mr. Quinn!*" She slapped her hand on the surface of her desk in an unusual display of emotion.

He stared at her blond hair, normally neat as a schoolteacher's, escaping the confines of her sophisticated twist. Her pretty face was scrunched into a frown. "What is it?"

"That detective guy is here, and he's got someone with him named Agent Campbell," she whispered dramatically, waving a hand at his cracked office door. "From the FBI!"

FBI. In his office.

Jesus Christ in a tutu.

He cleared his throat. "Thank you, Danielle. Did you offer the gentlemen some coffee?"

She nodded, serious as could be. "The detective accepted some, but the pinhead Fed declined. Guess that says something."

Yep. That the Fed was in no mood to socialize. Thank God.

And that he needed to have a talk with his new secretary about calling his visitors pinheads within hearing range.

Christ.

"Want me to go in with you?" Ryan asked.

"No, it's fine. Make yourself comfortable."

"Cool. Holler if you need me."

Shoring himself up for whatever was in store, Alex pushed into his office and closed the door behind him. "Gentlemen. I assume you're not here to vote me citizen of the year."

The two men occupied the plush visitor's chairs in front of his desk. Detective Lambert rose slightly and shook Alex's hand before being seated again. "Mr. Quinn, I wish it were something that pleasant. This is Agent Roger Campbell of the FBI. He's here because the second attempt on your life overlapped with the bureau's business on a couple of levels. Agent Campbell?"

The agent was a tall, skinny redhead who looked like he'd be more at home working for Bill Gates than the FBI. If not for the gun peeking out from under his jacket. Alex shook the man's hand and took his own seat, grateful for the barrier of his desk between them. An illusion of control.

"Thank you for making time for us, Mr. Quinn," the agent said.

As though he'd been given a choice. "I'm anxious to know how the attempted murder of an average attorney could possibly capture the bureau's interest."

"Simple. Dmitri Baranov wasn't your average assassin. To our knowledge, he'd never failed to take out a target, and he was wanted in so many countries it would be easier to list which ones weren't seeking him."

"Which the FBI didn't deign to inform us about until last night," Lambert said dryly, fiddling with his Styrofoam cup.

Professional international assassin. Alex absorbed this information. Bad. Real fucking bad. "Implications?" He already knew, but wanted to hear it from the agent's mouth.

"Baranov's services were expensive. Whoever hired him has serious money at his disposal, and is willing to throw around a load of cash to see you dead." The agent rested his elbows on the arms of his chair, steepled his fingers. "That's where we become involved. You have a connection to one of our high-profile under-cover operations, and with the hiring of someone like Baranov to kill you, let's just say we're real interested."

"Are you looking at one of my clients, or one of my employ-ees?"

"Henry Boardman. That man isn't the top of the food chain, as I'm sure you know, or at least suspect. The FBI was working on bringing down the entire racket when the local police fucked us over by arresting Boardman. Now your client is lying low with all the answers we need, content to keep his trap shut so his boss doesn't shut it for him."

"Agent, my conversations with Boardman are privileged—"

"Yes, I know. All I'm saying is you're in a helluva lot of trou-ble with some dangerous people, and your defense of Boardman is very likely at the root of it all."

"But that doesn't make any sense," he argued. "I'm his attor-ney. It's my *job* to provide him the best representation possible. He could walk away a free man."

But something teased the back of his mind. He'd been over this same train of thought before, right here in his office.

"It makes perfect sense . . . assuming you're not supposed to win."

The agent's statement hung in the air like a death knell.

Not supposed to win. And Alexander Quinn rarely lost.

"You're saying I'm some sort of figurehead to these bastards?" he asked through bloodless lips. "That I was hired to save face, so Boardman appears to have the best legal counsel on his side, when all along they intended for me to lose?"

"So that Palmer Hodge's boy goes to prison and the law is satisfied, yes. Only somewhere along the way, they decided not to gamble on your losing and opted to take you out."

Palmer Hodge. The name was new to him, but it proved his suspicions were on the money after all. Boardman, though involved to his ears, wasn't the top man. He was the fall guy.

"Then Boardman's case gets reassigned." Oh, God. "He's got someone inside the firm."

"Someone who possibly hired Baranov."

"Jesus Christ." He buried his face in his hands.

Ken Brock's hard, livid face rose in his mind.

"It gets worse."

He couldn't stop the bitter laugh from escaping. "I fail to see how."

"We've been screwed on this case at every turn and have ended up with jack except dead ends and an agent recovering from a breakdown. After a while, a guy starts to wonder why." Campbell stared at him, lips pursed, as though weighing how much to reveal. When he spoke, his voice was grave.

"Palmer Hodge may be calling most of the shots, but he's not alone at the top of the pyramid."

"He's got a partner," Lambert put in. "Positioned someplace in the know."

Campbell's jaw clenched in anger.

"And the FBI has a big motherfucking problem."

. . .

Alex pulled into a parking space in front of Jenna's condo and turned to Ryan. "Wait here. I won't be long."

"Gotcha covered."

He hated this. Ending a dangerous addiction was never fun. More so when the addiction wasn't something inanimate like drugs or alcohol, but another person, with sticky feelings involved.

He couldn't have explained his need to break off their brief affair, other than that the urgency to do so had nagged at him like a sore tooth for days. The bloom wasn't off her sweet rose. No, it wasn't the sex by any means. Her commendable talents never failed to get him going.

But the visit from Detective Lambert and Agent Campbell had left him jumpy. Pensive. His sexual antics with Jenna were potentially habit-forming—one addiction he couldn't afford to maintain, considering her involvement with the Boardman case.

Besides, if he were honest, he wasn't losing a thing. His true happiness stemmed from Liv's gift to him. She'd given him leave to explore untapped desires, and that bargain remained intact. A whole banquet of sins spread before him to choose at will. Or not.

He knocked and waited, listening to the rustle on the other side. Then she was smiling at him, pulling him inside. "I can't stay."

"Don't be silly. Why bother to come over, then?" She sauntered into the living room, short silk robe lapping at the curve of her ass, and sat on the sofa. Legs spread, so he was treated to a hint of her pussy.

His cock responded. After all, he wasn't dead. Yet.

He remained standing. "Jenna, you know I love my wife. I've never made any secret of that."

She rolled her eyes. "Right. But you've got the open-marriage thing, so what's the big deal?"

"True, but if you'll recall, I never intended for our indiscretion to last beyond that first night. I let us go too far."

Her gaze sharpened, and she tensed. "You've got your eye on another lover to fuck, is that it?"

"No." Thinking of the joy he took in Jason sharing his and Liv's bed, he knew that for a huge lie. But it didn't concern Jenna. "We just can't keep this up. The firm is under enough scrutiny because of the attempts on my life, without an office affair between the two attorneys on a big case becoming public fodder."

"That's a cop-out."

"If you like. But it's also the truth. So is the fact that I never lied to you."

Rising, she gave an unhappy laugh and crossed the short distance between them. Pressed her nearly naked body against him. "And what about Olivia? Do you lie to her, Alex?"

"Never. I tell her everything," he said, taking grim satisfaction from the stunned surprise on her face. *"Everything."*

"Y-you've told her about . . . us? The *details?*"

"Every word." He dipped a finger into the part of her robe, over the creamy swell of her breast. "Every caress."

"I don't believe that," she whispered. "What husband tells his wife about his sexual conquests?"

"One who's made a bargain to reveal all the juicy details in exchange for sexual freedom. One hoping to spice up his marriage."

Her voice rose, shrill and upset. "So, what? You, like, give her a blow-by-blow? A total rundown of your day whenever you've been with someone else? Whenever you've fucked *me?*"

He backed up a step. Her breasts heaved with anger, and her face was etched with...disbelief? "Don't play the woman scorned with me, sweetheart. You went after my cock like it was buried treasure, and you got it. We both got what we wanted, and now it's over."

God, how messy and awful. He should've been prepared for her to react badly, but he honestly hadn't thought she'd be so irate. This wasn't anything like the cool, poised barracuda he knew. That other Jenna, he could've sworn would be the first to agree with him now. Cold and professional.

He felt like a shithead.

With a visible effort, Jenna got her emotions under control. Her hands clenched into fists, but her voice was steady. "I assume this won't affect our working relationship—or do I assume too much?"

At least he could be honest in a way that might soothe her. "You're a fine attorney, Jenna. I have nothing but the utmost respect for your dedication and performance in the courtroom. Of course you have my continued support."

For several moments, she calmed herself.

"Thank you. And, Alex?"

"Yes?"

"Get the fuck out."

Gladly. "I'll see you at the office."

After he walked out, she slammed the door behind him. *That went well.*

He could not dredge up one iota of regret to see it finished.

His mind turned toward the two people waiting for him at home, and he smiled.

. . .

The sudden, insistent banging on his front door nearly gave him a heart attack. Each one struck the center of his chest like the bullets he was certain they were.

He had to check himself to be sure. No blood. Though that might change the second he admitted his visitor.

He crept to the peephole . . . and his jaw dropped in astonishment. Panic spurred him to yank open the door, grab Jenna's arm and look around for neighbors before pulling her inside.

"What in God's name are you doing here?" he croaked. "It's not even dark out yet! What if someone saw you? We can't be seen together!"

She stalked into his living room, unfazed by his tirade. "This is important or I'd be at home, licking my wounds." She stopped in front of his fireplace mantel and turned, hands on her hips.

"Well, it must be for you to risk half the county seeing you here. In jeans and tennis shoes, no less." He'd never seen her dressed down before, her wild red hair uncombed. For Jenna, this was a bad sign.

"Alex gave me the boot."

"What?" *Shit, shit.*

"Yeah. It's not as though I didn't know it was coming." She shrugged. "Lasted longer than I thought it would, and I earned every penny of what you paid me to get in his jockeys, so what do I care?"

"Then why are you here?" He crossed his arms over his chest, waiting. Wondering at the gleam in her eyes. What was her game?

"The open-marriage deal Alex has with his wife? Thought you might find it fascinating to hear the rest of their deal. Seems he confesses every little detail of his encounters with other lovers, and they get off on it together." She smirked. "Naughty bargain, huh?"

"Wait." He stared at her. Surely he hadn't heard right. "Alex tells her everything?"

"Mmm."

The sickness returned. Deeper than panic. More profound than fear. There was no way to know what Alex might've told Olivia. What clues the two of them might assemble if it ever occurred to them to do so.

Palmer's going to eviscerate me.

With a chain saw.

Jenna leaned against the mantel, acting very much like a woman in the driver's seat. "I would've done Alex for free, you know. I got to screw the blond hottie's brains out and work on a career-making defense, because *you* talked him into taking me on. Now you know what I think? I'll bet you've got a bigger agenda than merely distracting him. I want to know what's going on. What are you planning to do to Alex and who's paying for all of this?"

Cold sweat broke out all over his body. He moved to stand right in front of her and reached out to clasp her neck. Deceptively gentle, he skimmed the base of her throat with his thumb.

"Jenna, dear. Listen to me," he whispered. "You need to stop asking questions that will prove hazardous to your health. Do you understand?"

Her face went white. "Y-You! You're the one trying to kill Alex!"

"I don't *want* Alex to die," he said sadly. "I'm stuck in a situation over which I have no control. Just like you. Want to live? You'll be a good girl and be available to do what you're told."

"And if I go to the police?"

"By morning, you'll be at the bottom of the Mississippi River in a Hefty bag. We clear?"

She jerked her chin up and down, eyes huge and stark in her face.

"Good. I'll call you later with instructions."

Unless they were both dead by nightfall.

He saw her out, then went straight to the phone. His knees gave out and he dropped onto the sofa, running a hand through his hair. The hated voice answered all too soon, listening as he related Jenna's visit.

A nerve-racking silence followed. At length, Palmer spoke. Calm, as though murder was the last thing on his mind.

"We're out of time. Luckily for you, I have a plan in place to fix this, kill several birds with one stone."

He swallowed, praying he wasn't one of the birds.

"Tell Henry to invite our usual crowd to his estate outside the city for a party this weekend," Palmer went on. "Drinks, plenty of beautiful bodies to enjoy, all of the wickedness our clients desire. We're going to bait our hook. Have Miss Shaw get Quinn there, whatever she has to say."

"She'll be able to play upon their duty to make certain their client doesn't get himself into more trouble, I'm thinking."

"Precisely. And make certain Henry spreads news of the party through all of our underground channels. If Seraph is anywhere near, he'll attend because he needs me. Slaves don't survive well without their masters. When he shows, give him something to make him sleep during the trip home, but he's not to be harmed."

"All right. And Alex?"

"I don't care how you do it, just remove him permanently.

Something in his drink? An accidental overdose, perhaps? Tragic. Happens all the time at wild parties."

"I can arrange that."

"No," he said coldly. "You'll kill Quinn yourself or else answer to me when I arrive."

"You . . . you're coming here?" God help him.

"I'll be at Henry's before the party ends. Insurance."

The call was cut off with a *click.* Before he lost his nerve, he placed two more.

Soon, it would be over.

He'd be damned lucky if he wasn't sharing a grave with Alex.

.   .   .

"You're home early! What—"

Alex smothered Liv's impending inquiry with a hungry kiss, gathering her into his arms. She melted into him, all female softness, just the right curves. "Are we alone?"

"For now. Jason went home because I wanted to talk to you when you got home about—"

"Later."

Bending, he swept her into his arms and bounded up the stairs, carrying her like a baby, laughing as she squealed.

"Alex! What on earth?"

"I want to make love to my sexy wife," he growled, nibbling at the curve of her neck. "Is that so bad?"

"Mmm, you're at your best when you're bad."

"You know it, lady."

He placed her on the bed and crawled up her body, flicking open the button on her shorts and sliding them down her toned legs, along with a pair of lacy purple panties. After helping her off with her T-shirt and bra, he scooted to her feet.

"Lie back and let me spoil you."

"Works for me." She laid her head on the pillows and studied him curiously as he began to massage her feet. "What, no confession tonight? God, that feels good," she sighed.

"Actually, I do have one." She tensed some, but he kept rubbing, slow and easy. "I went to see Jenna after work. Not to be with her, but to break things off."

She blinked at him, surprised. "So, you didn't . . . you know."

"No, and I won't. Not with her."

Liv couldn't hide her happiness if she tried. "What brought about this decision?"

"Several good reasons, but mostly because she was starting to feel like a habit. Like she expected a regular thing, which was never what I wanted."

"Well, there are certainly other lovers to enjoy, if you're inclined."

"You're fishing. That's sort of cute."

"I am not! The bargain stands. I'm a woman of my word, handsome husband."

He kneaded the muscles of her calves and higher, to her thighs, lips turning up at her groan. "I know, and I'm the luckiest fool on the planet." Spreading her legs, he moved between them and began to stroke her sex with feather-light touches. "Will I indulge again? I don't know, but it makes me hard as hell knowing I have your blessing and you have mine. That we can tell each other anything and find quadruple the satisfaction we ever had before."

"Ohh, Alex." She let her thighs fall open, inviting him in. Needing him.

"Let me love you, baby."

He trailed his tongue along the inside of one thigh to her center. Laved her pussy lips, played with the tiny clit. He alternated between teasing and suckling until she writhed, pulling at his hair.

"I need you inside me!"

Kneeling, he pulled her closer and hooked her knees over his shoulders. Cupping her bottom, he lifted her up, parted her slick entrance, and slid home.

For a moment, he reveled in the mewling sounds she made, the sight of her impaled on his cock. He'd never get tired of this feeling, loving this woman.

"I love you," he said softly.

And began to thrust with sure, steady strokes. Parting her flesh again and again, burying himself in her heat. Making love to the woman who'd held his heart in the palm of her small hand for nearly twenty years.

Who'd hold it until the day he drew his last breath.

Fire gathered in his balls, licked at his cock. She met his thrusts by arching her back, totally wanton. Letting go, giving everything to him. His balls tightened and he tensed, holding himself deep, and he went over the edge.

"Ahh, yeah!"

The blaze shot from his spine down his cock and he filled her, jerking and spasming until they were both sated.

Withdrawing, he carefully lowered her and stretched out, gathering her into his arms. She settled on his chest with a happy sigh, one dainty leg thrown over his.

"My, that was fabulous." She gave his sweaty chest a peck.

"You sure were, baby."

"Flatterer."

"Nope, flattery is insincere. I mean every word."

She grew so quiet, after a few moments he thought she'd fallen asleep. But she stirred and rolled to look at him, chin propped over his heart.

"I'm sorry I left you alone so much that we grew apart," she whispered.

His throat tightened and he shook his head. "I'm just as much to blame. Sometimes it seems easier to let go rather than remember what you were fighting for."

"We almost lost each other."

"But we didn't."

"I love you." She bit her lip. "You know that, right?"

"I— of course I do. Why do you say it like that?" Ah, crap. "Are those postcoital tears of joy, or is something wrong?"

He smoothed away a stray drop with his thumb, waiting. Lungs suddenly devoid of enough air.

"Do you . . . could you find room in your heart for one more? I-I didn't mean for this to happen." She sniffed, regarding him with a mixture of apprehension and hope.

"You're talking about Jason." He kept touching her face, her hair. Reassuring. "We can discuss anything now, remember?"

She nodded. Took a deep breath.

"I think I'm falling in love with him."

Fourteen

✳

If she'd announced *she* was the one who'd hired men to kill him, Alex couldn't have appeared more shocked.

The emotions in his green eyes ran the spectrum from hurt and fear to desire and curiosity. "We don't know anything about him," he said, voice rough. "He won't share his past, doesn't seem to have a clue where he's going. How can we build on a lack of trust?"

"I didn't know *you* when we first met," she pointed out. "But it didn't matter to me because I saw the kind of man you are: funny, driven, successful, respected by your peers."

"You believe you can read Jason? And his secrets don't concern you?"

"Sure they do. I also believe he's a good man with a big heart, and he'll tell us his story when he's ready."

"What if he doesn't?"

"I don't pretend to have all the answers."

"Then try this one. . . . Am I losing you?"

Her husband was truly afraid. Even after their lovemaking, how special it was to both of them, she'd shaken his confidence.

She took his face in her hands, gave him a lingering kiss. "Never. I love you, Alex Quinn, and nothing will ever change the way I feel."

"What if I can't make room for another man, Liv? What then?" He paused, eyes searching her soul for the truth. "Would you let him go?"

"Would you ask that of me?" she returned quietly.

Stalemate. She knew what her answer would be, but did he?

His confusion was palpable as he lay holding her. The evening lengthened to shadows and finally to darkness, and sleep overtook her, chasing away the uncertainty.

The irony was that she, not Alex, might be the one to destroy their marriage with her bargain.

. . .

Alex eased from the bed and left his angel sleeping.

His angel who'd fallen for another man.

Feeling restless, he pulled on a pair of shorts and headed downstairs, thinking about how this underscored the difference between men and women since the dawn of the world. Men had forever been ruled by the drive to prove their virility, and to sample the forbidden where it could be found.

Women were creatures of the heart, ruled by their instinct to feather the soft nest of hearth and home for their men and children. They loved hard and forever, didn't take men to their beds lightly.

Well, Liv had never been one to nest, and the desire to have children had bypassed them altogether, but the last held true for his wife.

Despite their rich fantasy lives, she wasn't one to take a lover into her body and leave her soul out of the equation. She wasn't made that way, and he ought to know.

More than one man had tried. Ultrasophisticated men, movers and shakers power lunching in her restaurant. Until tonight, he'd always looked upon the occasional brave man's efforts with pride and no little amusement. His wife was a classic beauty. A man would have to be dead not to want her.

When she'd taken Jason as her lover, he'd been thrown. He'd been so caught up in himself, he'd believed her liberation to be more of a reaction to his own conquests. Tit for tat.

"The joke's on you, Quinn." He stepped outside onto the patio. Stared at the heavens.

And now she'd fallen in love. With a younger man. A stunning younger man who'd been badly hurt by someone, and had demonstrated no evidence of a job nor the desire to get one.

Fate was a tricky bitch.

Could you find room in your heart for one more?

Could he? To be honest, he found Jason charming, likable. The sex was fantastic, and they were definitely compatible.

The real question was whether he could be trusted. In light of everything happening lately—

A splash from Jason's pool interrupted his whirling thoughts. Drawn like a moth to a bug zapper, he drifted to the fence and watched the man swim laps with smooth, even strokes. Water sluiced off his lean back and pale buttocks, the line of his body pure poetry in motion.

A beautiful man who makes Liv happy.

Who makes me happy.

What if he chose to leave St. Louis?

A jolt of possessiveness and arousal hit Alex low and hard,

and something very much like distress at the thought of Jase walking out of their lives. A storm of emotions he'd never felt for anyone except Liv.

He refused to put a label on it. Would. Not.

He wasn't ready. Might never be.

Jason hoisted himself from the pool and walked over to a patio chair, grabbing his towel. He dried his hair and body while Alex appreciated the view, then suddenly straightened and looked toward the fence.

"Alex?"

Crap. "Yeah."

"Shit, you startled me." Wrapping the towel around his hips, he tucked in the end and crossed to where Alex stood staring at him.

"Damn, don't you ever wear clothes?"

"Hey, I'm in my own backyard. I can't help it if my neighbors are voyeurs."

"We can't help it if our neighbor is sex on a stick." Hell, what made him say such an asinine thing?

Jason grinned at him. "And you use your stick very well, I must admit."

Embarrassed, but pleased, he barked a laugh. "You're shameless."

"Pretty much. So, can I help you with something?" His gaze raked Alex meaningfully.

Oh, tempting. "Actually, I need to talk to you. Why don't you come over here."

Jason shrugged. "Sure."

In short order, the other man came through the gate, wearing nothing but the damned towel. "Don't have much modesty, do you?"

"Not really. My favorite T-shirt says *Go Naked*, so that should give you a clue."

"Not the one I'm after. Sit," he said, gesturing to one of the loungers. Jason got settled, elbows on his spread knees, the stupid towel hovering just above the essentials. "This is about Liv. And me."

"You're lucky; she's a special woman. I didn't know——" His gaze shifted to the patterned concrete under their feet.

Alex was patient, sensing the young man was about to reveal an essential part of himself. He wasn't disappointed.

"I never knew true joy in sex before you and Olivia."

Alex stared at him. "What *did* you know?"

"Pain. Humiliation. Servitude." He laughed, a harsh, bitter sound. "And let's not forget deviance."

"You, deviant? Jase, you're so young, you've barely lived." He shook his head, recalling the reference Jason made to his old lifestyle, right before their first sexual encounter. "I'm in the courtroom with unsavory people every day, and I've seen no evidence you have a single trait in common with them."

"You don't know me."

"I'd like to. So would Liv."

"Why?"

The simple question, so vulnerable, tugged at his heart. "Jason, my wife believes she's falling in love with you."

The other man was clearly stunned, his jaw dropping. And then his face filled with such wonder and hope, Alex knew he was one dangerous step from following Liv over the edge.

"And you?" Jason asked.

"I want Liv to be happy." Jason seemed to deflate a bit, so he couldn't help but add, "She's not alone in her feelings."

God help him, it was the unvarnished truth.

Jason clasped his hands tight, as though anticipating the answer to his next question. "What do you want from me?"

"The truth. Who—and what—are you?"

Crickets chirped, but there was no other sound as Jason looked away. "Soon I'll be able to tell you and Olivia everything, and that's a promise. I'm not a bum who only made good off my late uncle's inheritance, no matter how it might appear. Will you trust me?"

Ah, there it was again: trust. What was it about Jason that inspired it without cause?

"Until you give me a reason not to, yes."

"I can't ask for more. Thank you."

"Come inside and stay," he said, realizing it felt right.

"I wouldn't want to intrude . . . "

"For Olivia?"

"And you."

"Yes. Me, too."

The admission came easily, with the knowledge that he wanted to wrap himself around Liv and Jason. Keep them safe.

New and strange. But no less exciting.

"Let me grab some shorts and lock up," Jason said.

This is my gift to you, Liv, he thought, watching the other man go. *And if I'm honest, to myself.*

Jason was back in less than a minute, wearing cutoffs, probably commando underneath. In their bedroom, Jason stepped out of the shorts and Alex saw he was right. He swallowed hard, uncertain of how to proceed with these new and unfamiliar feelings. His cock had no trouble deciding, but damn.

"There's no shame in liking what you see, inside or out," Jason said softly. "No labels, remember? It is what it is."

"You're right. I'll stop thinking so much." He gave the younger man a small smile. "Let's wake Sleeping Beauty."

"Good plan."

Liv rolled to her back, stretching in naked, splendid glory, blinking at them. "She's awake now. What are you two hatching over there?"

"A plan to wake you up nice and slow," Jason said softly, giving her a smile. All of his feelings for her shone in his eyes. "But you caught us."

"Oh? Well, I'm sorry I ruined your surprise, then. Can I make it up to you?"

"No need, pretty lady." Jason crawled up the foot of the bed on his hands and knees, then stretched out beside her, combing his fingers through her dark hair. Liv gasped as he started nibbling her neck, palming a breast in one hand and playing with the dusky nipple.

Alex watched, feeling better already about having Jason come over. Liv needed this, and so did he. He joined them, kissing a path down Liv's tummy as Jason loved her breasts, nipping and grazing them with his teeth. Alex ditched his own shorts and moved between her legs, spreading her knees wide, and tongued her sweet little nub.

"Oh! God, yes . . . "

She arched into him as he suckled the sensitive flesh, tasting the evidence of their earlier passion. Her scent and responsiveness to both of them shot straight to his groin. He laved her slit, driving her insane, and when he knew she was poised at the brink, he eased away and looked to Jason.

"She's ready for you."

His brown eyes widened. "Me? I thought—"

"Don't keep the lady waiting," he ordered, mindful of Jason's preference for being dominated. "I expect you to make her scream while she comes."

Nodding, Jason fisted his cock and crawled between her thighs, pumping his erection a few times before covering her. He guided the plum-shaped head to her opening and sank deep. Began to shaft her with long, sure strokes.

Liv splayed her hands on Jason's back, holding him close, rising to meet him. Lost in the happiness of making love with him. Emotion clogged Alex's throat and he found himself wanting to be a part of them.

From the bedside table, he grabbed the bottle of vanilla-scented oil he and Liv used sometimes. Vanilla? How ironic. Prize in hand, he moved behind Jason, smoothed a hand over his flank. The other man slowed his tempo, making it easier for Alex to spread his cheeks and dribble the oil in his crease.

Alex inserted two fingers into his entrance, probing, preparing. Jason moaned, backing into his hand with each slow withdrawal from Liv. Alex worked his channel a bit more, then dribbled oil on his own cock, making himself nice and slick. He wanted to give them a smooth ride.

Tossing the oil aside, he lined up and pushed his length into that tight hole. Sank all the way into the hot passage.

"God, yes," he murmured, skimming a palm over Jason's spine. "You feel so good. So right."

"Damn, Alex, fuck me," Jason rasped. "Do it."

He did, gladly. Began to thrust, the forward motion sending Jason into Liv each time. The three of them established a rhythm, a perfect cadence, pumping faster and faster. Flying higher.

Alex's balls tightened and he couldn't hold back. He shot deep into Jason with a hoarse shout, filling him with his cum. His release triggered theirs, and Jason stiffened, rippling underneath him at the same time Liv cried out, clutching his back.

They remained locked together for some moments, letting the waves subside, floating down again. Alex withdrew first and flopped onto his back, content and sated. Happy with the world.

Jason did the same and snuggled on Liv's other side, practically humming with joy. How could he not trust a man who appeared as carefree and uncomplicated as their lover looked right now?

"Spoon," Alex said, pulling Liv's back to his front. She, in turn, pulled Jason to her, and Alex couldn't help but smile as he drifted off to sleep.

A Liv sandwich, with him and Jason as the buns.

Life didn't get much better than this.

* * *

Liv smiled into her mug of coffee. Waking up squished between two hot men had been beyond her fantasies.

Being loved by both of them? Out-of-this-world orgasmic.

The fact that Alex had fetched Jason sometime after their talk—and enlisted the younger man to make love to her—warmed her inside. Dare she hope this was a gesture of acceptance on his part? A true acknowledgment of her needs and his own?

Patience. She blew out a resigned breath, wishing Alex wasn't at work and Jason off to God knows where. Still, their absence gave her precious hours to think without all of that potent testosterone clouding her judgment. Alex had reservations about Jason, and rightly so. Bad shit was happening, and this bad shit coincided with their hunky new neighbor's arrival in the city. The hunk with secrets and sad eyes, who was not forthcoming about his past.

Which in and of itself wasn't unforgivable or altogether alarming . . . except that someone wanted Alex dead.

Her grandmother used to say the word *coincidence* was for natural disasters and damned idiots.

Setting her mug on the counter, Liv walked to the kitchen junk drawer and fished out the key Bill had given her years ago. The one Jason hadn't asked to be returned.

The very idea of snooping in someone else's home made her gut churn with guilt. Especially after last night.

The idea of her husband dying because of her own misplaced trust quelled it.

Before she could talk herself out of what she was about to do, Liv took the key, grabbed a fresh loaf of banana-nut bread wrapped in foil from the counter, and marched next door. Using an offering of food as a cover? Simple, but effective. Anyone watching, like the cop on the street, would see her knock. Wait. Then deliver the gift.

She figured she had five minutes, tops, before anyone became suspicious, but truthfully, she didn't require even sixty seconds. She had her goal set. Go in, take a look, get out.

She followed her course, not letting herself in until she'd waited like a good neighbor. Once inside, she made a beeline straight for Jason's office. She sat the bread on the corner of the desk and skirted it, pulse rushing in her ears, palms clammy. Lowering herself into the chair, she wondered how she'd explain herself if Jason caught her rifling through his personal effects.

He'd be disappointed, no doubt. Angry. Pissed enough to do bodily harm?

Someone's trying to kill my husband.

Resolve fortified, she yanked open the top desk drawer, half expecting to find innocuous pens, pencils, and paper clips. Which is exactly what she found. Frowning, she shut the drawer. She could've sworn he'd shoved something in this desk he hadn't wanted her to see.

She tried the top right-hand drawer, much deeper. And empty. What a bust.

She didn't expect to find much in the middle one, either. Whatever she'd seen, he'd probably moved. Or her overactive imagination had made too much of it—

Wait. A legal pad lay in the drawer, upside down. Why put it in there that way, unless you wanted to hide it? Nerves jumping, she pulled out the pad, tugging a little because something heavy was sitting on top of it in the depths of the drawer.

She turned it over and stared at the hand-drawn pyramid for several seconds before the import reached her horrified brain.

Names. A lot of names, layered from the base to the top.

Alex. Olivia.

"Oh . . . oh, no."

Jenna Shaw. Ken Brock. Kyle Murphy. Danielle Forney.

Me.

A helpless whimper escaped her throat.

Henry Boardman. Dmitri Baranov.

Palmer Hodge.

"Why? What's going on here?"

Flipping through the pad, she saw nothing else was written inside, and replaced the damning thing just the way she found it. But when she did, the top edge of the pad bumped whatever had been sitting on it before. Bending down, she reached to adjust the item.

Her hand, her entire body, froze.

Cold black metal glinted there. Belonging to a gun big enough to blow someone's brains to hell.

Many people owned guns. Few kept them stowed next to laundry lists for murder.

Liv slammed the drawer shut and fled the office without looking back. She locked the front, just as she heard Jason's garage door hum in the back. Close. Too close.

Safely inside her house, she stood in the foyer, legs shaking, hand over her mouth. Somehow she wobbled to the phone and dialed. Left a message on Alex's cell.

"Alex? Please, come home. I-I need you."

Next, she left a message with Danielle, who said he was in an important meeting. Once again, disjointed pieces of earlier conversations with Alex went round in her mind. Threads from his confessions that might be, at last, forming into something tangible. She should've spoken with Alex before, and now she'd have to wait.

An idea struck, and she made another call, making a simple request of a puzzled Detective Lambert. She opted not to tell him what she'd found in Jason's possession. Not yet. She needed to think.

Ten minutes later she had her answer, thanked the detective and huddled in a corner of the living room to ponder the implications of it all.

Only then did she remember the banana-nut bread she'd left perched on the corner of Jason's desk.

. . .

Alex sped home, calling Liv from his cell phone and telling her to hang tight. She sounded upset. And today, of all fucking days, he'd let his bodyguard go; after a lot of thought, he decided one man—even a well-trained one—wasn't going to stop a hit. Hell, they'd already gotten the drop on the man once. Next time, Ryan might not be lucky.

He could've used the guy now, but Liv insisted she wasn't hurt. She just needed his ass home, pronto.

His car screeched to a stop in the garage and he tore inside. "Liv!"

"In here." She rose from the sofa to meet him.

He gathered her into his arms, relieved that she seemed physically okay. "You're trembling."

"I have to talk to you. It's important."

"Yeah, I sorta got that part." The levity didn't work. "Come here, baby."

Leading her to his favorite chair, he pulled her into his lap. He took her hands in his, rubbing them, concerned by the chill of her skin.

"Alex, he's got a gun," she whispered.

Alarmed, he glanced around, making sure they were alone. "Who, sweetheart?"

"Jason. I walked in on him hiding something the other day, and I got to thinking. I knew it was wrong, but I used my key when he was gone earlier, and there was this huge gun in one of the drawers."

"Honey, lots of people have guns in the house. I have one in our bedroom closet, remember?"

"His was next to this." From her front pocket, she dug out a folded square of paper. "I drew this just the way it was on the notepad in his desk."

Taking the paper, Alex unfolded it and frowned at the pyramid. The names. He swore he actually felt the blood drain from his head. "My God. What the fuck is this? Some type of . . . laundry list?"

"That's what I thought at first, but it's a flowchart. And look— he put himself smack in the middle."

"It doesn't make any sense. Besides Jenna, how would he know of all the people in my office? Why are Boardman and Palmer Hodge on there?"

"He's involved in what's happening to you, somehow," Liv said. "All of these names below Boardman's are the people closest to you every day. And you know what's really weird? They're all people you've mentioned to me in your confessions."

"The police and the FBI think Hodge has someone in my firm. It's like Jason's trying to figure it out, too," he mused.

"Exactly! But he hasn't been present for all of your confessions, and I have." Pushing off his lap, she paced.

"I don't see how a string of naughty bedtime stories, even true ones, could be important to anyone but you and me."

Even as he said it he recalled Jenna's strong negative reaction upon learning that he'd been sharing every detail of his encounters. What had she called it? A *total rundown*. Odd word choice.

"Let's start with the fact that Jenna doesn't have a sister." She stopped pacing and crossed her arms over her chest.

"What?"

"According to Lambert, Jenna is an only child. The first time you were with her, she claimed she needed a ride home because her sister borrowed her car."

"I—shit. She used that excuse again the other night at the club."

"A simple lie. Something you'd never think to check . . . or perhaps weren't expected to live long enough to question."

"I can't believe Jenna's involved with killers," he said quietly. No, because that would make him a victim of his own stupidity.

"Then let's revisit the fact that you allowed a green junior partner to work on your biggest trial this year." Her expression was grim. Earnest. "Be honest, Alex. Besides catering to your cock, why did you risk alienating everyone in the office? You could've fucked her without giving her the case. *Why did you?*"

"Because Kyle said . . ." He went numb.

"He pushed you to take her on, didn't he? Just like he always pushes, and you caved, just like you always do when Kyle wants or needs something!"

"That's not true."

"What about when Bea retired? Who recommended this new secretary, Danielle?"

"All right, Kyle did. He thinks she's hot, and she is, but she also does a good job. Not the brightest bulb in the box, but enthusiastic."

"I'll bet," she muttered. Shook her head. "The point is, secretaries know everything. Bea was sharp, and you can bet she'd have gone to you the moment something smelled fishy in the office. You admitted Danielle isn't so smart. Once again, Kyle's suggestion."

"No. I won't believe he has anything to do with who's after me. He's my best friend, Liv." He stood and walked to the window, knees watery.

"Whom you've bailed out financially time and again. He leans on you."

"I've only lent him money twice, and he's square. I asked again a couple of weeks ago, and he doesn't need my help anymore."

"What convenient timing." He felt her hand on his back. "And why is that, Alex? Why is he suddenly so financially solvent?"

He rounded on her. "Don't. There has to be another explanation." If there wasn't, one of the biggest parts of his life had been a lie.

Liv's pretty eyes softened. She understood. Knowing someone close to him had sold him out was bad enough, but for that person to be someone trusted and loved like a brother?

Getting over the betrayal would take a lifetime.

"Have you seen Jenna and any of the others talking together, more than might be expected?"

"Hell, Liv. Everyone speaks with everyone else on a daily basis. It's a busy place, lots of clients coming in. But huddled in dark corners, whispering plots? That would be noticed."

"Maybe. What about Ken? You said he was royally pissed about the whole thing with Jenna."

"I'd hate to think it, but ... Brock's a possibility. He barely tolerates the sight of me. It's so bad, if I wasn't positive the second shooter was a stranger, I'd have to take a hard look at Brock. As it is, I think he'd sell me to the devil for fifty cents."

"We need to call Detective Lambert and tell him all of this." She walked into his outstretched arms, burrowed against his chest, seeking his warmth.

"Baby, we have to let him know about Jason, too," he said softly. "Show him your drawing."

Jason. What sort of man had they invited into their lives?

That would be the most painful betrayal of all. Because Liv loved him.

And so did he, in his own way.

"I know I was losing it when I called you—"

"I'll say, and with good reason." He kissed the top of her head.

"—but now that I'm calm and we've talked it over? I'm positive Jason's on our side."

"Liv..." God, he didn't want to see her get hurt. Emotionally or physically.

"Yes, it looks bad, especially since he's been so secretive about his past, but I'm a pretty good judge of character. At least I believe I am. He's had it rough, Alex, and he's here to lick his wounds. If he's involved, there's a good reason."

Lick his wounds.

Hang on. A snippet of conversation teased his memory. A comment, in passing, Agent Campbell had made in Alex's office. What was it?

Dammit, he couldn't grasp the words.

Neither he nor Liv wanted to believe they'd been betrayed by people they cared about.

One of them was wrong.

"It's just as well I'm home early," he said, pulling back. "I need to go out tonight, but it's not what you think. I just found out Boardman is having a private party, one of his risqué bashes, despite my strenuous protests. I need to go to keep an eye on my client and make sure he stays out of trouble."

Liv stiffened. "Is Jenna going?"

"Yes, but we're not attending together. In fact, since she's the one who brought news of the party to me, I want to keep tabs on her, too. All things considered."

"I don't like this," she said, rubbing her arms. "It reeks."

"I'll be careful, honey. Besides, I phoned Lambert, so he knows about it, too. He and Agent Campbell aren't happy, either, so they're going to slip someone on the inside as a precaution."

"I still think something stinks, but if the cops are watching, that's good." Worry clouded her blue eyes all the same.

"I'll be fine." He tipped up her chin. "Will you be all right here? I mean, Jason—"

"I will. He's not our enemy, Alex. I know it."

"Don't open the door for anyone while I'm gone. Including him."

Oh, he knew that stubborn look. His wife didn't take orders, never had.

"Tough shit."

"So I see. Do you kiss your mother with that mouth?"

"I could do a lot of wicked things with my mouth. If you were staying home tonight to benefit from them."

"I suppose I deserve that."

"Yep, you do."

"I love you."

"Back at'cha, Counselor."

Alex pulled her into his arms again and just held Liv for a long while. Clinging tight, a chill creeping into his bones.

How ironic it would be for them to find their way back to one another, only to lose in the eleventh hour.

The damned clock was ticking.

Fifteen

The afternoon melted into evening, the breeze perfect, the pool inviting. Liv had reconnected with her husband in these last couple of weeks, and life should have been good.

She was terrified.

Something was wrong with Alex attending this party, and he knew it, too. He'd held her so tight, then made love to her so tenderly, each caress had felt like . . .

Good-bye.

No. She was being emotional, that's all. This whole ordeal was taking its toll on both of them.

"Hey, babe? I have to go."

She turned in her lounger and had to suppress the urge to seduce her own husband into staying. Lord, he looked fine in a pair of dark, pressed jeans and a tight green T-shirt that made his eyes pop and blew the flabby lawyer-type cliché all to hell and back. The ribbed material defined his pecs and abs to mouthwatering perfection. He needed a haircut, the blond strands falling over his eyes and curling at his nape, but she wasn't about to remind him when she loved running her hands through it every time they made love.

He appeared every inch the bad boy, off to a wicked party where anything might happen. And she wasn't invited.

He leaned down and gave her a quick kiss. "Miss me."

"You know it. Hurry home?"

"Always."

But she knew it was likely to be dawn before that sort of thing ended. Then again, maybe it would die down early and he'd head home, satisfied nothing would be gleaned by staying.

Right.

She sat brooding after he left, how long she didn't know. An hour? Two? It wasn't until a shadow fell over her spot on the patio that she acknowledged she'd been waiting for Jason.

"I want to explain, but I can't. Not yet."

She digested this. Okay, so he wasn't going to deny what she found. "I'd suck as a spy."

"Like a Hoover. The dessert was great, though."

That's when she knew. If he could stand here and joke about her invading the sanctity of his home, his privacy, then he was no more guilty of subterfuge than Alex.

"I'm sorry," she said, looking up at him. Ashamed.

Lowering himself into the other lounger, he met her gaze. "Don't be. I'm the one who's sorry." He laughed, the sound hollow. "I thought I could come here and hide from my mistakes, just for a little while, before I had to make good. I didn't count on you and Alex. I didn't mean to lose my heart."

"Who are you? Tell me."

His throat worked, expression tormented. "Trust me for a bit longer. I know you don't have any reason to, but I'm begging you. Please give me more time."

"And then?"

"I have some issues to work out, and then maybe, if you two want . . . I'll put down roots."

A promise. She heard the truth in his voice, whispering what she wanted to hear. If only she could believe.

"You're not making this easy to understand."

"It will all make sense very soon. I'm not perfect, but I'm not the bad guy, Olivia." He sighed. "I'll talk to Alex, too. Is he home yet?"

Her laugh emerged as a sob. "Not until he's done playing Dick Tracy for the evening."

Jason's gaze sharpened. "What do you mean?"

"Henry Boardman's throwing some sort of kinky party at his place, and Alex has gone to make sure the dirty bastard stays out of trouble."

"Shit!" He bolted from his chair, fists clenched. "That idiot!"

Alarmed, she rose. "What?"

"He's walking into a trap, that's what. I'd heard about the party through a contact, but . . . goddamn, I have to get over there."

"I'm going with you!"

"Absolutely not. You don't know—"

"I understand that Alex is in trouble, and I'll get there whether I have to go alone or not. I'd feel safer with you, so it's your call."

He swore a blue streak, but she fisted her hands on her hips, completely unfazed. When he ran out of steam, he blew out an irritated breath and glared at her, 110 percent a man who meant business. She'd never seen this side of him before, and if the situation wasn't so dire, she'd take more time to appreciate the meta-morphosis.

"You'll do exactly as I tell you," he said firmly, straightening to his full height. A man who'd tolerate no bullshit.

"And here I thought you loved following orders."

"Only in the bedroom, sweet thing. Now go put on some-thing slinky so we can haul your stubborn shithead of a husband out of the fire."

· · ·

Alex wandered through the latex-and-leather crowd, sipping his Jack and cola, scanning the faces for someone familiar. Observing scenes of excess that far surpassed any of the sophomoric offer-ings at the Paddle and Whip and dodging invites to partake in each one.

Mountains of white powder. Pills of every color of the rain-bow. Hard-driving rock music and a packed dance floor. Toned, gorgeous bodies writhing in every room, in pairs or more. Some were tied, being dominated by various methods. Whipping, spank-ing, public humiliation. And nobody objected, least of all the sub-missives. Boardman's mansion was the devil's playground, filled with every forbidden pleasure known to man.

Drugs frightened him. He had no trouble staying far from those, but the sex?

A dull throb, a slow burn, settled in his groin. So easy to for-get why he was here, especially with Jenna and Boardman lost in the crowd somewhere, undoubtedly enjoying themselves.

Damn, what was he doing here? The cops and the Feds were watching Boardman and his cronies, and Alex was out of his ele-ment. Liv and Jason were at home, and that's where he belonged.

He turned, looking for somewhere to abandon his drink, just as a hand lit on his arm.

"Why, Alex!" Danielle stood in front of him, smiling. Wearing a sleeveless gold see-through tank top thing. "I'd hoped you would be here. Are you having fun?"

He blinked, trying like hell to keep his gaze on her face. Jesus Christ, she was . . . full. Pretty, rosy nipples gracing round, high breasts and a flat tummy. And the gauzy skirt? Answered the question of whether the lovely Danielle was a natural blond.

"I'm sorry, wh-what did you ask?"

"Are you having a good time?" She waved a hand at the room in general.

"Not yet." God. "I mean, it's fine, just not really my scene. I was thinking of heading out."

"Oh, but you can't! Things are finally starting to get interesting." Taking his hand, she tugged. "Come with me."

"I don't know—"

"Oh, come on, don't be such a party pooper. Is it always such a chore getting you to lighten up?"

Before he could chew on that, she took off, leading him across the room and into another one. A library, dark and quiet except for several couples and the unmistakable noises of people already having a fabulous time. He glimpsed naked backsides, spread legs, and tangled limbs—damn, it wasn't *that* dark—and he struggled to keep his eyes averted.

Wasn't easy. Didn't matter, anyway, because the effect was the same. He'd have to be a eunuch not to be hard and aching, his body coming alive, shushing the protests of the guardian angel on his shoulder.

She led him to a settee against one wall next to a tall bookcase and patted the spot beside her. The second he sat down, one slender hand slid up the inside of his thigh. Brushed the bulge in his jeans. "You sure look yummy in street clothes, Alex," she praised, tracing the ridge of his erection. "So sexy."

He covered her hand with his free one, inching it away from the danger zone. "I don't think you've ever called me 'Alex' before, even when I insisted."

"One, we're usually at work. Two, yes, I have." Undeterred, she cupped his sex, rubbed.

"When?" The question emerged as a croak. He cast about for a graceful way to extricate himself without embarrassing them both.

Leaning over, she whispered into his ear, "You look hot in a blindfold, boss."

The sensual information overload blew his mind. And his plans for escape. "Holy God. It was *you*."

"In the flesh."

He stared at her pleased expression, the kitten ready to lick the cream. Literally. She pressed into him, nipples grazing his chest through the nonexistent barrier, and nibbled his lips. Swept her tongue into his mouth, probing. Exploring. He let her, allowing himself this bit of pleasure. Telling himself he'd go no further.

Until she slid to the floor and pushed apart his knees, fingers digging into his thighs, thumbs brushing his crotch. "I could hardly believe my luck when Jenna told me about your openmarriage arrangement. The man I'd lusted after for weeks, available to play and possessing a wicked streak a mile wide. Imagine that."

Where Jenna was concerned, he knew luck had nothing to do with Danielle's fortune. "Danielle—"

"It *is* true, right? You have permission to play?" She cocked her head, narrowing her eyes. "I didn't think until later that one of you might have lied—not that I thought it was you."

"Yes," he said, glad this was an issue for her. Unlike Jenna, Danielle was someone he really liked as a person. "I don't keep secrets from my wife."

"Good." Clever fingers continued their mission, working on the fly of his jeans.

"We shouldn't."

She shrugged. "We already have. We enjoyed each other, and we can again, so why not?"

His silence, the heat of desire radiating from him, was his answer. Taking his drink, she placed it on a nearby table. He pulled off his shirt and bent, removed his socks and shoes, then pushed down his jeans and briefs. She tugged them the rest of the way off and shoved them aside, then knelt between his spread legs again.

He scooted to the edge of the settee, granting her easier access. She manipulated his testicles, squeezing and rolling them, creating a delicious pressure. A tingling that spiraled from his balls slowly up his cock to the tip.

Moist heat surrounded him. She took him in her mouth, sucked him deep, blond hair spilling over his lap. Head bobbing, little tongue working his shaft.

"Feels so good," he gasped. "Don't want to come yet."

She pulled off with a long, slow suck. "Fuck me."

Alex fished on the floor, found his jeans and the condom in the back pocket. Handing the packet to her, he stood with his erection straining toward her luscious mouth as though eager to burrow inside again. "Do the honors?"

She sheathed him quickly and spread her thighs, touching herself. "How do you want me?"

"Bend over the bench and spread your legs." She did, and he flipped up the material posing as a skirt, baring her to him. He smoothed his hands over her naked bottom. Lifted and offered up to him like a gift. His with which to do whatever he desired.

"Alex, please."

"Patience, beautiful." Wetting one finger, he parted her cheeks and teased her rosette. Pushed inside, nice and easy. "Good girl. What a pretty little ass, pink and spread for me. I'm going to finger fuck your hole while I slide my cock in and out of your pussy."

"Oh yes! More."

She shivered under him and his cock burned, desperate to find sanctuary inside her. First, he wanted her dripping, begging for it. Still working her ass, massaging gently, he slipped two fingers of his other hand between the folds. Probed into her slick channel, loving the scent of her arousal.

"Already so wet. Tell me what you want, baby."

"Please, Alex, fuck me!"

Replacing his fingers with the head of his cock, he pushed into her tight passage with a groan of pure ecstasy. Gripping one hip, he began to thrust, filling both entrances again and again.

In front of whoever cared to watch.

"God, yes," he growled, turned on beyond belief. "Anyone can see us. Does that make you hot, sweet Dani?"

"Oh! Oh yes! Harder . . ."

He fucked her hard and deep, balls slapping her pussy, his entire universe nothing but the wildfire between his legs. Sweeping out of control as he drove into her, sac drawing up. So close—

She arched her back, screaming her release, pussy rippling around his cock. That sent him over and he shot, thrusting once. Twice. Shuddering as he came so forcefully, he thought he might turn inside out.

Heaving, he kissed her spine, withdrew only his finger. "That was unbelievable. You were good, Danielle. Thank you."

"So were you, and the pleasure was mine."

He heard the smile in her voice, and chuckled. "I could tell."

She laughed as he withdrew, and he felt a pang of guilt. He liked Danielle and didn't want to hurt her. Or cause a strain between them at work. He discarded the condom in a nearby wastebasket and sat beside her, leaning his back against the bench.

"I liked when you called me Dani," she said, peering at him as though to gauge his reaction to their tryst.

"Really? It suits you. I'll call you that if you want."

"I do."

"Then it's settled." He studied her earnest face and found no trace of guile there. Simply a sensual person with whom he'd enjoyed an intimate connection. Oddly enough, he felt this might be the start of a friendship, despite the fact that she worked for him.

If Dani had been used by whoever was after him, she had no clue.

"I'm not going to get all weird on you at the office," she said, smiling at him.

"I appreciate your telling me, but somehow you didn't seem the high-strung type."

"Though I can't promise not to try and seduce you again, when you least expect it."

"I can't promise to resist, so we're even."

Her eyes darkened, and she licked her lips. They were plump

and inviting and he couldn't help but sample another taste. He drew her into his side and took her mouth, lowering her to the floor, covering her body with his. As his cock filled again, already reviving for another round, he thought maybe he should find his absent host later, thank him for the party.

Because, damn, his sixth confession would be one to remember.

.   .   .

Jason led Olivia into the throng, on his guard. The gun hidden in his waistband under his leather jacket was a small comfort. It had been too damned easy to crash Boardman's little soiree, which only meant one thing.

He wanted it to be crashed.

Sweat trickled down his spine and had nothing to do with wearing a stupid jacket in warm weather or the heat being generated by the press of bodies in full lockdown mode.

Fear rode him hard, left a bitter taste in his mouth. Not just because of what Boardman and Palmer would do to him when they discovered he was here. Or how many pieces Palmer would carve from his body when he learned who Jason really was.

Terror of failure was his real enemy.

He'd let everyone down once, most of all himself. He had to make it right, or he'd never hold his head up again.

First, they had to find Alex. "Go stand over there," he said to Liv, pointing to an alcove near the foyer. "Be on standby to get the hell out, but blend in. Be friendly; whatever you have to do to look like you belong here."

"I'd rather stay with you."

"We'll attract too much attention searching together. Besides,

I might be recognized. If I am, I don't want you with me." That last tidbit got him a startled look, but at least she didn't argue.

"Okay, just hurry."

He split off from her and dove into the crowd, wishing that he knew the layout, that Palmer had brought him here even once. He scanned the faces for Alex, the rock beat skewering his brain cells.

And he realized, with sudden cold in his stomach, that if anyone were to scream in this place, no one would hear. Or care if they did.

He moved faster, trying to shake the feeling they were almost out of time.

. . .

When he saw the good-looking kid with the shoulder-length hair, he nearly creamed his pants in relief. All the players were in place now. Just maybe Palmer wouldn't kill him now, out of gratitude.

He stepped out back, onto the patio, to get better reception. After making sure he was alone, he placed his call. Palmer answered on the second ring. Must be nice having a freaking private jet.

"Give me good news."

"Everyone is here, including that kid you've been so hot to find."

Palmer sucked in a breath on the other end. He could practically see the guy getting hard. "You're sure it's Seraph?"

He rolled his eyes. Couldn't he have named his slave something cooler, like Spike? "I'm sure. You had me study enough photographs. I could name his moles."

"Remember, keep him in the basement and prepare him for

transport, but don't harm him. That pleasure is all mine, or you'll answer to me."

"I know, you told me. Oh, something I thought you might want to know—he arrived with Olivia Quinn." He couldn't figure it out.

"Was her husband with them?"

"Nope. He got here earlier and is indulging in his extracurricular arrangement."

Palmer laughed, happy as shit. "One last piece of pussy before he dies. How poetic."

He felt sick again. But he could do this, as long as he didn't imagine Alex dead. *It's not my fault. They were going to kill him no matter what.* "Yeah. Fuckin' Robert Frost."

"Finish Quinn like we discussed. His death will provide a distraction while Seraph is dealt with. I'm less than forty minutes away."

Palmer hung up, leaving him holding the phone.

And carrying a heavy load of guilt for what he was about to do.

.   .   .

Liv huddled in the alcove, nervous and more than a little amazed at the open sex going on all around her.

Pairs. Threesomes. Foursomes! Good Lord, and Alex was here someplace, among this wicked crowd. Had he found a companion to play with? The idea lured her like the moth to the proverbial flame.

Glancing around, she left the alcove and bit her lip, hesitating. Okay, she'd stay close enough to check back in a few minutes, in case Jason returned.

The place was huge. Where to start? She glanced in some of the surrounding rooms, scanning for a familiar blond head. Now and then one caught her eye, but it was always a different man. She went down the main hallway, toward the back of the house, keeping the alcove behind her, glancing in rooms.

In one of the last rooms, she discovered a library, dimly lit like the others. Bodies writhed everywhere, moaning their enjoyment. Her nipples tingled and her sex heated, the atmosphere getting to her.

As she was about to leave, she saw him. Her heart pounded and her mouth went dry at being confronted with the evidence of her own bargain. Her handsome husband, basking in the freedom he'd been granted.

Completely naked, he sat on the edge of a padded bench, a goddess of a blond woman between his legs. Head bobbing, she sucked his cock in leisurely fashion, as though eating a stick of candy. Alex gripped the bench, totally into letting her do him.

A pair of masculine hands went around Liv's waist and pulled her close, startling her, and she craned her neck to find herself staring at an amused stranger with jet-black hair. A drop-dead gorgeous stranger, who nodded toward the pair she was observing.

"Your man?" he inquired in a lovely French accent.

Robbed of speech, she could only nod.

"You are shocked, but highly aroused," he murmured, sliding his palms to cup her braless breasts through the halter of her dress. "I can feel your heat. You have never seen him with another?"

"N-no." Except for Jason, but that was different.

"Oh, then you are in for a treat. Lean against me while we admire the miracle of beautiful people enjoying one another, yes?" The Frenchman kissed Liv's hair, parted the material over her breasts and pushed it aside. Pinched her nipples to peaks as she watched the woman bend over the bench and Alex rise to cover himself.

"This can be your pleasure, as well. Ah yes, look at them. The lady is presented to him, offering her body, everything that she is. And a man's desire to answer her call is older than time. Watch."

An earthquake couldn't have moved her. Alex positioned himself between the woman's spread legs as she said his name, begging for him. He murmured something low and soothing, then parted her ass cheeks and began to work her with one finger. She begged for more and he spoke to her again, gentle but driving her crazy with want.

The Frenchman slid one hand down to Liv's thigh, then skimmed upward. Found the silk of her panties and slipped underneath, finding the damp curls between her legs. Began to stroke her clit, sending whirls of delight all through her quivering limbs. "This is the gift he gives her now, and she to him. Nice, yes?"

"Yes." Liv melted against the Frenchman's hard body, his touch. All of the rioting sensations mingled with the awe she felt as the woman cried out Alex's name in a clear voice, begging to be fucked.

And then Alex sank his thick cock into his lover, inch by inch, saying something else to her, calling her *sweet Dani*. He thrust into her again and again, taking her hard. Head thrown back, face awash in glorious pleasure, fucking his partner, he was the picture of male beauty.

He was the act of sexual communion personified.

And she knew now she would never deny him this. When he confessed to her, *this* was what he wanted to share, the joy of sexual freedom that she'd given him and herself. The gift. She was glad she'd seen, and secretly hoped she would again in the future.

Liv panted in time with her husband pounding Dani's pussy, her sex throbbing under the Frenchman's skillful ministrations. Liv was no match for the waves flooding her and she exploded, coming hard, stifling a cry.

Alex buried himself deep inside his lover and they came, as well, shuddering together for some moments before he withdrew.

The Frenchman withdrew his hand from her panties, straightened her halter top, smiling warmly. "This was a good experience for you, yes? You see what I tried to tell you?"

"Yes." She smiled back. What an interesting man. "Thank you."

"No, thank you, sweet." With a brush of his lips against hers, he made his way into the crowd once more.

"Wow," she breathed. She looked to Alex and Dani again, while staying to the shadows. They were sitting against the bench, talking as though familiar—

She almost smacked her forehead. "Danielle! His new secretary!"

Well, now. This certainly made for a fascinating development. He liked Danielle, she knew. Knowing Alex the way she did, he'd want her again, too. Perhaps many times, from the chemistry that had nearly set the library ablaze—and he only had one more confession. Perhaps a different arrangement was in order next....

Whatever happened, she was glad Dani wasn't a stranger, but someone he cared for. A lot, apparently, because Alex rolled her to the floor and settled on top of her, between those long legs.

An idea teased at Liv's brain. What if she joined them? Oh, that could be mind-blowing!

But she'd been standing here a while, and Jason might be worried by now. She needed to go back to the alcove and find him first, let him know she'd located Alex, and that he was far from being in any danger. Then she'd return and get in on the action, too.

Excited about her plan, she started to sneak from the room when something round and small pressed into her lower back.

"Don't make a sound," the unfamiliar male voice instructed. "Just smile, go nice and calm, and I won't have to shoot the two lovebirds over there. Got it?"

Fear paralyzed her vocal chords. This man would do it, too. Smiling, terrified, she edged from the room, willing Alex to know somehow that they were all in trouble.

Then she was marched away to meet an uncertain fate.

Sixteen

✳

Jason had about given up on finding Alex when he spied his friend in a library on the main floor, laughing and talking with a familiar woman. Danielle Forney? Yep, that was her, gorgeous and blond. Barely dressed. And disheveled.

"You dawg," he muttered, annoyed. "I've been searching all over this damned mausoleum, and you're in here getting lucky with Miss Babe-a-licious."

Alex was zipping his jeans and Danielle was straightening what there was of her clothes, right there among a roomful of other partygoers who had been, or still were, doing likewise. Jason started toward them, ready to give his friend a piece of his mind, when another man pushed his way toward them, carrying a drink.

The room was dim, but Jason knew this guy was someone from Alex's office, too. Nice-looking, brown hair. What was his name? Kyle. That was it, Kyle Murphy. He was so wrapped up in trying to see Murphy's face that he almost missed the motion of the man's arm. One hand under the base of the glass, one over the top as though simply holding it steady.

Then the hand over the glass moved away, crumpled something small, and stuck it into his front pants pocket in one smooth motion.

Murphy had put something in Alex's drink!

He handed it to Alex, smiling, briefly joked with him about something, then moved off.

And Jason was too fucking far away.

"Oh, God!" He ran, shoving people aside, leaping over prone bodies. "Alex! Alex, no!"

Several people cursed, one made a grab at him, but he only saw Alex, lifting the glass, bringing it to his lips.

With a last push, he leapt, catching Alex in a flying tackle, sending the glass crashing against the bookcase and them to the floor. Lying half on top of Alex, the crisis temporarily averted, Jason rested his forehead on his friend's shoulder.

"Fuck me, that was close," he said, attempting to catch his breath.

"Since there are no rogue newspaper boys here, do you mind telling me what the hell that was about *this* time?"

"Poison. I saw Murphy poison your drink, Alex." Raising his head, he gazed into Alex's eyes, reading the shock and disbelief there. Then resigned sadness.

"Liv tried to tell me, and I wouldn't listen."

"I know, but it's going to be okay, buddy. He's not worth your grief. And now that we can play connect the dots from your office to Palmer's, we can get them all in one swoop."

"We?"

Jason shook his head and pushed up, offering Alex his hand. "Later. Let's find Liv first and get out of here so I can make a call."

Danielle glanced between them, wide-eyed. "Will someone tell me what's going on?"

"At the office, Dani," Alex said, giving her a peck on the cheek. "We have to go."

Jason shot his friend an arch look on the way out the door. "*Dani?* Boy, that was cozy. I can't wait to hear this confession."

"You don't know the half of it. And why'd you bring Liv here?"

"Do you honestly think I could've left her behind? She's a force of nature, my friend."

"Good point."

They got to the foyer, and Jason pointed toward the alcove. Olivia wasn't there.

Sick panic seized his bowels as he looked into Alex's grim face. She wouldn't leave willingly.

"Where is she?" Alex hissed, punching the wall.

"Hello, gentlemen. She's here."

They turned to see Jenna waving them to follow her down the corridor past the alcove. Exchanging a troubled glance, they went after her.

Alex leaned to him, keeping his voice low. "What's going on?"

"Two words. *We're fucked.*"

Jenna showed them to a set of stairs, descending into darkness. She turned to usher them ahead, face pale. "That's an accurate assessment. Olivia is in the basement, and if you want to see her alive again, you'll go without a struggle."

"You set us up," Jason said, stalling.

"I had no choice. Alex is going to die. And you? Palmer is on his way to take you home."

Alex gaped at him. "Home?"

"Not here, Alex. Not now, like this." Jason felt about a hundred years old at the moment, and had no clue how to get them out of this alive. He wanted so badly to come clean with the rest, but couldn't. Not if there was a slim chance of working surprise to his advantage.

"We get out of this, you owe me and Liv a confession of your own."

"I swear it."

Alex threw Jenna a glare of pure loathing over his shoulder. "They're going to kill you and Kyle, too. You're both idiots if you think they won't."

From her lack of a snappy comeback, Jason thought she might agree.

At the bottom, they drew up short, the scene more terrifying than any Jason had faced before. Henry Boardman had Liv by the arm, the muzzle of a gun pressed to her head.

. . .

Alex froze with fear and rage, both warring for top billing as he fought with the powerful need to tear Boardman, and everyone else associated with him, into unrecognizable pieces. He'd fully planned to defend this slime in a court of law. A few days ago, he'd actually believed every person was entitled to a defense.

Some didn't deserve to breathe.

Staring helplessly at his Olivia, the woman he loved, he wanted to cry, too. For what he'd gambled away. He'd been led to his own murder, literally, by his own dick.

If he had a single breath in his body to protect her, she wasn't going to pay for his mistakes.

Boardman smirked, the madness twisting his features. "You're quite a skilled attorney, Quinn. Under different circumstances, I'd love to allow you to get me off with no jail time. But my boss wouldn't like that. The cops need a fall guy." He shrugged before going on.

"By the time I get out in a couple of years, we'll be richer than ever. And you," he said, nodding to Jason. "Palmer can't wait to get his hands on you, boy. You know what the penalty for escaping your master will be? Torture. Long and excruciating. By the time he's finished retraining you, you won't be capable of a single thought except what pleases him."

"You sorry little bastard," Alex said, his voice low and dangerous. Oh, God. Now he understood at least part of what Jason had been keeping from them. "How will you explain our deaths? I was your attorney, and the authorities already know about you and Palmer. They'll know you helped to murder me."

A flash of uncertainty flitted across his hateful face, and the gun wavered. "No, they're going to find a messy murder-suicide. Seems your wife got tired of your affairs, and tonight was the last straw when she heard you had that busy dick of yours stuffed in your secretary's hot pussy. So she lured you down here. Shot you at point-blank range, then herself. A tragedy."

Alex clenched his fists, vibrating, thinking he might shake apart with the force of his rage. He caught Liv's frightened gaze, his own softening. Trying to tell her without words how sorry he was she had to hear something that should've been private spewed from this asshole's mouth. How sorry he was for all of this, and how much he loved her.

She knew. He saw the answer there and forced himself to stay calm. Wait for an opening. He risked a glance at Jason, who gave a slight nod. If they had one, they'd take it.

Footsteps sounded on the stairs, two sets, and he wondered

if one of them might be Kyle. The first man who stepped into the dim light Alex guessed to be Palmer Hodge. Medium height, dark hair. Very *GQ* and handsome if you didn't know he was a monster.

He was holding a gun and Alex bet his buddy in the shadows was, as well, sending the odds down the toilet. So, they'd make an opening and go down fighting. Of all the ways he'd envisioned his life would end, being murdered by a ring of criminals wasn't one of them.

"So nice of you to attend my party, Quinn," Hodge said, smiling. Smug. "And to bring Seraph to me? How wonderful. Unfortunately, I can't express my gratitude properly. Business, you understand."

"How did you get to Kyle? He was my best friend, and he's no killer." Well, that had sure as hell changed. He knew what Hodge would say, but he needed to buy more time.

"Ah, but he's a desperate man and they do desperate, and stupid, things. I'm sure you realize now that the money you lent him was just a drop in his ocean of debt. He was poised to lose everything, and I required a weak link in your firm."

"A question, if you'll humor me. Since Kyle was the weak link, why not just have him ask to be my second chair on Boardman's trial? He could've screwed up our defense just fine from the inside, with no need to involve Jenna."

"Perceptive man. I'm impressed." Hodge waved the gun at Alex's chest. "Very true, and I might have gone that route if I'd planned to use Murphy only once. As it was, I wanted to keep him free from suspicion and as far under your radar as possible. Because I have him well under my thumb and I can use him again and again, but he cannot get directly involved in each job I require without eventually attracting unwanted attention. Jenna, however, served one purpose, and unfortunately for her, is now dispensable."

"Her purpose being to get to me."

"Yes. Besides my desire to keep Murphy in the shadows, I enjoy playing games, as you can see. Your former friend certainly couldn't have distracted you as well as Jenna was able to do. Her job was to get you into bed and embroiled in a scorching affair, which she did quite admirably. At that point, you were to be blackmailed into tanking Henry's defense yourself, with no one the wiser about Murphy, who would walk away unscathed. In return, I wouldn't tell your lovely wife that you and Jenna were buried in more than just legal papers together."

Jenna, after him for weeks, weakening his resolve. All a setup from the start. Blackmail.

Unreal. "I wasn't meant to die."

"No. I only required your cooperation. Then Murphy overheard you telling Jenna about your open arrangement with your wife, and there went the blackmail option." He gave Alex a look of mock sympathy. "I had no other leverage, and I'm an impatient man. You've led quite the staid, boring life, Mr. Quinn. That it would come to this is what I'd call the mother of ironies."

Jason broke his silence. "I don't know how you think to get away with this. Nobody's going to buy whatever excuse you concoct to explain their deaths."

Anger darkened Hodge's face and he strode to Jason, swiftly delivering a blow to his face with his gun hand that sent the younger man to his knees. Liv cried out, and Alex started forward, but restrained himself. Boardman's gun was still aimed at

Liv's temple, and he couldn't launch a defense without Jason backing him.

Hodge loomed over Jason, sneering down at him. "You'll stay on your knees where I'll give that smart mouth better things to do. The sooner you remember that, boy, the better."

Holding his bleeding cheek, Jason lifted his chin, hatred in his brown gaze. Alex held out a hand. "Jason, don't—"

"Fuck. You."

His defiance earned him a hard kick in the ribs, breath leaving him as he bent double, holding his side. *Come on, Jase. Don't get yourself killed before we even have a chance to fight back.*

"Try again, boy."

"I-I'm sorry. *Sir.*" The last he spat with venom, but Hodge seemed pacified for the moment.

"Good." With his free hand, Hodge fished a long object from his pocket. A syringe. He tossed it to Jenna. "Tranquilize Seraph for the flight home. Quickly."

She started toward Jason, who pushed to his feet and gave Alex a meaningful stare. The last grain had fallen through the hourglass.

Hodge gestured to Alex with the gun, a nasty gleam in his eyes. "Who'll die first, you or your wife?" He straightened his arm, leveling the weapon at the center of Alex's chest. "You, I think. She can watch you bleed—"

Liv brought her elbow straight back into Boardman's gut, taking him by surprise, knocking him off balance. She leapt, tackling Jenna to the dirty floor, and they rolled, struggling for possession of the needle.

Seizing his chance, Alex threw himself at Hodge, hardly

believing his ears as he heard Jason shout, "FBI, freeze!" From the corner of his eye, he caught the motion of his friend producing a weapon of his own as Alex barreled for Hodge.

One gunshot exploded like a cannon in the closed space. Another shot, and Alex felt a punch to his chest as he took Hodge down. Falling, lungs burning. They hit the ground and Hodge rolled him like a sack of flour, pushed up. Alex tried to sit up but couldn't move. Had to fight to draw his breath, his chest on fire.

Hodge rose above him and aimed the muzzle between his eyes.

. . .

Jason fired at Boardman, striking the bastard in the chest. He heard the second gunshot and whirled. Saw Alex jerk, tumble into Hodge. Saw Hodge rise, level the gun at Alex's head.

"No!" Jason drew down and Hodge turned, swung his weapon in Jason's direction.

Jason got his shot off a split second before Hodge's, felt the burn graze his arm. His nemesis fell and didn't get up, but Jason saw only Alex. Lying motionless on his back, blood rapidly soaking his T-shirt.

Clutching his bleeding arm, he began to stagger toward his fallen friend, but heard a shuffle behind him. And realized his fatal error.

He'd forgotten about the man observing in the shadows.

. . .

Liv fought to gain the upper hand with Jenna, managing to get on top just as the gunshots erupted.

Bang. Bang.

Jason's cry of anguish was the most terrifying sound she'd ever heard, and she redoubled her efforts. Had to put an end to this, get to her husband.

Bang, bang.

Straddling Jenna, she drew back her arm and planted her fist in the other woman's face, gratified by her shriek and the gush of blood pouring from her nose.

"That was for Alex, bitch," she snarled.

Working fast, she grabbed the syringe from the woman's limp hand, ripped the cap off with her teeth, and plunged the needle into Jenna's neck. Emptied the contents.

"And that was for me."

Immediately, Jenna's eyes began to glaze. That threat removed, Liv pushed up, glancing at Boardman to make sure he stayed down. He lay still, his weapon next to his outstretched hand.

Her gaze went to Jason, stumbling toward—She gasped as a figure emerged from the shadows at the foot of the stairs. A huge black man dressed in an expensive-looking suit.

With a gun trained on Jason's back.

Before she could cry out a warning, Jason spun on his heel, raising his weapon. Then he stopped in midmotion, staring at the gun in the man's hand, stunned confusion on his face.

"Reginald," he whispered. "Why?"

The big man appeared almost sad. "Money, kid, why else? Palmer needed a man on the inside, and I wanted cash. Lots of green to supplement my shitty retirement from the fucking bureau. You were my gift to Palmer, Jason. You see, he knew all along you were an agent, and he didn't care. He had it bad for you, and you couldn't hide how much you liked it, could you?"

Liv gasped. She'd heard Jason yell out his ID as an FBI agent, but it hadn't registered. This was Jason's supervisor. Jason had been undercover as Hodge's sex slave, and that explained so much. The pyramid list, his pistol, the secrecy surrounding his past. Everything he'd promised to tell them when this was over.

And he'd been set up, too. Just like Alex.

"You motherfucker," Jason said, mouth trembling. Blood seeped from between his fingers, and his cheek had begun to swell. He was a mess, but those injuries couldn't compare to the ones Reginald had dealt him.

She inched toward Boardman's weapon.

"You were just a casualty in a war you were never supposed to win, Jase. You were a good kid. I'm sorry."

Liv dove, but couldn't reach the gun fast enough. A gunshot exploded and she screamed, covering her ears, whipping around to see Jason still standing.

Reginald sank to his knees, then flopped prone onto the floor. A few feet away, Alex was leaning up on one elbow, holding a pistol in his shaking, bloodied fingers. Closing his eyes, he fell backward, dropping the gun. Jason kicked Reginald's weapon into the darkness and started toward Alex, yanking his cell phone from his jacket.

Liv scrambled to her husband's side, tears streaming down her face. "Alex? Please, please hang on!"

His lashes fluttered and he looked up at her, those beautiful green eyes filled with love. He gave her a half smile, his mouth tight with pain. "Baby, I have a sixth confession, but . . . I think I'll skip straight to seven . . . if it's all the same to you."

"Oh, honey," she sobbed, shaking her head. "Don't talk, all right? Jason's calling for help."

Blood everywhere. So much of it, soaking his chest. Pooling around his body. *Don't let me lose him.*

"I love you, Olivia Quinn . . . and I always will. I'm just sorry it had to end this way."

"I love you and you can't leave me, do you hear? Stay with me." She wanted to cradle his head in her lap, hold him close, but was afraid of jostling him. So she settled for clinging to his hand, rubbing his cold fingers against her cheek.

"Jason?" he rasped. His lungs wheezed, every intake of air a battle.

Jason knelt, tucking away the phone, and laid a hand on Alex's shoulder. "I'm here, buddy."

"You tried to tell me . . . there's always a price. Should've listened."

"Oh, God, Alex—"

"Take care of her. Promise me."

Jason's breath hitched and he visibly fought not to cry. "You know I will, but you're gonna be fine."

"Good. And Jase?" He was fading, voice barely a whisper.

"Yeah?"

"No mushy shit . . . but you're pretty special to me, too. Wanted you to know . . . "

"I do know, and—Alex?"

Helpless, Liv watched as her husband's lids drifted closed, lashes settling on waxen cheeks. "No, please don't go. I love you so much."

She laid her head on his shoulder and cried, clinging to him, willing him to stay. She was hardly aware of Jason tugging on her. The paramedics moving in, working on Alex, racing against time.

Vaguely, she knew someone was screaming as Alex coded. Horrible and rending, the soul being ripped from someone's body.

Jason, holding her tight. Rocking her.

Her hands, her face, covered in Alex's blood.

A paramedic, placing pads on Alex's chest. Shaking his head.

A sting in her arm.

Then the screams were sucked from her lungs and lived only in her brain. Somehow that was worse.

And then, blessedly, she knew nothing at all.

. . .

Jason watched Olivia sleep, held her hand, stroked her cool fingers. He'd insisted the nurses clean her as best as they could, and thank God for that. She didn't need to awaken with Alex's blood all over her.

He didn't even try to think about the tangle of lies. The betrayals.

The losses.

He couldn't help Alex now, couldn't dwell on the man he cared about so much without breaking down. So he concentrated on Liv because she was the only person he had to cling to. The one who needed him like he needed her.

She stirred, licked her chapped lips, coming around. Tense, he watched her emerge from the safe, protective fog, saw her open those pretty blue eyes. The confusion giving way to awful realization.

That she might have awakened to a world without Alex.

When she spoke, her voice was that of a small child. Needing the truth, yet afraid to know.

"He's dead, isn't he?"

He brought her hand to his uninjured cheek, nuzzled her, trying to lend her strength for what was to come. "I don't know," he said honestly. "He made it here, so they rushed him into surgery."

She'd never know about the battle to restart his heart, how they nearly called his time of death after giving her the shot. How Jason had bawled like a baby instead of a grown man, holding her while Alex lay dead on the dirty basement floor.

Most folks didn't need that much reality. It would hit her soon enough, how tough his fight would be, even if he survived surgery.

"His chances. Tell me."

God help him, he wanted to lie. But Alex never had, so neither would he. "Not good, sweetheart. But they improve every hour, and he's not leaving us if he can help it."

The tears welled, slipped down her cheeks. "Thank you. For being honest, for being here."

"Shh, I've got you."

Leaning forward, he pressed a gentle kiss to her lips. One of comfort and friendship. Promise.

After a while, he helped her into some sweats and a St. Louis PD T-shirt Detective Lambert had in the trunk of his car. The man was a little sweet on her, wanting to assist in the aftermath, and he was glad. The dress she'd been wearing had already hit the incinerator.

After a while, Jason escorted her to the waiting room, since the nurses needed the ER bed. Hours passed, excruciating, both of them jumping every time a doctor or nurse emerged from the restricted area beyond the double doors.

Once Liv said, "He always jokes that he wants to die at home in his lounger outside, with a beer on the table next to him."

And then he held her while she cried until she had no tears left. She hadn't said much since.

Near dawn, the doors opened and they jerked upright. This time, a sandy-haired doctor in fresh scrubs headed their way, eyes tired. Expression solemn.

"Mrs. Quinn? I'm Dr. Alan Chapman."

She leapt to her feet. "Yes! Please, how's my husband?"

"Why don't we go in here, where it's private?"

Liv paled and reached for Jason's hand.

The doctor ushered them into a nearby family crisis room and waited until they'd taken seats before continuing. "Mrs. Quinn, it was quite a battle, but your husband made it through the surgery."

Praise God.

Liv clapped a hand over her mouth, seeming to fold in on herself. Jason put an arm around her shoulders, letting her lean into him. Chapman gave her a moment before going on.

"I'm not going to lie to you; Alex is extremely critical. The bullet came so close to his heart, a sheet of paper wouldn't have slid sideways through the space. It bounced around, did internal damage, and lodged at the back of his spine between the shoulder blades."

"Oh, my God."

"We removed the bullet. We'll have to wait and see about possible spinal injury, but that's the least of our worries right now. He's got a real fight ahead of him, especially these first few days."

"Doctor Chapman, what are his odds?" she asked quietly.

His eyes were kind but firm. "I don't deal in percentages. They aren't scientific or useful, and they don't factor in a person's will to live. And believe me, Mrs. Quinn, your husband wants to live very badly, or he wouldn't still be here."

Jason prayed he was right. Alex was going to need every ounce of that will, and then some.

. . .

He hurt.

He hurt so fucking bad, maybe he should've stayed dead.

And he *had* died, right?

He'd always thought that floating-above-your-body bullshit was just that. A load of crap. Then he'd closed his eyes, felt the world slide away. The pain disappeared, and suddenly he was above the scene, watching his Liv cry. It made him sad and he wanted to get back to her, but didn't know how.

So he'd just sort of hung around. Waited until he was pulled back in to fight again. Several times this had happened, Alex yo-yoing back and forth between Here and There, and he wondered if he'd be able to go another round.

And now? Definitely awake inside his shot-to-hell body.

He'd probably dreamed all of that woo-woo shit.

"Alex?" Liv's voice, her sweet perfume filling his senses. "I think he's waking up!"

"Thank God," Jason muttered, sounding exhausted. "I'll buzz the nurse."

How did she know? He tried to open his eyes, but it seemed like the wire between his brain and body parts had been snipped in two.

Okay, not cut, just stunned. He blinked his lids, feeling like he had a fine coating of ground glass on his eyeballs. His vision was fuzzy and the white light killed his eyes.

"Damn." Sounded like his voice box had been scraped with a rusty nail, but everyone else thought that one curse was the greatest event on record.

All at once, people were chattering, poking, and prodding.

A doctor, a couple of nurses. Where were Liv and Jason?

Was he hurting here, here and here? Yes, yes and *hell* yes, dammit! This information seemed to please the shit out of everyone, too.

The doctor was telling him stuff about getting shot, the bullet missing his heart. His spine healing, and taking it easy, as if they were in danger of his leaping from the bed to run laps. Spine? What the hell? He couldn't take it all in, and wanted everyone out except the two people he needed most.

At last, blessed silence. Liv's delicate hand holding his. On the other side of the bed, a masculine palm on his shoulder. "Better," he sighed.

Opening his eyes, he tried to focus again, but they were blurry. His limbs so damned heavy.

"Rest, big guy," Jason said. "You're going to be fine now."

"If you . . . say so."

He let go. This time, he wouldn't have to fight to wake up again.

Seventeen

A lex had fallen into a normal, healing sleep. Finally. After nearly two heartwrenching weeks of watching him struggle from the brink of death, cheating the Reaper three more times, he'd won, running on nothing except willpower for fuel.

Jason had begged her to go home and get some sleep in her own bed instead of the cot she'd been living on. Maybe tonight she'd feel easy enough about leaving him to do that. Besides, Jason had offered to take her place.

Alex twisted, blond hair tousled on his pillow. He opened his eyes and this time, clear green stared back at her. "Hey, beautiful."

His sleepy, drugged smile broke her heart. He'd been through so much. "Hiya, handsome," she said, stroking his hair. "Welcome back."

"Mmm. Feels good. Dreamed I was outside my body. Wouldn't leave you."

Oh, God. "I'm so happy you stayed. You scared us, honey."

"Scared me, too." He closed his eyes for a few minutes. When he opened them again, he was more lucid. Worried. "Jason's all right?"

"He's just fine. His arm was grazed by Hodge's bullet, but nothing more serious than scratches and bruises. He's almost healed."

"What happened with the others?"

"Henry Boardman's dead. Hodge is facing serious prison time for attempted murder and illegal sex trafficking. Kyle, the lily-livered pissant, tried to skip the country, but the Feds caught him at the airport. He and Jenna are being charged as accomplices in everything."

"Who was that guy I shot? A Fed?" His gaze clouded with worry. "I didn't quite catch all of what was said, but I know he was about to kill Jason."

"He's Reginald Paige, and he was Jason's supervisor in Virginia, or was before he got placed under arrest."

"I didn't kill him." Alex sank into his pillow a little. "I'm glad I don't have that on my conscience."

"Me, too. Besides, he was dirty and deserves to go to prison. He sent Jason on an undercover assignment with Hodge to bring down the sex racket, and, well . . . Jason got caught up in the lifestyle. He had a breakdown over what he perceives as his failure, and Paige was forced to pull him out for a while to keep anyone from knowing what was up."

"And so Jason shows up in St. Louis, licking his wounds." Alex blinked, remembering. "That's it. Agent Campbell mentioned one of their guys having a breakdown on the case. Paige pulled him, and Hodge was looking everywhere for him."

"Right. Because Hodge didn't know he was FBI. Paige claimed he knew and that they'd had a good laugh over it, but Jason said

Paige was just trying to hurt him more. Hodge didn't know, or he'd have tracked him down long before that night."

"Christ, what a fucked-up mess."

Leaning down, she brushed his lips with hers. "Well, it's over, and I'm incredibly lucky to be able to sit here, to talk with my husband and kiss him if I want."

"Are you? Lucky, I mean?"

She noted the smudges under his eyes, the shadows in their depths. He wasn't simply tired and in pain. At least not just physically. "Yes, I am, Alex Quinn! Don't you dare blame yourself for any of this. The bargain was my idea."

"I was the one who was tempted to stray." He looked away, raw anguish on his face. "And that's what I did. What's more, I involved us with people who nearly killed us."

"You had no idea Jenna was out to seduce you because of some sort of secret agenda," she said firmly. "The way things were between us, I didn't blame you. I don't, and I never will. And you weren't the only one who gave in to temptation."

He thought a moment, apparently deciding to drop that part of the discussion for now. "Jason is a good man. He's special, and he fits us."

"He is. I love him, and I love you."

"Would you . . . want him to stay?"

"I do. He won't say much to me until he talks to you, though."

"Sounds ominous."

"Not really. I think he doesn't want to make plans regarding the three of us behind your back."

"I wouldn't feel that way, but I'm anxious to talk to him."

"I know. Rest right now and he'll be by later."

She couldn't stop touching him. Reassuring herself that he

was alive. Her strokes and caresses lulled him to sleep in minutes.

For the longest time, she watched his chest rise and fall.

And wondered what would happen with the three of them.

. . .

The last person Alex expected to see walked through the door a couple of days later. Decidedly less hostile, but far from warm.

He sat up in bed, hating to be at a disadvantage. Then again, he had been for some weeks where this man was concerned.

"Ken. How are things at the office?" He couldn't very well say it was nice to see Brock, so that pretty much left work stuff.

"Morose. Everybody's acting like you died, man. Never seen so many glum faces."

"Except yours, I'll bet."

Ken snorted, sticking his hands in his pockets. "Shit, if it was up to me, I'd beat your sorry ass again one more time. For good measure."

"Can't say I blame you." Might as well get it over with, see if crow tasted good. "I owe you an apology, Ken. I should've chosen you, and I know that. I was used, but that's no excuse, and I'm sorrier than you'll ever know."

"I accept, but I don't think I can stay at the firm. Too much water under the bridge."

"You don't believe that and neither do I. Do you really want to start over where nobody knows you or the incredible attorney I know you are?"

"Not really, but I'm too old and I've worked too hard to put up with the crap I did from you."

Alex put every ounce of sincerity in his voice he could muster. "It won't happen again. You have my word. And I'll tell you a secret about why."

Ken sat down, interested in spite of himself. "Yeah? This I gotta hear."

"I've got a newfound appreciation for life, and I'm here to tell you, it really is too short. I'm going to be cutting back on my caseload, so I'm going to need you more than ever. The other partners count on you. They look up to you, Ken. So do I. What do you say?"

Alex stuck out his hand, hoping Ken would accept his peace offering. For several heartbeats, he thought the man would refuse; then Ken reached out and shook his hand.

Withdrawing first, Ken said, "For what it's worth, I'm glad you're not pushing up daisies."

"Thanks. Me, too."

"You're something else, man."

"So I've been told, in prettier company."

"Jackass."

. . .

Alex wiggled in the hospital bed, flipping channels, bored out of his freaking skull. Yeah, he was grateful to be alive to get bored at all, but *Oprah*? Still not his favorite afternoon pastime, and it was too early for the news.

And goddamn, his chest itched. A while ago, one of the nurses caught him red-handed with the bandage peeled back, scratching up a storm on the healing flesh. She'd lit into his ass like his sainted mama would've done if she'd been alive, swabbed and taped it back, then marched out again, leaving him thoroughly chastised and wishing for a Jack and cola.

Maybe Jason would sneak him some—

As though he'd conjured the man, Jason sauntered into his room, face lighting up on seeing him. "Man, you're looking better every day." The younger man pulled him into a bear hug, drawing back quickly at his grunt. "Crap, I'm sorry!"

"It's okay." Christ, the guy was strong for being so lean.

Jason took the seat by his bed and laughed at the television. "Dude, *Oprah*? That's *so* not right."

He flipped off the TV and tossed aside the controls. "Wasn't watching it."

"Sure you weren't." He grinned. "Must be boring as hell, stuck in here. Have you played the pipe organ yet?"

He laughed, wincing at the pull in his chest. "God, you're a piece of work. I'll never tell."

Jason sat back, crossing his calf over one knee, relaxed but sobering some. "I have to go back to Virginia."

Oh. He'd been expecting that. So why did it feel worse than the bullet to his chest? "Permanently?"

"Depends. I have to get my shit together, find out where I stand at the bureau. Get reevaluated, and with any luck, reassigned."

"Oh? What do you want to do?" There. Casual. Not like he was holding his breath, hoping to hear any promises.

He plucked at his jeans, watching Alex from under his lashes. "I'd like to apply for a transfer to the St. Louis field office. . . . If you and Liv wouldn't mind having me next door."

Pretense failed. He knew the younger man could read the emotions on his face, but he didn't care. "You didn't even have to ask. There's nothing we'd love more than having you here. How long will it take to make the move?"

Jason smiled. "A few weeks. Months at most. But I'd visit in the meantime."

"We'll count on it." Something else was bothering him, and he had to get it off his chest. "Jase? I'm sorry we doubted you. Your notes and the gun, they were scary in light of what was happening. Liv was the first to trust you, but I wasn't so sure. I had no idea what you'd been through, and hope you can forgive me."

"Nothing to forgive, Alex. You didn't know, and I wasn't forthcoming. In the secrets department, anyway." He wiggled his brows suggestively.

"I'd better get going." Jason stood, gently laid a hand over Alex's heart, careful not to hurt him. "You'd make a terrible agent, you know that? Your poker face sucks."

Jason bent and kissed him right on the mouth. Slow and lingering. A little tongue, a sweet sigh. A hint of pleasures to come. "I'll be in touch."

"You'd better." He cleared his throat. "Liv will miss you."

Jason didn't reply, just gave him a knowing smile before turning on his heel and walking out of Alex's life.

For now.

I'll miss you, too, he added silently.

Picking up the remote, he flipped on *Oprah.*

Maybe the lady had some advice today for someone with an aching heart.

⋅ ⋅ ⋅

Home.

Holding Liv's hand, Alex walked into the kitchen and inhaled.

"I wasn't sure I'd ever see this place again," he said softly. "Wasn't sure I'd be granted a reprieve to be with you in this world for a while longer."

Turning in to him, she hugged him close. "I prayed every day, something I haven't done in years. I don't know what I would've done, how I would've survived if—" She couldn't finish, but held him close. Telling him with her soul what no words could ever express.

"Baby, we don't have to think about it now. I'm home, on the mend, and all yours." He nuzzled her hair, pulled her closer, his cock beginning to take notice. Lord, it had been so long.

"You still need a lot of rest. Two more weeks, minimum."

That, on top of four boring weeks in the hospital. At least he was home, where people weren't constantly poking him. Where he could eat real food—he'd lost fifteen pounds—and have a drink that wasn't fruit juice.

Where he could make love to Olivia.

"You'll be my nurse?"

"Absolutely. Can't have you wearing yourself out."

"Unless it's for a good cause."

"I'm all about good causes."

He wanted to sweep her into his arms like he'd done weeks ago, but he wasn't quite up to playing Conan the Barbarian yet. So he settled for taking her by the hand and walking together to the bed where they'd shared so many happy years.

They removed their clothing, crawled onto the mattress. Alex pushed his wife onto her back, cupped her breast. Rolled the nipple between his thumb and forefinger, loving the way she gasped and arched into his touch like a feline being petted. He drank her in, wondering whether she missed Jason's touch, as well.

"You never did answer my question, you know," he said casually. "The one I asked you weeks ago, about Jason."

She cocked her head, midnight hair fanned across the pillows. "Which one?"

"Would you have let him go?"

"Oh, Alex," she said, reaching up to run her fingers down his face. "You've been my heart and soul for most of our adult lives. You're the first man I ever loved, and despite my feelings for Jason, yours is the last face I ever want to see. So, yes, I would have. I'd hoped you knew."

"I suppose I did." He smiled, never more in love than at this moment. "But I never would've asked you to."

"I know."

"I love you, Liv. More than anything on earth."

"Prove it, Counselor."

He kissed her soundly, tongue sweeping between her lips. His fingers found her little clit, circling, dipping into her passage. Making her wet and ready for him. She whimpered, and he positioned himself between her legs, the head of his eager cock pushing inside. Then all of him.

"Ohh, Liv. God, it's good to be home."

They both knew he meant here. In their bed, joined together, alive and happy. Loving each other without fear or uncertainty.

He made love to her slow and sweet until they quickened, in perfect tune with one another. Flying toward the edge and over, before floating down to earth once more.

He'd never take this for granted again.

After, he rolled to his back and pulled her onto his chest. One of her hands rested over his scar, fingers tracing the ridge. Instead of hating the puckered flesh, he considered it another reminder to count his blessings.

"My turn to ask a question," she said.

"Shoot." He winced. "Sorry, bad choice of words."

That stupid joke earned him a punch in the arm. Not a very hard one, though. "Idiot." She gave him a faint smile. "We reached the end of our bargain, so it's time for us to make a decision. Bring some closure."

"Seems to me we already made that decision, sweetheart. Jason will be back before we know it, and I, for one, can't wait."

"You really want him with us, don't you?" She hesitated. "You love him, too."

"I couldn't help but love anyone who makes you happy, but yeah. I do. He's a great guy."

She was quiet for a moment, toying with one of his nipples. "No more confessions? I know you enjoyed them. So did I."

"Well . . . I never did get to confess about the night of the party with Danielle."

Reaching down, she brushed his semierect cock. "The new blond secretary who looks like a Victoria's Secret model," she observed, her body growing warmer against him. "I have a confession of my own. I saw you together in the library."

"Y-you did?" he stammered. "You never let on!"

"Yes, while this handsome man pleasured me. Thinking of you fucking another woman turned me on, but seeing it—my God. I wanted to join you, but then—" Boardman had found her. No sense in going there again. "Did you enjoy her? Was she good?"

"Oh yeah, twice. Her pussy is like silk and she loves her backside to be finger fucked at the same time. And I learned something else—she was the mystery woman at the club that night. We'd already been together, and I didn't even suspect."

Her fingers closed around his cock, which had perked up with the memory of Danielle. "When you go back to work in two weeks, she'll be a temptation, my sexy husband."

"Shit, yeah," he moaned, arching into her hand. "She's responsive and fun to be around. And she's already warned me she'll be difficult to resist. What will you and Jason do if I give in?"

"Punish you, of course," she murmured, trailing her tongue down his abs. "We have all of that equipment downstairs; it would be a shame never to use it again."

"Damn, you drive me wild. I'll have to be sure and confess. From time to time."

She gave a husky laugh, treated him to a slow lick.

"Kinky man."

"All your fault." He winked. "You've created a monster."

"Why don't you prove it, big boy?"

Not a problem. As her lips sheathed his cock, he did just that.

. . .

One hot afternoon in July, the doorbell rang. Liv dabbed the last of the icing on the Italian cream cake she'd made for Alex and hurried to the front door. Where was Alex, anyway?

Always cautious these days, she looked out the peephole. Blinked and looked again, to be sure her eyes weren't deceiving her. "Oh! Alex, come here!"

Throwing open the door, she launched herself into Jason's

arms, squealing as he hoisted her up and twirled her around. "You're back! Please say you're here to stay."

"I am, gorgeous."

He took her mouth in a blistering kiss that curled her toes, then held her shoulders, smiling like he'd won the lottery. She stood and gaped at the man on her threshold. Still their Jason, but one she'd never seen before.

He wore a crisp thousand-dollar suit and polished shoes. His sun-streaked hair had been trimmed to his collar and combed away from his face in a futile attempt to tame it. Dark, wraparound sunglasses completed the effect.

"Wow, very *Men in Black*." She whistled. "I like."

"I'll say," Alex said from behind her. "Welcome home, Agent Strickland."

"Are we going to stand out here, or can I come in?"

They trooped inside and Alex grabbed beers for all of them. Jason tossed his sunglasses on the coffee table, got rid of his tie, and plopped onto the sofa with a contented sigh, taking his Corona from Alex and twisting off the cap.

"Thanks, I'm parched." He took a swig, and Liv admired his tanned throat and hint of chest at the part of his collar. "Damn, it's great to be back. Frigging bureaucratic red tape involved in every single step along the way, let me tell you. Being put through the wringer after all of that shit was over, securing the transfer, moving. And I missed you guys like crazy."

"Poor baby," she sympathized, settling on the sofa next to him. "I suppose we'll forgive you for not being able to visit. Sounds like you need some TLC."

Poking out his lip, he gave her exaggerated puppy dog eyes. "Like you can't imagine."

"Oh, I think I can." She went to work on the buttons of his white shirt, revealing a strip of his lean, muscled chest bit by bit. She tugged out his shirttail, then slid her hands under the fabric to peel it away, starting when she bumped the holster hidden under his suit jacket.

"Sorry," he said, contrite. "I didn't think about the gun. I mean, I know guns will always bring back bad memories of what happened to Alex, but I have to carry one, sweetheart. More often than not, you'll see one with me. Is that going to be too much of an issue?"

Would it? She hadn't really thought about it before now.

"Is that the same gun?" she asked, lifting his jacket to peek at the weapon. "The one you used to shoot Hodge when he was standing over Alex, getting ready to put a bullet in his head?"

"Yes," he said softly. "The same."

"Then I'm fine. You saved our lives, Jase, and without that gun, none of us would be here. Being an agent is your job, and you're one of the good guys. One of *my* guys."

"For as long as you want me."

She helped him off with his jacket and holster, laid them on the coffee table. She kissed her way along his jaw, nibbled down the strong column of his throat, his chest and flat tummy. Next, she unbuckled his belt and undid his pants. He shoved them down, lifted his hips, and they were off.

Jason was spread naked on her sofa, fully aroused and fisting his cock, lips parted slightly. "Feels like I've waited a lifetime to return. I've wanted this so much . . . with both of you."

She smiled. "Well, you're here, and none of us has to want any longer."

Peeling off her tank top, she freed her braless breasts, exposing them to two feral pairs of eyes. One female taming a couple of wild beasts—or perhaps they'd tame her. Her pussy clenched at the thought.

Alex stood and pushed down his cutoffs, the only clothing he'd been wearing, and she did the same. "Let's go over to the rug by the fireplace," she said, taking Jason's hand. "We'll all be more comfortable."

They padded over and Jason lay on his back, grinning, legs spread. The man didn't possess an iota of modesty, a trait she intended to enjoy to the fullest. Every day.

"Look at that lush mouth, Alex," she said, tracing Jason's lips. "Have you ever wondered what it would be like to kiss him together?"

"Yeah," he admitted, scooting close. Eyeing their prize. "I have. In fact, I was fantasizing more along the lines of *devouring* him together . . . before we both stuff you full of our cocks."

Oh, my! "That sounds fabulous."

"Jesus," Jason murmured. "Yes."

She and Alex stretched out on either side of him and bent, angling their faces close to his. At first, they took turns nipping and licking at his lips. Jason's tongue darted out, flicking against theirs, brushing each one. Drawing them in to his hot mouth, closer, more urgent, until all three of them were locked in one passionate kiss. Tongues sweeping, eating each other's mouths. Electric.

More than sexual, although certainly arousing, it was also an affirmation. An acknowledgment of their union, a loving home-coming.

They moved from his mouth, exploring his throat with nips and kisses, to his chest. Liv grazed one of his taut male nipples with her teeth while Alex did the other, coaxing a rumble from their lover. They journeyed lower, all the way to his flushed sex, ready and eager for whatever they wished to do.

Liv crawled between Jason's thighs, lay on her stomach, and lifted his heavy sac. She rolled the velvety balls, manipulated them, and when she began laving and suckling them, both men groaned in unison.

"God, Liv, that looks so damned good. Show him who he belongs to, baby."

"Join me," she said, winking. "We'll show him together."

Alex going down on their lover's beautiful cock while she nuzzled his soft skin was the sexiest, most decadent thing she'd ever seen. Alex's lips slid along the slick flesh, making Jase shiny and wet, nearly driving him out of his mind.

"Oh, my God! Oh, don't . . . you two are g-gonna make me come too soon," he rasped.

"Can't have that, can we, baby?" Alex gave the weeping slit a last lick. "Why don't you straddle our boy and let us take you some place special."

"Shit, yeah," Jason panted.

Liv placed her knees on either side of Jason's hips. Her sex was so hot, already moist, her entire body needing her men. Off to one side, Alex steadied the base of Jason's cock, eyes burning.

"Sink onto him slowly, sweetheart. I want to watch as he fills you." He nudged her folds, rubbing with the head of Jason's penis as she lowered her body. "Shit, yeah. That's so hot, so fucking sexy. All the way, baby, that's it. Feel every inch of him."

Ohh, she did. Every bit of skin sliding into her, the delicious hardness overlaid with soft. Alex's naughty talk, cloaking her in a haze of pleasure. She felt desired, cherished, powerful.

Bracing her palms on Jason's chest, she began to ride. Not too fast, savoring the friction that fanned the flames. She was hardly aware of Alex moving away, rustling for something, then crawling behind her, between Jason's legs.

"Keep fucking him, nice and slow. I'm going to get you ready for me, real easy since it's been a while."

Yes, it had. And she'd never had two men inside her at once, wasn't sure she could take them both. Didn't know how they'd fit.

Cool fingers, slick with lube, parted her cheeks, massaged her entrance. "Oh! Alex, yes."

"More?"

"Please . . ." He inserted a finger into her channel, riding her motions up and down as she fucked Jason. Preparing her gently, driving her mad. Then two fingers, stretching, creating a burn that streaked to her pussy. "Inside me, now. I need you."

"You've got me."

The fingers were removed, and she stilled for a moment, angling forward to give him access. The blunt head of his cock spread her tight opening, and he began to push inside. She tensed some at the pain, and he murmured soothing words, stroking her spine.

"Doing good, just relax. Let go and let us love you."

Love you. Magic. She felt herself enter the right head space and she did just that. Let go for him, for all of them.

Alex sank into her, slid all the way in. They moaned together, soaking this in. So dark and wicked. And wonderful.

"I'm so full," she gasped, beginning to move on Jason's cock again. Alex moved with her, pumping. "Oh yes! It's so good."

"Fantastic," Jason managed, eyes fluttering closed. "I can feel you both fucking me."

Liv set the pace, pumping Jason's cock as Alex thrust deep into her ass on every down stroke. Both cocks, plunging into her at the same time, setting her nerve endings on fire. They rode faster and harder, the tempo increasing until both her men were fucking her with abandon.

Wild and raw, flesh pounding, the three of them soaring higher, higher . . .

Jason gave it up first, stiffening and shooting into her with a hoarse cry. Liv went over next, tremors wracking her, pussy juices flooding his cock. Alex came with a shout and they writhed together, vibrating, wringing out every last bit of the orgasm they could.

Liv collapsed on Jason's chest and he stroked her hair, whispering, making her feel even more special than they'd promised.

"Love you." He paused, throwing a meaningful look over her shoulder. "Both of you."

"Love you back," she said, smoothing her palm over his sweaty chest. "Welcome home."

Alex pulled out carefully and stretched out beside them, his feelings for both of them shining in his green eyes. "Yeah, welcome home, Jase. I'm damned glad you're here."

Liv smiled. When it came to expressing feelings out loud for another man, that was as close as her husband would get for a while. Newfound sexual freedom or not.

Jase laughed. "You guys sure know how to make a guy feel wanted. This is way better than banners and balloons."

"This is nothing. Just wait for what we have in store next," Alex said, obviously pleased with himself. "We've had weeks to plan. Hope you brought your vitamins so you can keep up with this old man."

"Ha, you *wish* you could keep up with me. So, I guess this means Liv tamed you for good, huh? Man, I'm going to miss your confessions—and her creative punishments, too."

Alex's lips tilted up in a secretive smile. "Who says I don't have one to give?"

Liv eye's widened. Why, that sneaky rat. "Alexander Quinn, you're so good when you're bad."

"You wouldn't have me any other way, baby."

And wasn't that the truth?

"All right, stud," she said with a smile. "Start talking."

About the Author

Jo Davis spent sixteen years in the public school trenches before she left teaching to pursue her dream of becoming a full-time writer. An active member of the Romance Writers of America, she's been a finalist in the Colorado Romance Writers Award of Excellence and has one book optioned as a major motion picture. She lives in Texas with her husband and two children. Visit her Web site at www.JoDavis.net.